PENGUIN BOOKS

**ALPHABET CITY**

Steven Knight was born in Marlborough in 1959 and grew up in Birmingham. After studying English Literature at University College London, he worked as a radio producer and then as an advertising copywriter, winning several industry awards. In 1987 he began his career as a television scriptwriter and has written extensively for some of Britain's leading performers, both alternative and established, and he has also devised a series of successful TV game shows. He now runs his own TV production company in Covent Garden, writing and producing comedy and drama for the BBC and the independent networks. In 1994 he won the Writers' Guild award for Best Light Entertainment.

Steven Knight's first novel, *The Movie House,* also published by Penguin, was selected for the 1994 WH Smith Fresh Talent Promotion.

# ALPHABET CITY

Steven Knight

PENGUIN BOOKS

PENGUIN BOOKS

Published by the Penguin Group
Penguin Books Ltd, 27 Wrights Lane, London w8 5tz, England
Penguin Books USA Inc., 375 Hudson Street, New York, New York 10014, USA
Penguin Books Australia Ltd, Ringwood, Victoria, Australia
Penguin Books Canada Ltd, 10 Alcorn Avenue, Toronto, Ontario, Canada m4v 3b2
Penguin Books (NZ) Ltd, 182–190 Wairau Road, Auckland 10, New Zealand

Penguin Books Ltd, Registered Offices: Harmondsworth, Middlesex, England

First published by Penguin Books 1995

10 9 8 7 6 5 4 3 2 1

Copyright © Steven Knight, 1995
All rights reserved

The moral right of the author has been asserted

Filmset by Datix International Limited, Bungay, Suffolk
Printed in England by Clays Ltd, St Ives plc
Set in 9.75/12pt Monophoto Baskerville

PART ONE

# Lies

## Chapter One

**1**

The six o'clock news reporter was pulling her moose-fur boots over her studio shoes. She wiped her hair from her famous face, exhausted with the effort of dressing for the ferocious blizzard that was raging outside. Inside the little hospitality room, the last light in the place was burning. The TV output had been switched onto monitor-automatic, re-runs, cop shows, old movies, overseen by some station ghost who would sleep until the pale Alaskan sun rose, late next morning.

Steven Hawthorne was fretting on the phone in the corner of the hospitality room, beside the TV, which was playing with the sound turned all the way down. He was trying to put a phone call through to Anchorage airport, but the information desk wasn't answering.

'Like I mentioned, Mr Hawthorne,' the reporter said, zipping up her boots, 'you don't need to worry. Blizzard or no blizzard the planes always fly out of Anchorage. They grill the runway from underneath. You could fry an egg.'

Steven was booked onto the eight o'clock flight to New York, the city where he would find out for sure if his enterprise would stand or fold. His anxiety to discover if the planes were still flying was more than half dread. More than half of him hoped that the airport had disappeared under an avalanche so he would have a few more days to prepare. New York City, the axis of his tour of the United States, had come around too quickly.

The reporter waited while Steven held the line and then put the phone down. She was already sweating in her thick quilt coat. The moment he replaced the receiver it rang and a security guy said sleepily that there was a cab right outside the door. When they stepped out into the reception area, the reporter shrugged at how crazy this was and closed down the station switchboard herself.

'Up here, we all do three jobs,' she said. Steven had noticed how the darkness and the endless cold made everyone in Alaska bright and resourceful. 'Hey, I almost forgot,' she continued. 'I need you to sign my copy.' She unzipped the pocket of her quilted jacket and held out a copy of Steven's book. 'Put "to Julia",' she said.

'Julia.'

'My sister. She'll go crazy for this book. She's really into crime.'

Steven took out a pen and wrote 'to Julia'.

'She'll go crazy when I tell her I met you too. Really, she's worse than a guy. She's so into guns and gangsters. She goes to those conventions . . .'

Steven handed back the book and said, 'You're sure they'll be flying in this.'

'Double sure.' She tucked her copy of *Alphabet City* back into her pocket. Then she said that she really meant it when she said that it had been a privilege to have interviewed him today. For half an hour, Steven had been telling her the same story he had told to a dozen other TV reporters, DJs, magazine journalists, feature writers in California, up through Oregon, then across Canada and on to Alaska. The story of how he had spent a year living undercover as first lieutenant and quartermaster for an Hispanic crack gang in Alphabet City, one of the most

4

dangerous square miles of territory on earth, tucked into the belly of Manhattan Island on New York's Lower East Side. More dangerous, corpse for corpse (Steven had the statistics) than the malarial jungles of Africa or the cholera-infested river basins of India. He had gone to live there, the preface of the book said, to research a sociological paper on the structure of street gangs, drawing parallels with the structures of tribal societies. But the diary he kept while he was there was now attracting interest far beyond university campuses.

The true-life drama of *Alphabet City* was selling faster than the Bible all along the West and East Coasts. Part of the publishing deal was that he would do an extensive publicity tour of the whole of the United States, grazing on little shoots of airtime, moving from place to place to catch the briefest ray of media light. He'd been given a chance at the local news in Anchorage because there was an angle. When Steven had been growing up, he had lived for three years up near Bristol Bay, where his father had been based at one of the USAF's early-warning and tracking stations.

The reporter had her hand outstretched. They shook and she said she'd send a video cassette of the piece they had just recorded on to his publisher in New York. She said it would be the second item on the local bulletin next day, unless a polar bear ate some schoolchildren or a plane fell out of the sky.

'Only kidding, Mr Hawthorne.'

'About what?'

'About a plane falling out of the sky. You'll be fine. This is just a squall.'

When she opened the door, the wind roared like a mighty bear. The wall of ice and snow, the smell of outer space that could only be experienced here at the top of the world, reminded Steven of the time he'd spent living here on the bristling tip of America, among the radars and electronic whiskers. His only memories were of the cold winds, the rumble of the jets on the military airstrip, and the way his father used to look out at the snowy horizon and say, with awe, that the Russians were so close you could smell their bacon frying.

A taxi somewhere out in the blizzard flashed its headlights and Steven trudged through the thick fresh snow with his suitcase. A few shirts and shoes, a lot of dirty laundry, two dozen copies of *Alphabet City* to plant like seeds in two dozen cities.

When the cab arrived at Anchorage airport, he found out that the planes were taking off just as if this roaring bear blizzard was routine, and his flight to New York left right on time.

**2**

Steven finally fell to sleep somewhere over the Yukon. There was nothing to see out of the window except clouds of snow and his own reflection. Night flights always made him dream that he was back in a Hercules, the kind that his family had used as a government-paid removal service when he was a kid, when his father had been shipped from place to place, from hemisphere to hemisphere.

He was born at Fort Hays, North Carolina, among the 82nd Airborne, and his father had done a victory roll over the Carolina Outer Banks in his Starfighter jet when they radioed to him that it was a boy. When he was three they moved for the first time, to an airbase in England where he spent eight years until his mother died. After that, when his daddy was transferred, it would be just the two of them who would board the creaking, roaring C13 transporter planes, with their little stash of furniture and clothes stowed at the back along with the jeep spares and black kerosene barrels and pin-up photos. First it was North Africa, then Thessalonica, Korea, Alaska. Sometimes, when they were moving house, his daddy would fly the plane and Steven would sit in the greasy cockpit, a tiny bubble of light with the smell of aviation fuel and mint gum and sweat. His daddy would let him touch the controls, let him feel the huge swell of the trade winds, the spin of the earth, and he did it because he was sure that someday Steven would be doing this for real. Someday he'd be flying these birds around the world just like the big, bone-headed co-pilot, who would smile nervously when Steven banked the plane off its flight path.

Instead he'd gone away to college to study with professors who were the kind of guys who made his father thump the breakfast table when he read his morning paper. Steven swopped the high-wired Air Force compounds for the freedom of campuses in London and New York, and set about systematically and deliberately erasing his past, re-creating himself from scratch. It was a corny, predictable kind of rebellion until *Alphabet City*. The publication of the book had changed everything, and even his father would have been impressed, if he hadn't got himself killed on the day when his manuscript was accepted for publication. Ever since then, Steven had had a prickly, uneasy feeling about coincidence.

When Steven woke up his ears hurt and the plane was bumping down giant steps of turbulence towards LaGuardia airport. The stewardess whispered that he should fasten his seat belt. His publishers, Anton and Zucker, had arranged that there would be a limousine and a publicist waiting to meet him, to take him on to his hotel. In every city they gave him a different escort to make sure he showed up for appointments and interviews, and always the first few hours with them were the hardest. The escorts

7

would have diligently read his book beforehand and they'd
always try to prove it by talking about specific details, the
drug-store hold-up, his love affair with Lucretia the
hooker, the ritual gang murder he'd witnessed in the
basement on Avenue D. Steven always had to make it
clear early that he didn't discuss these things unless the
red on-air light was glowing. They were usually college
students making a little extra money, and when he grunted
at them, or simply refused to answer their questions,
they'd get embarrassed and launch into some detail of the
itinerary and the subject would never be raised again.

As the plane swooped down over the East River, Steven
consulted his New York schedule. His New York publicist
was called Natalie; she was a sociology graduate. He
closed his eyes and waited for the thud of the wheels on
the tarmac, filled with dread at the idea of an escort who
was also a sociology student. His copies of *Alphabet City*
nesting down there in the hold, hurt like a sore place on
his body.

### 3

'I majored in sociology,' Natalie Kishon said, as they
splashed down the airport slip road in the limousine
Anton and Zucker had hired for him. 'You should have
seen my old professor's face when I told him I was going
to meet you in person. He's recommending your books
to all his students now.'

Steven wiped a hole in the condensation on the limousine window and stared out at the streets of New York. He
hadn't been back for almost a year. A blizzard had just
blown over, and the last of the snow was glistening like
brown sugar in doorways and in gutters. There was a light
drizzle falling and New York looked feverish, like a city in

a cold sweat. As the limousine climbed the arc of the Queensboro Bridge, Steven narrowed his eyes and the lights of Manhattan looked like the inner workings of some fantastic electrical machine.

'I'd just like to say right now', Natalie said quickly, 'that I loved your book and when I got to the end I cried for a whole day. I guess you'd think I'm saying this because it's my job but I really mean it. I believe that what you did was so right. And so . . . necessary.' She took a deep breath and smiled. 'There, I said it.'

'Thank you. Which hotel am I staying at?'

'The UN Plaza,' Natalie said, still with misty reverence in her voice. She was staring at the side of Steven's face in the half-light. 'And I know this sounds like, aaaagh, but I feel like I know you already. Like I've known you for a long time.'

The limo got held up in a bad-tempered queue on FDR Drive. Horns began to blare. Steven turned to Natalie and put his hand on hers. She had big round glasses, a neat, open face.

'Well, let me tell you something, Natalie,' he said. 'You don't know me at all. Not even remotely. Whatever you read about me in the book you can forget as of this second. The more you find out about me, the more you'll find to dislike.'

Steven could see that Natalie was mistaking his honesty for cute modesty, that what he was saying was only making things worse, but he continued anyway.

'It would be a great help to me if, while we're together, you treated me just like anyone else, like someone who writes recipe books. And you should know that my least favourite topic of conversation in the whole world is *Alphabet City*. My second least favourite is sociology.'

They drove in silence after that until they arrived at the door of the UN Plaza hotel, opposite the United Nations

9

building. A doorman in ear muffs opened the door of the limo and welcomed Steven to New York. At the check-in desk, Natalie fussed with her papers and gave Steven an updated itinerary with lots of new appointments added. She said that she'd see him next morning at ten at the studios of Radio WK210 in Murray Hill for his first live interview.

'You want anything else, Mr Hawthorne, anything at all, you just call. Call me at home too if you need to. I volunteered for this assignment and I just can't wait for it to start. I'm treating the next four days as part of my education.'

Steven thanked her with a smile that he tried to hide, and then took his case to the elevator. When the elevator doors closed, he took a deep breath, like a man about to submerge himself in cold water for a very long time.

# Chapter Two

**1**

The beat of the music sounded like a wooden hammer beating on hollow metal. The DJ danced in his chair and then pulled the fader down.

'*This* . . . is Radio WK210.'

The DJ smiled at Steven then at Natalie and let the music swell. He dipped it again.

'Coming up my special guest is Steven Hawthorne, the man who took it to the wire . . .'

The DJ whooped. The music was making him vibrate like a bean on the skin of a drum.

'Hey, and if you think I'm sounding just a little weary this morning it's because I was up till way past four reading this guy's book. The last ten pages I cried like a little baby. If you live in New York you'd better listen to what Steven has to say. We're going to meet him, right after these.'

The DJ pushed a cartridge button and an ad began to play. He took off his headphones and his body deflated, like a surfer beached on a wave. He eased down a fader then he stretched out his arms and gasped.

'Did they give you guys coffee?'

Natalie nodded her head, with her folder clutched in her lap. Steven lit a cigarette. The ad had the soft beat of a drum and the voice of a stage Red Indian.

'You want to give me some level?' the DJ asked.

Steven leant into a microphone, tugged it into position on its stiff steel arm and counted aloud. He flicked the first of his ash onto the carpet. The studio looked like the scene of a party that happened twenty years ago, and then was left to rot.

'It's true about the book, Steven,' the DJ said with a grin, adjusting Steven's level as Steven counted eight, nine, ten.

'I'm glad you liked it.'

'One more time.'

'I'm glad you liked it,' Steven said, a little louder. The DJ played with Steven's fader then hit a button on his stack and another ad began to play. A Chinese voice. Pancakes.

'Hit me right between the eyes,' the DJ said. 'I guess New York is just eating you up.' He looked directly at Natalie. 'You taking him to WNK2?'

Natalie consulted her schedule.

'Day after tomorrow,' she said, glancing at Steven to get his permission.

'They know you brought him here first?'

Natalie blushed and smiled and shook her head.

'Ooooh, those guys hate to be second with a story,' the DJ said and he used his elbow to hit another button. There was a huge explosion. It sounded to Steven like the sound of a B52 bombing run heard from a long way away. He'd heard lots in the North African desert. It was an ad for a discount furniture store in Poughkeepsie. Pushing buttons was an effortless punctuation in the DJ's conversation.

'I used to have a place down by Stuyvesant Square Park', he said, angling a shiny CD against the half-light to read the track number. 'Took a stroll into Alphabet City myself a couple of times. It was daylight but my ass was like a camera shutter. That place is pretty fucked up.'

'I'd like another coffee,' Steven said. 'If that's possible.'

'Sure it's possible.'

The DJ picked up a phone and ordered coffee. The next ad had a woman screaming and moaning, faking an orgasm, while a voice-over talked about cream cheese.

'I used to see a guy down there,' the DJ said, with a sly smile. 'A guy called Polka. This is six, seven years ago. He wore military stuff on his coat, medals from Vietnam. He used to beg for quarters . . .'

A voice from somewhere in the ceiling, bored and flat, said, 'This is the news room. You got thirty seconds you can give me?'

The DJ flicked a switch and said wearily, 'News room, go to hell.' He grinned at Steven, as if Steven would know how crazy that was. 'The guy I remember used to have like a wooden stick. Used to use it like a phoney flute. I saw him begging for quarters every day. That the same guy?'

The DJ settled the CD into its slot and the machine sucked it in. The DJ got himself ready for the red light, the next big wave.

'Same guy as what?' Steven said.

'Same guy as the guy in your book. The guy you call Polo. It sure sounded like the same guy. You say Polo wore the Purple Heart and used to sing cowboy songs. Old Polka used to do that too when he was begging for quarters. Is that him?'

Steven nodded his head but shrugged at the same time. He could feel Natalie's eager stare on the side of his face.

'Didn't tell this guy about my promise of confidentiality,' he said softly.

Natalie stammered that Anton and Zucker had made an undertaking that actual identities of the people described in the book would remain confidential and that no

13

attempts would be made to identify any of the real protagonists.

The voice in the ceiling said, 'Five seconds.'

The DJ put on his headphones. 'I was just talking off the record,' he said as he caressed a fader.

'On or off the record, I don't use real names,' Steven said quickly.

The DJ raised a fader and the air was filled with the sound of a jet-engine and the rasp of electronic machine-guns, the station ident.

'Steven Hawthorne, welcome to the show.'

'Hello.'

'Well, Steven, shit, you are one brave guy.'

Steven was about to laugh and say whatever came into his head but the DJ pressed a button and there was a round of applause, people whooping and stamping. It lasted for five seconds.

'Sure,' the DJ said, softly, 'one brave guy. This is the guy who lived a whole year in Alphabet City, dealing crack cocaine and he lived to tell us his story. You were down on Avenue D, that right Steven?'

'Avenue D, then East 14th.'

The DJ suddenly dropped his chin into his chest and his voice dropped so low it was almost inaudible.

'That's the . . . baaaaaadlands,' he growled.

According to Natalie this station had a good reach, good coverage in the white suburbs, *Alphabet City*'s target market. The morning slot had a good profile because this guy had a reputation for being crazy and people liked to hear him being crazy every morning. To secure your piece of air-time in New York City, to be sure of an audience, you had to have an angle, you had to be insane. Natalie said it was a good, solid start to the assault on the city.

'I mean, the real badlands,' the DJ growled. Then he smiled. 'So how d'you survive in the badlands, Steven?'

'Like I say in the book,' Steven said, pulling the steel arm of the microphone closer to his mouth, 'it was kind of like I had to change all my preconceptions. I had to . . .'

The DJ broke in.

'If you haven't read *Alphabet City* for yourself, Steven changed his name. Got himself a street name. What d'you call yourself, Steven?'

'I called myself Thomas Bolivar.'

'And a buddy of yours got himself shot, that right?'

'That's right,' Steven said. The DJ waited and the two seconds of silence throbbed like an eternity. Silence was an obscenity.

'Guess it still hurts to talk about it, huh?' the DJ said.

'Sometimes.'

More silence.

'OK, OK, we got more from Steven Hawthorne and the story of his odyssey into the underworld of the big Alphabet, right after this . . .'

The DJ hit a CD cartridge and took off his headphones.

'You OK?' he said after he had dimmed the sound of the music.

'Yeah, I'm fine.'

'You OK talking about the dead guy?'

Steven looked at Natalie who was biting her lip.

'Whatever. I'll talk about whatever,' Steven said.

The DJ cooed, 'Good, good,' as he inspected another CD. 'After the record I'll ask you some shit about the gang hierarchy. What's that stuff I read . . .' The DJ found a copy of *Alphabet City* under a pile of CD sleeves and cartridges. In the half-light, only the silver lettering shone out. The copy looked unread. '. . . some stuff on the back . . . you're a sociologist, right?'

'That's right.'

'So we'll do some stuff about the structure of the gangs.

15

Like an academic angle. Then I'll ask you some more about the Haitian guy who you saw being shot. Pilot?'

'In the book I call him Pilot . . .'

'OK. Sure as hell would like to know if your guy Polo is that guy Polka. He was a real fucking character.'

Steven looked at Natalie. She shrugged. The DJ looked up at the clock on the wall and made a fast calculation.

'I just got time to take a piss,' he said and he inelegantly extricated himself from a tangle of wires, shook his hair and whooped. Before he pulled open the air-lock door he turned to Steven and said softly, 'You got something to say, Mr Hawthorne. Don't you clam up on me now. You want to sell books, you've got to open your mouth and speak.'

## 2

After Steven and Natalie had finished their interview at WK210, they took a cab to the head office of Anton and Zucker, a twenties tower block on Madison Avenue. The plan was that Steven would meet Foley, the editor-in-chief who was overseeing the publication of *Alphabet City*. They arrived early because the interview at WK210 had been cut short by mutual agreement, and now Steven and Natalie sat like intruders in the huge, exquisitely furnished boardroom on the 34th floor that was booked for an hour in Steven's name.

Natalie poured two coffees and sat down opposite him at an enormous varnished desk which had seats for twenty people. The view from the office window was of boats and islands on the East River and across to the shoreline at Greenpoint. There was a fleet of rusting barges with dislocated cranes taking waste out to the ocean, moving as slowly as the current. Natalie blew into her fringe.

'That was a pretty bad start,' Steven said.

Natalie seemed startled. Steven hadn't spoken at all since the end of the interview.

'You think so?' she said.

'Yes I think so.'

After the DJ had returned from taking his piss, he had whooped and hollered and showered Steven with praise and then he had drifted back onto the topic of his old buddy Polka from Stuyvesant Park, live on air. He'd done it with a smile on his face, while Natalie had cut the air with her hands, waving at him that this topic was out of bounds.

'I can't promise,' Natalie whispered – the boardroom had a spotless grandeur that made raised voices sacrilegious – 'but from now on I'll make the point about confidentiality right off and I'll get it in writing. But I think you should understand . . .' She seemed to be having trouble getting to the point she wanted to make. She pushed her hair away from her face and looked at him with a pained expression. 'Now you're back here in this city, it's kind of inevitable that people are going to start making connections.'

Steven checked his watch. Foley was due at twelve. Then there was another live radio at two, something else at four and the *Village Voice* at six. Then at seven he'd try to make it to his grandmother's place on Long Island early enough so that he could leave before ten without being impolite. He needed to see her because there were some things that he had to get straightened out with her. The thought of going back to his grandmother's place after so much had happened had been bothering him all day. But getting off the island of Manhattan, even for a few hours, would be a relief.

'Connections,' Steven said. 'That's why New York bothers me so much.'

Natalie gave him a look of deep compassion, a look which he diverted by staring out of the window. To the south, before the curve of the East River, he could just see the jumble of stained clay and sand that made up the rooftops of Alphabet City. In the book he'd made the point that the distance between Madison and the ghetto was a flight that wouldn't exhaust a mosquito: shared blood on the insect's jaws.

'I guess a lot of these guys don't understand,' Natalie said softly. 'For them your book is just another cop show. They just want the body count.'

Steven said nothing. Outside a light drizzle had begun to fall. When Foley arrived, his beige macintosh was stained grey with rain around the collar and shoulders. He wiped his hair dry and shook his sleeves and cursed the weather.

'Steven, welcome to New York,' he said with a grin. The air around him smelt of freezing air. He took off his coat and helped himself to coffee from the jug. 'So how you making out? I heard you this morning. Sounded pretty good. That guy is crazy isn't he?'

Foley had thin, wispy, blond hair that was plastered to his head, and his eyes glistened with false emotions.

'Could I speak to you alone?' Steven said. Foley had hardly sat down.

'Alone?'

'Natalie, could you just give Mr Foley and me a second?'

Natalie hesitated. Foley shrugged and nodded and she collected up her papers before she left the office in silence. After she had closed the door, Steven stood up and looked out of the window across at the barges drifting on the river.

'If you people can't give me cast-iron guarantees,' Steven said, 'then the publicity tour is off.'

He turned around to see Foley's face struck by lightning.

'Say again, Steven?'

'I need guarantees.'

'Guarantees of what?'

'Every page of *Alphabet City* has detailed descriptions of friends of mine breaking the law. Every law. Don't you understand that?'

'Steven, I don't know what you are talking about.'

Steven looked out of the window again.

'The first fucking interview I have in this city, some guy starts pumping me for names. Real names. If people start to make what Natalie calls "connections", then I will be putting those people in real jeopardy. Not just from the police but from the enforcement of the laws that they live by.'

He turned around and Foley was blushing scarlet. He was looking down at his folder and blinking quickly.

'It was the first fucking stipulation I made,' Steven said.

Foley puffed out his cheeks and tried to gather his thoughts. He hadn't even had chance to deliver his well-rehearsed (mock bashful) little speech about how *Alphabet City* was the finest work of non-fiction he'd read for ten years.

'You're talking about the interview this morning? WK210?'

'Whatever the fuck it was called.'

Foley examined his papers as if there were an explanation written there.

'Well I heard the interview myself, Steven . . .'

'Sure you did.'

'And I have to say I think you're being a little unreasonable.'

'I *am* unreasonable. You'll find that out. This is how this thing is going to be. I have to have guarantees of absolute confidentiality.'

What seemed to puzzle Foley was that Steven had sounded tranquil on air. He had arrived at the offices of Anton and Zucker thinking that at last he had an author who could handle crazy DJs like the one at WK210.

'Then I can give you those guarantees,' Foley said. 'Unequivocal. Maybe Natalie didn't make the point strongly enough before you went on air. She's kind of inexperienced.'

'It wasn't Natalie's fault. She's OK.'

Steven was still staring out of the window. He drummed the glass with his fingers for a while. Foley checked his watch and hoped that a few seconds' silence would seal the matter. Finally he said, 'Steven, I've booked us a table at a Japanese place around the corner.'

Steven instantly turned and grabbed his overcoat from the back of the chair and began to put it on.

'Is that OK?' Foley said.

'Let's go.'

Steven headed for the door and Foley quickly collected his papers and followed.

'There are some things I need to talk to you about over lunch,' Foley said.

'What things?'

When they emerged into the reception area, the two women who were operating the phones, and the post boy who was flirting with them, all fell silent. Steven Hawthorne was a hot item in Anton and Zucker, and the heat had penetrated all the way down to the temporaries and the desk staff. Foley was trotting along behind as Steven headed for the elevator.

'I need to talk about your personal biography,' Foley said. Steven hit the elevator call button. 'Your CV. The details we have on your background. There seems to be some confusion.'

The elevator arrived and they both stepped in. The back wall of the elevator was a full-length mirror and Steven examined himself in it.

'What do you mean, confusion?'

As the elevator began to fall through thirty-four floors, Foley wiped his brow and said he'd prefer to talk about it over lunch.

## Chapter Three

**1**

Foley ordered food for them both as he walked into the restaurant, before he had even taken off his coat. He did it out of Steven's earshot, with his hand clutching the tiny Japanese waitress's arm, as if the business of ordering food wasn't something that Mr Hawthorne should be troubled with. Then he ushered Steven to a reserved table with the earnest obsequiousness of a waiter on his first day. Steven's outburst had had the effect he'd hoped it would.

They had both been soaked by a fine, freezing drizzle, but Foley's anxiety had made him waterproof. He didn't seem to notice the rainwater dripping from his hair. He spread some papers out in front of him.

'OK, let's see here,' Foley said. His nervousness had increased but he was trying to make out that this was something routine. 'Like I say, there are some points about your . . . personal details . . . which I need to clear up.'

He approached the words 'personal details' like someone hopping over an anti-personnel mine.

'What about them?'

'Well, Steven, it's like this . . .'

Two glasses of iced water arrived just in time for Foley to take a few extra seconds to prepare for his next leap. Foley would have dealt with pain-in-the-ass authors before. He kept his job because he never looked them in the eye and told them to go to hell. He kept his job because he was genuinely eager to please, desperate to avoid unpleasantness. Steven decided that Foley would be a breeze.

'I have here the personal history that your agent in London sent through to us.'

Foley handed Steven a photocopied sheet. *Alphabet City* had been picked up first by a literary agent in London called Warren Kanavros, a friend of a friend who knew gold when he saw it.

'And we sent it out to all the magazine editors who we thought might want to run a feature on you.'

Foley began to shuffle through some more papers. When he wanted to hide, he hid in his papers. His face had turned scarlet again. Finally he 'found' a sheet he'd had in his hand all along.

'And you see, Steven, one of the magazines we sent this to was a magazine called *True Society*.'

An alarm bell began to ring in Steven's head.

Foley handed Steven the sheet he had in his hand. It was a photocopy of the biog, but this copy had scribbles all down the margin. Steven recognized the spidery handwriting straight away.

'This is what the editor of *True Society* sent us back. He says he knows you. His name is . . .'

'Anderson,' Steven said.

'That's right.'

Steven looked at the scribbled comments. There were a lot of exclamation marks and question marks and a rash of profanities at the end. Steven stared at the sheet for a long time with horror, and then he made a fast decision and began to laugh out loud. He laughed for a long time and then handed the sheet back to Foley.

'That little shit, Anderson,' Steven said with a broad gesture of contempt and affection.

23

'So you do know him?'

'We were at college together. Same class.'

Two plastic dishes of raw fish arrived, pink and white and brown, glistening with oil. Foley's face had the same sheen from rainwater and sweat.

'So what, this is some kind of joke?' Foley said.

'You could say that.'

'I don't understand.'

'What don't you understand?'

Steven took a sliver of fish in his fingers and put it in his mouth and smiled again. Foley was more nervous than ever.

'I don't understand if what this guy Anderson says about you is true or if what the biography your agent sent us is true.'

Steven wiped his hand on his trousers. The alarm bells were ringing louder this time.

'Please don't worry about Anderson,' Steven said.

Foley tried to pick up some fish of his own but the raw salmon slipped between his chopsticks. He looked down at the defaced biography.

'Anderson and I were rivals,' Steven said. 'From way back when we were studying together at Dartmouth. He just can't stand the idea that I got a book published before he did. He can't stand the idea that he's still editing some crummy magazine . . . what the fuck is it called . . .'

'*True Society*.'

'Right. *True Society*. Believe it or not, Mr Foley, sociologists are worse than divas. Long nails. Bitches.'

Foley and Steven began to eat in silence. A whole minute passed while Foley tried to think of a way to frame his question. The weight of it was like a mudslide waiting to engulf the table. Finally he took refuge in his papers. He turned the defaced biography around and frowned at it.

'So . . .' he squeaked, 'I can just . . . go ahead with the biog we have?'

'Yes.'

'And this stuff from Anderson about you not actually getting your MA and the stuff about your father and your wife is all untrue?'

'It's all irrelevant,' Steven said, with the first trace of irritation.

More silence.

'But is it true?'

'It is beside the fucking point. I did what I did. You think the guys down in Alphabet City wanted to see my academic qualifications? Anderson is just pissed off because I put into practice what he can only theorize about. Sociability theory, changeability theory, it's all bullshit. I did what I did. If Anderson wants to write fucking graffiti then that's his problem.'

Foley had begun to fuel his anxiety with raw fish. He was shovelling it into his mouth two, three strips at a time.

'And the stuff he says about your father being a fighter pilot, not civilian ground crew . . .'

'What the fuck difference does that make?'

'It's just the class thing. You talk about class a lot. A feature writer is going to want these things nailed. If your father was a fighter pilot then that's something we should get right.'

Steven thought about standing up and leaving the restaurant. Instead he sighed heavily and peered up at the ceiling. Foley consulted his notes again.

'Maybe you should take this stuff away with you and go through it and maybe check that the details we have are all correct,' he said, unhappy even with his own compromise.

Steven thought about it for a while and then took hold of Anderson's sheet, folded it up and put it in his pocket with great purpose, as if he had been mortally offended. Foley was emboldened by the way Steven had co-operated.

'Especially the stuff about your wife,' Foley said quickly, hoping he'd get away with it if he said it fast enough. 'The feature people will want to know either way about your wife. We have you down as single.'

Foley finished up his fish in silence. After he had guzzled some water and cooled his throat, he said that in spite of what Anderson at *True Society* had said, he had still wanted to give Steven an interview.

'He was very insistent about that,' Foley said. 'He said that he can't wait to meet up with you again. It's not a magazine we would normally suggest but as he's a friend of yours . . .'

### 2

The reporter from the *Village Voice* wanted to know how Steven felt about people describing him as the Dickens of New York, the chronicler of the New York underclass.

'What people?' Steven said.

'Me.'

'This is your analogy?'

The reporter from the *Village Voice* smiled. She had long, cherry-coloured hair and lips like an Italian tomato. They both had their elbows on the table of a café in Greenwich Village. Natalie had collected Steven from the Japanese restaurant in a cab and Foley had taken her to one side and spoken sharply and quietly to her while Steven waited in the back of the taxi. Now Natalie was sitting at a far table, reading the papers that the café left out for customers to read. The lady from the *Village Voice* had insisted that she conduct her interview with Steven in private and had sent Natalie out of earshot. She read her papers diligently on the edge of Steven's vision, trying hard not to exist. Occasionally she glanced up at the cherry-coloured hair of the reporter. Outside the air had turned misty grey, with a steely wind that promised snow.

'I was considering the Dickens analogy as a way of nailing you down,' the reporter said and her smile turned into a grin. She had put her face close to Steven's face and he could smell her perfume. Steven was good-looking, handsome enough for his face to make an overwhelming first impression, and his diffidence attracted women's curiosity like a letter marked 'confidential'. All through his life he had somehow managed to inspire recklessness in the women he met, especially women he'd only known for a few hours. When they got to know him better, when they realized that beyond his silence there was more silence, like the endless Arctic wastes, they usually abandoned their quest, planted their flag and left. For the moment the feature writer from the *Village Voice* was still as curious as hell.

'It's just that you're not what I expected,' she said, curling her legs around the table leg. 'I read your biography and, I don't know, I expected someone a little more weird.'

'I'm pretty weird.'

She snorted into her coffee and said that she had to keep reminding herself what it was that Steven had done. She said that it was just too unrealistic, that not only was he a hero but he looked like a hero too. She wanted to make sure that Anton and Zucker would provide photographs for the article, because otherwise no one would believe it. Then she asked why a guy like Steven had never married.

'Are you gay?' she said. He guessed that she had a

27

reputation for getting right to the head of the nail. Steven shook his head.

'I *am* married,' he said, stretching his arms and studying the polite street life of Greenwich Village through the café window. The lady from the *Village Voice* looked puzzled and consulted her photocopied sheet of Steven's personal biography. Steven looked at it too.

'I told Anton and Zucker that I was single because I wanted to cut loose from all the crap that went before,' he said casually. 'I wanted to enter this arena with no past at all. I wanted to just be a body and a face. Like I was an ingredient in an experiment. I didn't want people like you asking me questions about it. I didn't want the focus to be something like "What kind of person would do something like that?"'

It was the most he had said during the entire interview. He'd worked out his explanation after his lunch with Foley, realizing that Anderson's intervention meant he would have to tell the truth and he would need to be consistent in all his interviews. For some reason, before New York, the subject had never arisen. Anderson had presented Steven with a bump in the road, but it was nothing Steven couldn't handle, nothing he couldn't turn to his advantage.

'So you don't take questions about your past?'

'That's not what I'm saying.' The lady from the *Village Voice* shook her cherry-coloured hair and made a temple of her fingers over the table. She became mock serious.

'You sure know how to make a person curious,' she said and Steven laughed. There was stuff he could reveal, stuff he would keep to himself. Maybe Anderson had done him a favour.

'My wife was English. We lived together in London before I came over to New York. She was a sociologist too. We graduated together and married when we were just kids and naturally when we both grew up the marriage kind of wore off, like 'flu. We're still married legally but in reality it ended way before I decided to go down into Alphabet City.'

She automatically began to scribble on her notepad. Steven grabbed her hand.

'Do you really want to trivialize this whole thing?'

The lady from the *Village Voice* looked at Steven's hand on hers then she smiled.

'Whatever you say, Mr Hawthorne.'

She crossed out what she had written with an elaborate gesture and a shake of her mane.

'Ask me again about Dickens,' Steven said.

'You like that analogy?'

'No I hate it. But ask me about it and I'll give you a hundred reasons why I hate it.'

For the rest of the interview, they talked about Hawthorne as a latter-day Dickens, as the conscience of a whole city, venturing where no other white New Yorker would dare to go. She asked about guns and drugs and prostitution and Steven gave the same answers he'd given a dozen times before, a kind of animated mantra which by now had lost all meaning. After it was over, the reporter from the *Village Voice* left and Steven flopped down in a chair beside Natalie. She carried on reading her paper.

'How was she?' Natalie said, as if she didn't really give a damn.

'She was fine.'

'I didn't recognize her. Last time she interviewed one of my clients she was blonde.'

'Is that right?'

'It looked from here as though she liked you.'

'Am I finished for the day?'

Natalie folded her paper and said that he was. Then she said casually that he had the rest of the evening free and that if he wanted, if he didn't have anything else to do, then maybe they could go and eat somewhere and they could go through his itinerary one more time. She blinked at him, her soft brown eyes full of longing. Steven said that he was tired and that he needed to rest and that Natalie should go home.

'OK. It was just a thought.'

'Another time.'

'Sure. Do you need a cab anywhere?'

'No. I'll just take a walk around.'

Natalie tore a page from her clipboard and then quickly went through his next day's appointments. She seemed reluctant to leave but Steven finally told her that she should go home. She left the café and he waited a long time to make sure she'd disappeared before he hailed a cab and asked for Penn Station. He hadn't told Natalie that he was going to visit his grandmother on Long Island because no one at Anton and Zucker even knew that he had a grandmother. He needed to keep it that way, for as long as possible.

### 3

The train from Penn Station to Southampton, Long Island, passed over some of the toughest neighbourhoods in New York. The train line was raised up above the bewildering jungle of sandstone tenements and flooded basements and burnt-out cars. The burnt-out cars were like monuments, the black, scorched grills and hoods sneering at their own fate. The parallel streets, swept of rubble, looked like footage of Berlin in 1945.

'. . . the rotting molars at the back of New York City's smile . . .'

Steven had been pleased with some of the work he had put into *Alphabet City*, at least with the language he had used. He put his head against the train window and looked out at the decaying city through his own reflection. Then, as the sun set, the tenements turned into steelyards and docks, and then rotting suburbs, and then neat lines of white-wood one-storey houses. The journey to South-ampton had been one he'd made many times when he had been living at his grandmother's place.

His grandmother was expecting him and when he ar-rived at her door a little after seven-thirty, she stood on tiptoes and hugged him around the chest. Her lively blue eyes sparkled with tears of joy. Steven had lived with her for a year and a half and his stay at her house had been a brief but joyous interlude for her amidst twenty years of solitude. Her bungalow was dark and smelt of age and baking. On the mantelpiece there were photographs of Steven's father in his Air Force uniform, photographs of his father and his mother on their wedding day, photo-graphs of Steven's graduation. On the TV set there was another portrait of Steven's father, looking stern, on the day they made him into a Major, and behind that a cute little full-length shot of Steven as a six-year-old, in a home-made blue uniform all of his own, saluting the camera. The living room had been turned into a shrine to the family, his father and mother now saints in heaven, Steven a living reminder of his father's glory.

'Steven, it's been so long. So long. Come on. Come and look. See . . .'

She hurried Steven into the kitchen, past the study which she had made for him when he was living there, his desk and typewriter still in place, waiting for Steven to resume his studies. She pointed out into the little, over-grown yard at a pine bird-house which had been nailed to the apple tree that was twisting, unpruned, over the patio.

'Mr Librevsky made it for me. I had two finches in there the whole summer.'

It had been a ritual every morning that his grandmother would put out cake crumbs and strips of bacon fat for the brightly coloured birds that used to swarm in the garden. Steven had often watched them without seeing as they quarrelled for the food, sitting alone at his desk, tap-tapping away like a stone mason at the monolith that would become *Alphabet City*.

Steven's grandmother was so overcome at Steven's return that she was trying to do six different things all at once. There was a cake to be taken out of the oven (she was a famous baker), there were photographs of the beach to be shown, there was mail which had arrived after Steven had left. Steven took hold of her around the shoulders and said that if she didn't sit down and relax right now he'd get right back on the train to New York. She sat down in a huge armchair, which engulfed her. Steven sat down too and took out a large brown envelope, the purpose of his visit.

'When Dad died,' he said, 'Air Force welfare sent me this.'

He kept the envelope on his lap while his Grandmother prepared herself for the subject of her son's death. Steven could see that she had promised herself she wouldn't cry. The accident had happened nine months before, when Steven's father had been instructing trainee pilots over the desert in Saudi Arabia. His jet had hit a dune in a fireball sixty miles from Riyadh. Steven had only ever spoken to his grandmother about it over the phone. Now the house seemed darker than he remembered it, and his grandmother seemed smaller and more ragged. He knew that the death would have hollowed her out and that in nine months since it happened it had eaten away at her like a cancer. Finally, when she was composed, he handed her the envelope.

'It's some of his personal things. It feels like there are some medals in there too. I didn't open it. I thought it would be better if you had it.'

She took the envelope without fuss and placed it on the mantelpiece, as if it were some inconsequential piece of correspondence. Steven's grandmother had never taken sides in the disputes between Steven and his father, which first started when Steven went to college instead of enrolling on the USAF induction. His father had paid his fees and grumbled intermittently for five years, but when Steven wrote and told him that he was leaving college before his MA examinations, there was silence, like the silence between lightning and thunder, except the thunder never came. There was just more silence, which lasted until his death.

In that time, his grandmother had taken Steven in and fussed over him and tried to help him make up his mind what he wanted to do with his life and she even once profaned family tradition by trying to get Steven and his father to talk to each other. Nothing ever came of it, but she had always stayed scrupulously loyal to both of them. When Steven thought about his paternal family he thought of a small group of stone statues, close together but never quite touching. If you wanted to know about them, you had to read the inscription. Steven had to guess that his grandmother didn't want to open the envelope in his presence in case Steven saw that as taking sides. He wanted to take it off the mantelpiece, rip it open and pour the contents into her lap and shout out loud: 'You see what that bastard did to me, you see what he made me do just to prove that I was brave too.'

'Are you OK, Grandma?' Steven said.

She said that she was. Then she said quickly she had made up Steven's bed and that she knew what he had said but that if he'd changed his mind he was welcome to stay there with her for as long as he liked. Steven said that he'd like that but that they both knew it wasn't a good idea.

'I have a lot of appointments in the city,' Steven said. 'The book . . .' The mention of it chilled the air.

'I heard you on the radio,' she said, pretending that she was pleased.

'Yeah, you'll be hearing a lot of me on the radio, Grandma. That's the other reason I came here.'

She gave him a look of great pity and for a moment her features were exactly the same as his father's features, except the expression wasn't one he'd ever seen on his father's face. Then she struggled out of the armchair and said that she could smell something burning in the kitchen, even though the cake was only half baked. She wanted to avoid the subject of the book, because she was the only other person in the whole world who knew the truth. The only person in the whole world apart from Steven who knew the truth about Polo and about Pilot, the drug-store hold-up, the murder in the basement. Steven stood up and took her by the arm as gently as he could.

'Please don't worry, Grandma,' he said. 'No one knows about you. No one knows who you are or where you live. I won't let anyone get you involved in any of this. You won't have to say anything because no one will ask. I promise.'

She smiled up at Steven with tender forgiveness and they spent the next two hours eating cake and talking about the birds and the blizzard that was due and everything else that had no relevance to what they were both thinking.

## Chapter Four

'*As I looked down from the train compartment that morning across the wasteland, I saw Alphabet City for what it is. A slab of concrete tundra, and the people who inhabit it are survivors, people who have had to learn how to survive in this human harshness, harsher than any extreme of climate. Remember those plane crash survivors who ate each other? Well Alphabet City was suddenly a piece of Andean mountainside and the only way to survive is to tear the guy next to you into pieces and roast his flesh over your zippo lighter.*'

Steven turned the pages of his book and read with his head bowed. He didn't care to look up and face the audience but he could hear them sniffing and coughing and occasionally whispering. This was his first reading in New York, and he was standing on a podium on the second floor of the Barnes and Noble Bookstore on Broadway and 82nd. There was seating for eighty people, hardbacked chairs placed in rows, and every seat was filled. There were also people squatting on the floor and perching on the window ledge, and beyond them, Steven could see the bright early-morning sunlight that was dazzling the street outside.

'*Most of Manhattan is a stockade. Just as surely as when the Dutch and the British, dissolute renegades and free thinkers, lived their desperate lives behind walls of sharpened timber. Beyond those walls live the untamed tribes of Haitians, Hispanics, Jamaicans. And we inside the stockade know as much about the lives of those people as the first settlers knew about the lives of the Wampanoag and Narragansett Indians.'*

Steven thought he heard someone near the back whisper 'bullshit' but the sound was masked by the horn of a taxi cab outside. He buried his head in his book again. There were fifty copies of it on a rack beside him and the silver lettering and the maroon covers made a larger pattern all of their own. Later he would take each copy and sign the inside. The sunlight outside was being magnified by the windows and he had begun to sweat.

*'In* Bonfire of the Vanities, *Tom Wolfe has the Mayor of New York declare, "Go to the frontiers you gutless wonders!" He was of course talking about the Bronx, Washington Heights, Alphabet City. His appeal inspired me. That is why I set out on my own odyssey into the violent, violated underworld of New York City.'*

Steven closed his book. There was silence for a few moments followed by polite applause. Natalie was standing at the back of the seating area with her clipboard in her hand. Beside her was the manager of the bookstore who had been listening to the reading with his lips squeezed between his fingers, his curtain of blond hair falling over his eyes as he angled his head to look more intently. When the reading finished he encouraged the applause and then hurried to join Steven on the podium.

He put his hand on Steven's shoulder and whispered in his ear. 'What's it to be, you OK to take Q and A?'

When Steven had arrived at the bookstore, ten minutes late and weary from lack of sleep, he had horrified Natalie and the manager by saying that he wasn't sure that he wanted to take questions and answers after the reading.

He'd been through Q and A in every other city, dealt with it a hundred times, but in New York it was going to be different. They persuaded him that he should make up his mind after he had finished the reading so he could get a measure of his audience.

'Sure, why not,' Steven said. He'd seen that the chairs were filled mostly with people who looked like students. That had relaxed him a little. Foley had called the previous night and said that he'd heard a rumour that there were some 'activists' sniffing around the book. Foley didn't explain what kind of 'activists' they were but he made them sound like a virus.

A hand was raised.

'Mr Hawthorne, did you go to Alphabet City as a researcher or as a tourist?'

'I went to Alphabet City as a human being. I went to find out what it was like.'

The girl who asked the question was sitting cross-legged on the floor. Steven had learned that the first question always set the tone for the rest. Hostility at the start soured the air, because audiences hunt in packs. An audience was a many-headed beast capable of only the simplest emotions.

'Did you ever cheat?' said a stout, short guy with a beard, who appeared to be in charge of a group of half a dozen students.

'Cheat? Cheat in what way?'

'Like they say George Orwell cheated. When he researched *Down and Out in Paris and London* they say he used to go home at weekends to get cleaned up. They say he used to borrow money from his friends.'

He looked around for approval. Steven had heard over the past few weeks that his book had developed something of a following on certain campuses. Students admired his courage. There was even talk that *Alphabet City* would become a set text as early as the fall semester. The short, stout guy probably wanted to prove that he was way ahead of them, starting the backlash early.

'No, I never cheated. And I'm not so sure that you have your facts right about Orwell. The way I remember it, writing that book killed him. He picked up a disease in a flop house and it killed him. How genuine do you need it to be?'

Steven didn't care to continue but someone picked up the thread and asked Steven how close he had come to death.

'Close enough.'

'Did you ever feel that you were cheating other people? Lying to them?'

'I had to lie to survive. Don't you lie to survive?'

'What I mean is, the part where you swap your stash of crack cocaine for the baking soda. You almost got your friend killed for doing that. Page 110.'

A few people began to flick through their copies of the book. On page 110, Steven described how he had been given an envelope of crack cocaine by a gang leader called Emilio while he was hanging out with Polo and Pilot on Avenue D. To keep his head, he had swopped the stash of crack for baking soda but Emilio had found it and blamed Polo for cheating on him.

'And on page 115 I saved Polo's life,' Steven said. 'Like I say, how genuine do you need me to be.'

After that, questions on specifics faded away. The audience sensed that Steven was still bruised, and that if they asked about specific people, he'd spit flames at them. His controlled venom, the idea that certain parts of the book were no-go areas, served to raise his credibility, as he knew it would. The questions came thick and fast about police corruption, state housing policy, immigration policy, the fourth wave, drug law, gun law. Steven had a stock answer for questions about firearms control which usually raised a smile.

'Guns and drugs are a lethal mixture. Self-fucking evidently . . .' A pause to let the profanity fizz in the air like a firework. 'Except we have it the wrong way round. Drugs should be legal, guns should be illegal. Without guns we'd have to express our rage in other ways. We'd have to resort to cutlery like they do in Europe. There is only so much damage you can do with a soup ladle.'

The answer, the mention of Europe, provoked an unexpected question. A lady in pink with a black felt hat pulled down over her eyes sitting near the front asked: 'Mr Hawthorne, you weren't raised in the United States were you?'

Steven explained that he was born in the US but had been raised all over the world. England, North Africa, the Middle East.

'And before you wrote the book, you only lived six months in New York.'

'That's right.'

'So do you think that gives you the right to pass comment on our beautiful city?'

There was a lot of sniggering from the students.

'I'm not passing comment. I am merely reporting what I experienced.'

The lady in the black felt hat looked slightly crazy. She had been fidgeting all through the reading. She looked around at the rest of the audience and mumbled: 'I don't know why we have to listen to him when he's not even a real American.'

She stood up and fussed with three Barnes and Noble plastic bags full of books, shaking with rage or embarrassment. The time it took her to leave made the rest of the audience smile behind their hands, and when she finally walked away, they were more on Steven's side than they

39

had been before. There were further questions about the cover Steven had used (he adopted the identity of a Cuban, the son of a refugee) and about the way in which justice and punishment were dispensed within the gang structure. Then a young guy lounging in the front row asked how it had felt to smoke crack cocaine for real.

'Can't describe it in words,' Steven said. 'To describe it I'd have to make a noise. It's like . . . whooooosh . . . like taking off in a jet fighter.'

The audience shone with awe.

'Habla Español?' said a lady three rows in. She had black hair, Hispanic features.

'Un poco. A little.'

'How come you survived in Alphabet City? How come you could pass yourself off as Hispanic?'

'Most of the chicanos I hung out with spoke very little Spanish. The Haitians spoke French. Besides, when I say "a little", I'm being ironic. I speak Spanish very well. And my colouring and black hair make it feasible that I am of Spanish descent. Indeed if you read my biography you'll see that my father was half Bolivian. He was adopted by an anglo family.'

The Hispanic lady then asked in Spanish if Steven was happy with the idea that he was now making vast amounts of money from the sale of a book which he had only been able to write by deceiving people, by exploiting people who lived on welfare. He answered in perfect Spanish that a percentage of the profits from the book were being donated to organizations working in the barrios. Steven then said in English that he didn't care to go into any more detail than that.

Steven could see that the Hispanic lady was shaking her head into her lap and when he had finished she looked up at him with disgust. He thought she was going to leave but he guessed that she didn't want to go the same way as the lady in the black felt hat. The audience were *his* gang now. After a few moments silence, another hand was raised. It was guy in a suit, late forties, with sandy-coloured hair and a face that looked like it was made from dry, cracked saddle leather. It struck Steven that this guy didn't belong here. It was a lightning impression that stuck.

'Mr Hawthorne,' the guy said, his voice a dry hiss. 'I'd like to ask you a question about the incident you describe on page 117 of your book.'

'One one seven?'

'Yes, Mr Hawthorne. The part where you witnessed a murder. The part where the guy you call Pilot is shot dead.'

Steven began to blink quickly and looked down at the podium. Some people in the audience began to flick through their copies again. Steven didn't need to refer to the book since he knew this particular page almost by heart. The moment when a dispute between Pilot and Emilio ended in Pilot being shot dead in a basement in Avenue D. On page 117, Steven watched from behind a heating boiler while Pilot was shot twice through the head, then burnt. The guy with the sandy hair stood up. He was tall and lean and powerfully built.

'What about it?' Steven said, changing the register of his voice, summoning his venomous and grave indifference.

'Well, Mr Hawthorne, I'm curious. You say that the guy with the deformed face . . . what was his name . . . ?'

'In the book I call him Emilio.'

'Emilio, that's right. You say the guy Emilio was one side of Pilot and the other guy . . . Polka?'

'Polo.'

'Polo. You say Polo was the other side of him holding

41

him by the left arm. Then you say that Emilio pulled his gun and shot Pilot twice through the head. That right?'

'Yes.'

'Through the side of the head?'

'I guess so.'

'I mean the killer is here, the guy Pilot is here and the other guy is here.'

The guy with the sandy hair placed each one with his hand, chopping out distances with his hand as a blade.

'That's about right,' Steven said. Outside a taxi cab screeched to a halt.

'And Emilio shot Pilot through the side of the head like this?'

The sandy-haired guy put two fingers to his temple and clicked his thumb like the hammer of a pistol. Steven nodded.

'That how it happened, Mr Hawthorne?'

'Yes.'

'So how come the bullet didn't pass through Pilot's head and into the other guy, Polo?'

There was an earnest look on the guy's face that almost made Steven smile. The intensity of his theatrics made Steven think that this guy was crazy like the lady in the black felt hat.

'Well I really don't know,' Steven said, 'maybe Polo ducked.'

There was a ripple of nervous laughter around the audience which Steven fed on. They were laughing at the big intense guy, not at the answer Steven had given. The guy with the sandy hair scratched his head but he wasn't embarrassed by the laughter at all.

'Polo ducked,' he said and he nodded his head. 'OK, I guess that makes sense. Just one more thing, Mr Hawthorne. Did you manage to get a good look at the gun Emilio used?'

42

Steven adopted a look of incredulity, hoping the audience would laugh again.

'I'm sorry?'

'What make of gun was used in the murder of the guy you call Pilot? In the rest of the book, you seem to have an admirable eye for detail, Mr Hawthorne. And you seem to have some knowledge of firearms . . .'

All through the book, Steven had been meticulous about detail when it came to weaponry, since in the pages of *Alphabet City*, Steven had been able to rise through the ranks of the gang because of his ability to repair and adapt firearms. His father had put Steven through the USAF firearm drill course when he was growing up, part of a special curriculum that his father had devised for him to pass the time behind the high-wired Air Force compounds. Steven could identify most hand guns just by feel, and he could disassemble and assemble most European- and American-made assault rifles in the dark. He also had what his daddy called a 'steel arm', which meant that he was a steady shot.

'You want to know the make of gun that was used to murder my best friend?' Steven said with disbelief in his voice.

'I was just wondering if you managed to catch sight of the gun. I realize that it must have been a pretty intense experience, Mr Hawthorne, but sometimes, when people are afraid, they tend to notice everything. Even the tiny details.'

Steven said nothing. The guy with the sandy hair had a cold stare that seemed to empty the room.

'It was dark down there,' Steven said finally and for the first time since he'd arrived at the store, he used his own voice, his own natural voice, not the one used for readings and for Q and A, which was cool and dismissive and weary.

'In the basement,' the sandy-haired guy said. 'You're saying that it was dark in the basement.'

'Yes.'

'Well was it an automatic? You say in the book that you were only, what was it, ten yards away when the guy was shot . . . so you must have been able to see if it was an automatic.'

Everyone had stopped shifting in their seats.

'Yes it was,' Steven said at last. 'Now you mention it, it was a 9mm automatic pistol.'

'A 9mm automatic.'

'Yes.'

'You sure about that? I mean, in the dark . . .'

'Yes I'm sure about that. Jesus.'

'Thank you, Mr Hawthorne.'

The guy was about to sit down and Steven pretended to laugh and said, 'That was a pretty strange question.'

The sandy-haired guy straightened up and smiled. 'Oh I guess it's a kind of hobby of mine. Guns. Ballistics.'

Steven nodded at him and then at the whole audience.

'Nice hobby,' he said. The sandy-haired guy cleared his throat. His stare was suddenly deadly.

'It's also my work,' he said softly.

The sandy-haired guy bent over to pick up his raincoat from between his knees. After he had ducked out of sight, there was silence, apart from the sound of taxi cabs hooting and the gentle tread of footsteps out on Broadway. Steven wiped a film of sweat from his face and looked across the lines of seats at Natalie and the manager of the store. They read his look of panic and the manager hurried to join him on the podium.

'OK, does anyone have any more questions for Mr Hawthorne?'

No hands were raised. The sandy-haired guy had already stood up and was putting on his coat.

44

'Then I guess that's it,' the manager said and there was a sparse outbreak of applause. The sandy-haired guy had raised his collar and he shuffled between two rows of seats and headed for the escalator down to the ground floor. Steven followed his progress all the way to the escalator, and watched as he slowly descended and then disappeared.

'Hey, you did fine,' Natalie said with a huge grin, pinching Steven's arm. Steven was still looking at the empty escalator.

'Yeah. It was OK. Who the hell was that last guy?'

The manager had left the podium and was shepherding people towards the rack of books. Steven's next task was to sign copies. Natalie laughed.

'We get all kinds of people at readings. Sometimes they're just people who want to get warm. In summer it's people who want to get cool. Maybe he was a gun nut. You should see this place when there's a book that's even within half a mile of anything to do with sex. With books like yours, we sometimes get gun nuts, or gang nuts.'

Steven could see a queue forming in front of a small desk which the manager had set up near to the escalator. Everyone in the queue had a copy of *Alphabet City* in their hands. The manager skipped back onto the podium and took Steven by the arm.

'You ready to give us some signatures, Mr Hawthorne?' he said with a smile. 'I know what a pain in the ass this is.'

'Jesus that's the biggest queue I've had so far,' Steven said.

'This is New York, Mr Hawthorne,' the manager said and Natalie rubbed Steven's arm as if she'd known him for years and was proud of him. When they set off towards the front of the queue, Natalie laughed and told the manager that Steven had been freaked out by the last guy who had asked all the questions about the gun.

'You mean the cop?' the manager said casually, as Steven took his seat.

'He was a cop?' Steven said.

'Sure. He was the first here. He introduced himself and said he was real anxious to hear you speak. I guess cops read books too.'

Natalie and the manager took their positions, flanking the desk, and Steven began to sign copies of his book, not even hearing all the nice things that people said to him.

## Chapter Five

**1**

Steven and Natalie had to get to Houston and 6th on the fringes of SoHo by eleven a.m. A documentary film crew wanted to interview him as part of a piece for *60 Minutes* about gang violence. Steven had been sought out as an expert with first-hand experience and to give the piece an academic angle. They wanted to interview him walking around the streets of one of Manhattan's most fashionable neighbourhoods, a kind of visual irony. They arrived and found a small film crew waiting, sipping steaming coffee from paper cups and taking turns sitting in the cab of their truck while they waited for the reporter to find the location ('She gets lost easily').

Foley arrived a little after eleven. The director told Steven he could relax for a while because they'd had word that 'Her Majesty' had been having trouble getting her car to start in the cold. He gasped at the biting wind and offered Steven brunch from the truck. Instead, Steven, Foley and Natalie decided to hold an impromptu progress meeting on the pavement, among the arc lights and generators. It was a fine, freezing New York morning and their breath hung in clouds in the air.

'I got a couple of things before I hand over to Natalie,' Foley said, stamping his feet and blowing into his hands. His corporate manner seemed wildly out of place in the street.

'First, the business with the biog.' He gave Steven a confidential look. 'Did you have chance to go through what we discussed yesterday?'

A make-up girl yelled out that her face spray had frozen and all the crew in the truck hooted with laughter. Foley took Steven to one side. 'You OK to talk about this in front of Natalie?'

Steven said that he was. He then explained that most of what Anderson had scrawled on his biog was true, but that it was written from a pretty jaundiced angle. He said that he was married, technically, but that he hadn't included it in his personal details because he hadn't thought it was relevant. He then gave Foley the same speech he'd given the reporter from the *Village Voice* about wanting to enter this thing with as little baggage as possible. Natalie had begun to take notes and her pen slipped around in her gloved hand, as her papers blew in the biting wind.

'Some of the profile people will think it's relevant,' Natalie said. 'Sure, they think it's their territory.'

Foley gave her a sharp look, as if she'd spoken out of turn. Steven knew that Foley was handling him like gelignite and he found his anxiety amusing. Steven spoke direct to Natalie.

'Then if they think it's relevant and if you think it's relevant then sure, I was married. What can I tell you? She was called Fiona. We got married young. We split . . .'

'Did you say you were divorced?' Natalie said, with pen poised.

'No. Just separated.'

Natalie looked vaguely disappointed. Foley said firmly and quietly to Natalie that they didn't need chapter and verse on this thing, just the straight facts.

'Hey, I have nothing to hide,' Steven said.

'It's really not an issue,' Foley said, and Steven grinned at Natalie.

'Natalie is just curious,' Steven said.

Steven laughed out loud and that gave Foley permission to laugh too. This really was a beautiful morning, Steven thought, and even the mention of Fiona hadn't dampened it. He had married her when they were both still freshmen. In '77 Steven Hawthorne and Fiona Van Draken were the king and queen of sociability theory at Dartmouth and later at University College London. She was the daughter of a Dutch shipping merchant and when they met she had recently and theatrically become a Marxist to spite her father, just like Steven. The two of them shone in seminar groups like beautiful distant stars. She was slim and blonde with a complexion like butter gold and he was dark and beautiful and when he spoke at all he was terrifying. He put it around at college that his father was in jail, then when that wouldn't hold up he said he was a GI in the army. Either way he always spoke in seminars as if he had first-hand knowledge of what used to be called 'the struggle'.

In those days, even Fiona didn't really know the truth about Steven's background. When they were alone, they hardly spoke at all.

If Steven and Fiona were the king and queen, then Anderson was their surly prince and part-time court jester. The three of them had been a cogent, united force within the faculty and even the weaker professors (of which there were many in both cities) feared their disapproval. When Steven and Fiona got married, at Chelsea Register Office when they were both just twenty-two, they did it as a kind of double flip rebellion. The last thing on earth that the footmen and ladies-in-waiting within the department would have expected was that Steven and Fiona would endorse the discredited institution of marriage. Like almost everything they did, they did it just to see the look on certain people's faces. Their acolytes, Anderson, their fathers. Naturally, no one, except a perfect stranger who happened to be passing, was invited to the regal ceremony.

After five years of study, agitation, preening, the final examination approached and like a bright phosphorescent beam it shone through the cracks in the royal marriage. Fiona had already been offered three research posts, Steven had been offered nothing. He had neglected to fasten himself firmly enough to any one professor. He couldn't bear the indignity of failure and that was why, three weeks before his examinations were about to begin, he dropped out of college.

After that, his marriage to Fiona turned into a race. Fiona fast and agile, slipping from one research post to another, then studying for a professorship, while Steven took a job working for her father, shipping Lignite around the world from an office in London. While she worked on taking the inner workings of society to pieces, had papers published, wrote for prestigious journals, he organized the movement of rusting hulks, filled with brown sludge, which took their poisonous cargo to ports all around the world. Anderson, the vicious prince, took his chance to make an assault on the throne. He never slept with Fiona, that wasn't the issue, he simply became her academic wife, her other half in their joint manoeuvrings. He also began a retrospective damnation of all the work that Steven had ever done, watching as his beautiful, dark opponent was gradually stripped of all his power and all his glory.

Then, one night, Fiona had been working at her desk in the study of their London apartment and she had turned to Steven and yelled, 'Stop watching me!'

'What do you mean, watching you?'

'You're always watching me. You're turning into a fucking spectator . . .'

Steven always thought of that exchange, soon buried in apologies, as the moment when his marriage to Fiona became impossible. From then on, Steven decided that he would do anything, anything at all, to get even with her. His first recourse was the most obvious and the easiest. His face and his build meant that it was the simplest thing in the world to begin affairs with other women. Soon his infidelities had become so regular that they had become a burden and a chore. He became lazy in his deceptions, even began to hope that he would be found out, and one night Fiona discovered an airline ticket from an outing to Paris with a Turkish air stewardess. A week later, Steven had packed his belongings, boarded a jet and left. The only place he could go was his grandmother's place on Long Island. There, he sat at his desk and brooded, watching the beautiful-coloured birds fighting for scraps of food in the yard. And it was there that the idea of *Alphabet City* had come to him, rising up from calm blue waters like the humped back of a whale.

*Alphabet City* was the perfect solution. It would leapfrog him way ahead in Fiona's academic circles, and it would prove to Daddy that you didn't have to leave your jet trail in enemy skies to show you had balls.

A make-up girl had pushed herself between Natalie and Foley and was dabbing his face with zinc powder to take away the shine. Steven crouched down a little so she could reach him.

'Now this is a face I could work with,' she said with a lascivious smile and she glanced at Natalie. Everyone laughed and Foley seemed to have decided that it would be OK if he relaxed a little.

'Any other little secrets we should know about?' Foley said with a big grin. Steven frowned.

'The MA is phoney,' Steven said and Foley quickly said, 'OK,' as if it really didn't concern him. The make-up girl was putting the finishing touches to Steven's eyes and flicking his black hair from his face.

'There was some confusion when I first made my approach to my agent in London. He got the wrong information and I never got round to putting him right. Does that bother either one of you?'

Natalie and Foley both shook their heads. The make-up girl said, 'There now', zipped up her cosmetics bag and hurried back to the warmth of the truck. It was bizarre that it had been the intervention of Anderson which had forced this much of the truth out of him. It seemed that their fates were linked by sheer purpose of will and Fiona's too. Foley clapped his hands together.

'What else do I have for you ... let's see here. I just had a call from a lady working on a Spanish-language paper wants to know the split on your royalties. She wants to know how much you are donating to the barrios.'

'She sure didn't waste any time did she?' Steven said and he pushed back his hair. 'Tell her it's twenty per cent.'

'Twenty per cent,' Foley said and he wrote it down.

'Is that really true?' Foley said, hoping to sugar the question with a gust of nervous laughter. Steven glared at him and he looked back at his notebook.

'Well OK,' he said at last, dotting the page hard with his pencil as if he were carefree. 'That's all from me. Natalie, over to you.'

Natalie said that as far as she knew, all the appointments she'd set up were still going ahead. After the documentary film crew, there were two more radio stations, two magazines. Steven felt buoyant.

'What about *True Society*?' he said.

Natalie consulted her list. 'I have that down for the day after tomorrow,' she said.

Steven grinned at Foley, who was in on the joke.

'Now that we've cleared the air, call Mr Anderson at *True Society* and have the meeting brought forward,' Steven said. 'Tell him I only have a space in my diary this evening at six. I'm in the mood for him today. I want to give him a signed copy.'

Natalie made a note. The crew began to emerge from their truck, their ears glued to mobile telephones. Then Foley said that he'd almost forgotten but his office had a call early that morning from someone called Tom Pettman at the NYPD. A beaten-up Volkswagen Beetle pulled up behind the truck.

'NYPD?' Steven said. 'What the hell did they want?'

Foley tried to look unconcerned. 'I was kind of curious about that myself.'

An elegant lady in fur stepped out of the beaten-up Volkswagen and the director and the crew began to fuss around her. She yelled loudly about the fucking weather in this city, before seeking out Steven, introducing herself as the host of the show and saying that she really loved his book.

## 2

Steven was leaning against a bench outside a bar. The camera was trained directly on his face. The bright arc light above his head warmed the air. The lady reporter had swopped her fur for a windcheater as they had walked through the streets of SoHo, talking about the darkness of Alphabet City. Now all they needed were some reaction shots from Steven to put into the finished edit.

'OK, this is the part where I ask you about the drug-store hold-up. Just nod your head like you're remembering it.'

Steven composed his face and nodded his head at the reporter's raised hand. She had her elegantly manicured hand raised to give Steven his eye-line. Then when the director said, 'Next,' the reporter flicked through her sheet.

'OK, this is the question about prostitution. I've just said the stuff about cocaine and sex, about the way no one uses money as currency any more.'

Steven rubbed his chin. Then the reporter wiggled her fingers.

'Hey, hey, keep looking at my hand . . .'

Steven had glanced over her shoulder and seen that a car had pulled up directly opposite where they were filming. A small crowd had gathered to watch the crew at work and it made way for the car as it slowed and then stopped. Steven couldn't be sure, but the guy in the passenger seat who was looking over directly at him looked a lot like the guy in the Barnes and Noble bookstore who had asked all those questions about the gun. But why would Detective Tom Pettman from the NYPD want to follow Steven Hawthorne around New York?

'Mr Hawthorne?' the director said. 'Look at the hand.'

The car pulled away and Steven couldn't get a good look at the driver or the passenger. So he looked at the lady's hand and nodded his head gravely.

**Chapter Six**

1

Steven sat at a table in Slovo's restaurant in Little Italy, the only customer. Outside, the sun was setting early, as if it had grown tired of trying to light and warm the New York cold. All the buoyancy that Steven had felt that morning had gone. The radio interviews had been hard and ill-tempered and Steven had felt that there was one enormous question that was waiting to be asked, that was hovering in the air like a huge bubble that needed to be burst. One of the interviewers had said softly between red lights that he'd heard there had been 'questions about veracity'. Steven couldn't get that dry, sandy face out of his mind.

The street was filled with Chinese, hauling boxes and pushing trolleys laden with green vegetables and twisted white roots. On the other side of the street there was a dark shop front with a rotten door, and all around the door there were cages with rabbits inside them, and stacked above the rabbits there were cages for cockerels. The waiter had already told Steven that Slovo's was the last Italian place still operating for five blocks in any direction, that Little Italy was more like Little Peking since City Hall changed the rent system and forced all the Italians out of the neighbourhood. The waiter brought Steven a glass of water and with it delivered his short, well-rehearsed assault against City Hall rental policy.

'Tourist like you comes to Little Italy,' the waiter said, 'and all he finds is chinks.'

'I'm not a tourist.'

'Whatever. You eating alone?'

'No, I'm expecting someone.'

Anderson had agreed to shuffle his appointments and meet Steven at six. It was now ten past. Steven expected him to make one small gesture of defiance by being late and he knew that having to change his schedule would annoy the hell out of him. But now, Steven was taking no pleasure out of the prospect of meeting Anderson. He had a bad feeling that reflected the growing darkness outside. He had sent Natalie home because this dark feeling was like a premonition.

'You see that old guy in the street,' the waiter said, drifting past Steven's table. 'The chink with the pigtail. You watch him now. Watch.'

Steven watched as the old Chinese man paused in the doorway of Slovo's, put his hand on the door frame for support and then heaved a mouthful of phlegm from the blackened roots of his lungs. The old man spat the phlegm out and then tottered across the street.

'Bastard does that every fucking day of the week. Same fucking place. Goes out of his way.'

The waiter glared out into the dark street for a few moments and then began to dump two sets of cutlery on the table with sudden force.

'You see they got family,' he said, breathless with anger. 'Like the Italians used to have family. They got the whole family working their places for nothing. Italian kids don't want to follow their fathers no more. They want to be movie stars. So the Italians move out and the chinks move in.'

Steven saw a taxi pulling up outside the restaurant. A guy with grey, fuzzy hair and hunched shoulders got out and paid the driver. Steven hadn't seen Anderson for five years. If that was him . . .

The waiter fussed with the placement of Steven's knife and fork, his hand trembling. 'That's just how it is,' he said, breathing hard, getting mad. 'And after the chinks move out it'll be the Koreans or Vietnamese, all the way down the evolutionary chain until it's monkeys running the restaurants. You want coffee while you wait for your friend?'

'No, I prefer Chinese tea,' Steven said.

The waiter straightened up. 'Say again?'

'I prefer Chinese tea. From China.'

The waiter was already angry and it didn't take long for him to divert his anger to Steven.

'You trying to be funny, smart ass?'

Steven stood up and threw his napkin on the table. The waiter's fists began to fold and Steven brushed by him. He met Anderson in the doorway and almost pushed him over.

'Steven? . . .'

'Come on, Anderson,' Steven said loudly, 'let's get out of here. This guy's a fucking racist.'

## 2

Because Steven's anger had been real, he found it hard to talk for a few moments. He had often pretended to get mad but he was unaccustomed to genuine anger and it overwhelmed him. He'd lost count of the number of times he had absorbed the casual racism of the city – white, black, Irish, Italian – but this time something had snapped inside him. He had hailed the same cab that Anderson had just stepped out of and they both climbed into the back. If Steven had meant it as some piece of theatre to throw Anderson off his guard or to impress him, it would have been perfectly executed. But this time, Steven hadn't been calculating. It was the kind of thing that would have happened in the book. It belonged in the pages of *Alphabet City*.

'Shit, Steven, what's wrong with you?' Anderson said as the cab pulled away. His hair had receded to two bunches of grey around his ears, his lips had grown crooked and he seemed smaller than Steven remembered. 'Like what happened to "hello",' he continued, 'what happened to "how are you, nice meeting you again after all these years"? Or maybe a punch in the mouth for the stuff I sent to your publishers.'

Steven smiled and nodded his head. 'Hello Anderson, how the hell are you. You look terrible.'

'That's better. Where are we going?'

Steven shrugged and then told the driver to take them to the UN Plaza hotel. Then he shook Anderson's hand awkwardly in the cramped rear seat.

'I mean it, Anderson. You look so fucking old . . .'

Anderson grinned because this was how they had always talked to each other. At college Anderson had a reputation for brutal honesty but like a lot of people with that reputation, he was only honest when he had something bad to say.

'Screw you,' Anderson said. 'Why would someone of my age want to look like a teenager, answer me that? It stinks of fear. I don't want to be healthy. It's the new morality, Steven, you know that, don't you? Health is heaven, cancer is hell. You live a clean life you live forever. This fucking country. Bullshit. You want a cigarette?'

Anderson offered Steven a cigarette and Steven took it. They both lit up as if this were an act of huge defiance.

Steven was startled to discover that it actually felt good to see Anderson again, because for years he had hated him for his success and his notoriety. After leaving college Anderson had written articles for every left-of-centre journal in the world and features for every magazine that felt it needed a little action to boost its circulation. Any magazine that wanted its mailbags fattened with human excrement and razor blades. Editors would lay their disclaimers, turn their heads, open the gate and let Anderson into the ring, kicking and bucking like a bull. And all around the crowd would howl and scream and yell for his severed ears.

In the past three years things had changed. People had come to realize, even people as slow on the uptake as university professors, that Anderson wasn't a devil or an angel but a showman. They realized that he wasn't seeking converts to any particular cause, he was only seeking attention. And once Anderson had been unmasked, it left only a kind of wry affection for him amongst his old enemies and a measure of sympathy and embarrassment from his few old friends. Lately he had taken to railing against political correctness and the health lobby, because he wanted to be the first to kick against the fashion. Once upon a time, he would come riding in on the breakers of a new movement, waving to his darling on the shore. Now he seemed to be drifting on any tide or current that came his way. His fall from grace had given Steven a measure of pleasure but now that they were together inside the taxi cab, isolated in their little pools of cigarette light, Steven wanted to cling to him. He envied him his obscurity.

'Hey, Steven,' Anderson said, 'I'm sorry about sending that stuff back to your publishers. I'd been drinking.'

'That's OK, Anderson. You did me a favour. They would have found out eventually.'

'I did you a favour? Shit, I didn't mean to.'

Steven laughed. There was an old habit that Anderson had from college days. When he was about to step over the line, when he was really going to hit someone between the eyes with something, he'd always start shaking his right hand rhythmically over his hip. He glanced up at Steven, his hand shaking, then the moment passed. Steven couldn't believe that Anderson had apologized to him, even if he had made a joke about it straight away. Anderson never apologized for anything at all. He really had grown old. His vicious, milky blue eyes looked pale behind his spectacles.

'So should I ask?' Steven said.

'Ask what?'

'Ask you what you thought of my book.'

Anderson said nothing. The cab had reached the fringes of Greenwich Village and the streets were just beginning to fill up with young wanderers and prim middle-class locals with their air of faded radicalism. Steven had written in *Alphabet City* that the Village was a like a museum these days, or a monument to something that never happened. Finally Anderson said: 'Steven I know you. I know you inside and out. Please don't ask me about the book and don't try to bullshit me. No one knows you like an old enemy. That's a cliché I made up myself.'

Anderson's hand began to shake. Steven had forgotten how intimate they had once been, drawn together by their intense and pointless rivalry. Anderson was right about old enemies and Steven was afraid of what he was going to say next.

'So how come you want to interview me?' Steven said.

'Interview you? Come on, Steven, give me a break.'

It was dark outside now and it was hard to make out Anderson's features but Steven was sure that Anderson was nervous about something, actually trying to think of ways of making this easier.

'So why were you so anxious to see me? Is this social?'

Anderson finally bit on what he wanted to say. 'I'm here because I had a phone call from Fiona.'

'My Fiona?'

'"My Fiona" he calls her. Let me tell you, Stevie, when I spoke to her she wasn't your Fiona. She was sucking the devil's dick when I spoke to her.'

The cab was held up by traffic lights and the streets had begun to sparkle with rain. Steven was sure that Anderson was pausing because he really didn't want to say what he had to say.

'So Fiona called you. So what? What did she say?'

'Well, Stevie, first she told me about the other women. Told me about the Turkish woman. She called her . . . what was the word she used? . . . English word. "Slag". I like that word. I'll use that word . . .'

'Please, Anderson, what else?'

'OK, it's like this. When you left London my friend, you left a pot on the stove. You left Fiona just boiling over. Then when she reads your book, reads what people are saying about it . . .'

Steven felt a coldness creeping up from his feet. His premonition had been right.

'Steven, no one knows you the way I do and the way Fiona does. You can bullshit everyone else but you can't bullshit us. So Fiona has decided to put together a diary of her own . . .'

The cab was pulling into FDR Drive, where the rain was thick from the river. Steven was clenching his fists so hard his hands hurt.

'She's putting together dates, times. She's calling everyone who knows you, to find out when they last saw you. She says to me, "When did you last see old Stevie?" and if I'd known right off what she was doing I would have told her to go to hell, I really would. Believe it or not, I always

61

liked you. I always like people who tell lies more than people who believe them. But Fiona is meticulous. How do you think she got straight As? She's putting together a diary on you to prove for a fact that there was no way you could have spent a year living in Alphabet City. She's going to prove that *Alphabet City* is a lie.'

Anderson sighed with cigarette smoke. Then he mumbled, 'Jesus, I knew you were up to your old tricks the minute I opened the fucking book. But I would have kept my mouth shut. The stuff I sent to your publisher was just to shit you up a little. But Fiona, she's scary. She won't rest Steven. When she's got this diary finished she says she's taking it to *The New York Times*. And you know that if Fiona is working on something it'll be as tight as her ass.'

The cab pulled up outside the UN Plaza and a uniformed doorman hurried to open the door. The rain was falling heavily. Steven stepped out of it as if he were stepping out of a dream. He hadn't said anything to Anderson because he knew that he didn't have to. Anderson was leaning into the open door.

'If I was an ordinary guy, Steven, I'd tell you that you've gone too far this time but that's bullshit. You tell a lie often enough, it'll become the truth. It's a good book, Steven. You've got something to say. It takes more balls to lie and carry it off than it does to do it for real. I have no advice for you my friend, I just come riding across the prairie with dire news. And it shames me to say it gives me no pleasure. It's her I always really wanted to nail. So long, Steven. And good luck.'

Steven closed the cab door without a word and Anderson was driven away, a grey, fuzzy head in a little pool of yellow light. The ice cream-faced clerk on the hotel check-in desk handed Steven his plastic key and also handed him a folded note. The note was marked 'most urgent':

'For the attention of Steven Hawthorne. Please call Detective Tom Pettman at NYPD Precinct 7 (Avenue D).'

There was a phone number and a three-digit extension with the word 'Homicide' beside it inside brackets.

## Chapter Seven

### 1

'It began as a misunderstanding,' Steven said out loud. The TV was on but the sound was turned down. His hotel room was empty and it was early morning. He was speaking softly out of the window, which was pulled up as high as the suicide blocks would allow. The panoramic view of New York City was his only audience. 'I told Warren it was fiction but the guy got the wrong idea. It was Chinese whispers.'

This was a rehearsal for Steven's speech from the gallows, which he had always prayed he would never have to make. There were two pigeons roosting on the window ledge, staring dumbly at him, not prepared to be afraid this high up. Steven was on the 37th floor.

'And by the time it got to publication it was out of my hands.'

Steven couldn't even tell the whole truth to himself any more. The truth was deep down and with Steven that was deep as a diamond mine. He turned from the window as the phone rang. He let it ring.

After he had left Fiona in London and gone to stay with his grandmother, he had found himself with no home, no income. His grandmother's endless patience and sweet ambition on his behalf only made things worse. He knew that this state of affairs vindicated everything his father had ever said to him about nailing down a real career. When he had been studying, he had often played around with the idea of writing fiction and now that he was drifting in the dark lagoon of his grandmother's study, the idea of writing a novel returned as an hilariously unlikely last throw of the dice.

He contacted an old friend of Fiona's in London who was a literary agent. He'd met him once at a party and the agent had been drunk, as rumour had it he often was. Steven had put his number in his address book and shortly after arriving at his grandmother's place, Steven called him. Warren Kanavros hadn't been there but his deputy had taken a message. Warren had called back the next day. It was after lunch in London.

'Steven Hawthorne?'

'Yes.'

'This is Warren Kanavros. I got a message . . . Should I know you?'

Steven broke in. He had his finger in his ear. The idea he'd had for a novel was a kind of fictional revenge on the entire world which had been brewing up in his imagination ever since he'd left London. Specifically it was a fictional revenge on Fiona Van Draken's world. He had cut and cropped it inside his own head so that he could deliver it in one sentence. He remembered Warren Kanavros as being vaguely dissipated, with a questionable attention span. When he listened to other people speak, he would mouth words to himself at the same time.

'That's right,' Steven had said. 'I have an idea for a book. Do you have a moment . . . ?'

Steven described it as a diary. It was a diary kept by a sociology graduate who goes to live in a tough barrio in New York and discovers that everything he was ever taught at college was bullshit. Steven dressed it up with detail but it was still a thin and absurd project, as projects fuelled by dim vengeance always are. He threw in a few lines about the closure of mental institutions, an act of madness which had been legitimized by sociability theorists like Fiona and which had led to anarchy in certain parts of New York. Steven knew this for a fact. He'd seen it from his train compartment window.

Warren had seemed distracted and said that he would need something on paper. But by chance, a few days later, Warren had mentioned the idea in passing to a publisher over lunch in London. She had said that it sounded interesting. Steven hadn't realized at the time that Warren Kanavros had built whatever reputation he had in London on the strength of an excellent list of non-fiction. The publisher had assumed that Warren had been talking about a factual account.

Warren called Steven and said that he might have someone interested. While Steven worked on the first sixty pages, the publisher in London spoke to someone in New York. The people in New York phoned Warren and said they'd heard that some middle-class sociology graduate had spent a year living in a New York ghetto and had kept a diary. Warren phoned Steven and told him the news.

'You mean someone's done this for real?' Steven had said.

Warren had thought about that for a while then said, 'I think they were talking about you. Steven I have to go, my other phone ... my PA is off with irritable bowel syndrome again and it's like Custer's last stand in here.'

The rumour about the diary reached Anton and Zucker and someone called Warren to get Steven's number. Anton and Zucker called Steven at his grandmother's place and suggested that he send them the first sixty pages direct, with Warren's permission. He'd written it in the first person and to his surprise it had turned out well. His anger had put some juice into his use of language.

Steven heard nothing from Anton and Zucker for two months, then a new editor picked it up. It was floating around the editorial department and she had just arrived at Anton and Zucker, a publishing house with a rather sniffy, highbrow reputation, from a small radical press. She wanted to establish her new priorities early and the book seemed to have possibilities. She called Warren who called Steven.

'Steven, I must be losing my fucking marbles or something. I didn't realize that you did it for real. I've got some woman screaming for you down the phone . . .'

Steven met the new editor from Anton and Zucker at a café in the Lower East Village. She said that the old guard who had their heel on her head were saying that the potential for controversy was just too great but that she was going to fight them. Finally, it was Foley who backed her, with the proviso that they get film rights as part of the package.

Steven took the radical editor to lunch and drank some wine and then she invited him to her apartment and they slept together. Steven had known six phone calls back what was happening to this project. He'd picked up from Warren that he usually dealt in non-fiction and he could trace the misunderstanding all the way back to there. All it needed for Steven to do was to open his mouth. All he needed to do was blow the bugle right there and then, on the phone, in the café, in the bed. He didn't do it and it seemed better to stay silent because silence wasn't a lie, it was just silence, which meant nothing at all. The morning after they had slept together the radical new editor offered Steven a hundred thousand dollar advance.

All night, when she had asked him about the little details in the first sixty pages, he had said nothing, he had grunted, he had shrugged his shoulders. She took his reticence as evidence that all of this was still too painful to talk about. When they were lying in bed in the editor's huge SoHo apartment, she said, 'Hey, Steven, you did take a test didn't you?'

Even her accent was different when she was afraid.

'Test for what?'

'You know what I'm saying. The part where you slept with Lucretia in the disused train compartment. She was a hooker. She used needles. I mean you did do the sensible thing and take an AIDS test when you left Alphabet City.'

Some parts of those first few months still made Steven laugh. At first he told himself that this was a smart ass trick that he was playing on the publishing people who began to swarm around him. He was still so mad with Fiona, for no reason, that his anger was like a machine-gun which he couldn't disengage, it just kept on firing at whoever came his way. He told himself that it was funny that people who worked in Madison Avenue knew so little about what life was really like just a few miles away that he could construct this absurd fiction from TV shows, newspaper articles, even sociological research and get away with it. Then the radical new editor was fired and someone else took up the baton. The new editor had more pull, wanted Steven to hurry up with his final draft. He began to hang out in the Lower East Village, read every book in the Southampton Library about the New York gangs. He would even interrogate taxi drivers, if they were black or Hispanic, about what life was really like in their neighbourhoods. He put all his notes together in a leather folder, the one he used to use when he was still a freshman at college, when he had been king and Fiona had been queen.

Steven had imagination, a solid track record in deception and a fierce motivation stretching all the way back to London. He finished his manuscript right on time. And it was once the manuscript was accepted for publication, the day his father had been killed, that this hoax stopped being funny. But by then Steven had banked fifty grand and he had appointments all over the United States. The publicity tour was arranged even before the book cover had been designed and Anton and Zucker's tentacles stretched all the way to Anchorage, Alaska. When his first itinerary arrived, he knew that he would have to take a deep breath and see this thing through to the end. Just so long as he avoided getting caught up in detail, so long as he managed to stop people making any connections to the real Alphabet City, then he would maybe survive. But he had figured without Fiona.

The phone rang again and this time he picked it up. It was Foley.

'Steven, we're down in the lobby. Get down here right away. Man have we got some news for you!'

## 2

Foley said that almost overnight, New York City had exploded. They were walking quickly down East 44th Street, with Natalie trotting along with them, checking her watch. The air was five degrees colder today and the weather report said a blizzard was rolling down from Alaska and would be hitting New York in the next two days.

'The *Village Voice* piece was fucking dynamite!' Foley rarely swore. He grabbed Steven's shoulder to stop him stepping in front of a taxi cab. 'With the *Voice* on our side we don't have to worry so much about radicals. And listen to this, Steven . . .' Foley checked the street for on-coming traffic on Steven's behalf and then led him across the road as if he were blind. Steven felt precious.

'We've had word, unofficial, that you've gone straight to number six on the non-fiction list in *The New York Times Review of Books* this Sunday.'

His grin was too big for his face. Natalie gave Steven a look of devotion and then skipped to keep pace.

'Excuse me,' Steven said softly, 'where exactly are we going?'

'Natalie?' Foley barked and she checked her itinerary.

'Book-signing on East 53rd. I figured it would be quicker to walk.'

They continued their frantic pace through the early-morning rush hour. Everyone had found a new layer of clothes to wear, fur and quilted cotton, apart from the beggars who hopped up and down in doorways in their thin, worn-out jackets, holding out plastic cups and mumbling thanks.

'This thing is taking on a buzz,' Foley said, 'just like I knew it would. It's like they say when you're selling books, either you catch the wind or you paddle real hard. *Alphabet City* has caught the wind.'

The wind blew like a frozen blade down Park Avenue. The street was a solid stream of ice-cold metal. Steam billowed in great clouds from the underworld, as if beneath the pavement there was a seething cauldron.

'Something else too,' Foley said beneath the hooting of car horns. 'We had a call from Eliot at Eagle Studios. That his name, Natalie?'

Natalie checked her clipboard and nodded.

'Eliot is head of development, New York. He sent the coverage on *Alphabet City* to Hollywood overnight and they're interested. He wants to talk about movie rights . . .'

They had stepped into a river of humanity which was

flowing in the opposite direction to the way they were walking. Natalie's head was lost in the crowd and Steven could just see it bobbing up and down. Steven and Foley were pushed together.

'There's a meeting late this afternoon at Anton and Zucker. Don't worry, Steven, we won't bore you with it. It'll just be exploratory stuff at the moment but Eliot did say he'd need to speak to you about rights of portrayal slips . . .'

Foley was pushed into a doorway and Steven found himself mid-stream. The people rushing by were all too cold to look up from inside their steaming collars. Foley danced back to the middle of the stream. Natalie rejoined them too.

'What rights of portrayal slips?' Steven said, raising his voice against the sound of the traffic.

Foley turned into East 53rd and they escaped the Park Avenue avalanche. East 53rd was quiet. 'It's just routine,' Foley said. 'The movie people get jumpy about litigation. Any movie based on real events they have to get the permission of all the people who are featured before they can make up a contract. Like I say, it's still early but they won't move without signed permission.'

'I don't understand, signed permission from who?'

Foley had walked on ahead and Steven caught his arm and stopped him.

'It's early yet, Steven.'

'Permission from who?'

'From the people portrayed in the book. The real people. The ones that are still alive at least. It's just a piece of paper that they have to sign giving the studio permission to portray them any way they please. Without it there can't be a deal . . .'

Natalie had spotted Steven's alarm. He had stopped walking and she hovered at his side.

'Mr Foley,' she called out, and Foley turned around. 'I think Steven has a problem with that?'

Foley looked incredulous.

'With what?' He laughed. 'With the rights of portrayal? Steven, really, it's just a formality for the legal people. It's all off the record. No one outside of the studio's legal team would need to know the real names, I swear. We're talking about two, maybe three lawyers, sworn to secrecy. And we'd only need permission from the major players, like Polo and Azole the landlord and maybe Lucretia.'

Foley took Steven by the arm and led him forward.

'We're not talking about cops or journalists here, Steven,' Foley said. 'And hey, we could be talking about a deal worth five million dollars. More.'

## Chapter Eight

**1**

The question and answer session in the bookstore on East 53rd went badly. Steven became irritated by a woman in the second row who kept asking insanely detailed questions about Pilot, the guy who Steven had seen shot in the basement. She asked questions as if she had written them down in advance.

'You say that the guy you call Pilot lived for a time on the Big Farm Estate in Salvador, Brazil . . .'

Steven had got the name of the estate from a TV documentary about child prostitution.

'He'd been in New York three years . . . that right?'

'Yes.'

'And the guy Emilio who shot him had a scar down the left side of his face . . .'

'That's right.'

If Steven hadn't been so preoccupied he would have spent some time wondering about the lady in the second row. It crossed his mind that Fiona might already have tipped off *The New York Times*. But he was too busy rehearsing his argument with Foley. After the Q and A had finished, Steven picked up where he had left off before he stepped up to the podium. He said that it was out of the question that real identities could be revealed to anyone, even corporate lawyers. Foley suggested that they could restrict it to one other person, chosen by Steven. Steven countered that he would only agree to proceed if an arrangement could be made where Steven went back to Alphabet City alone and secured the signatures of his friends himself.

'Besides, Polo and Azole can't read or write,' he said desperately. Foley had said again that it was still early days but that if Eagle really wanted this thing, ten million dollars was not beyond the realms of possibility. For the first time he showed his corporate teeth. He'd tolerate Steven's pathological desire for secrecy as regards the media but when this kind of money was at stake, then his job was at stake too. He said he'd report back with Steven's suggestions and then he left Steven and Natalie alone in the street outside the bookstore.

'OK, where next? Shoot, let's get it over with,' Steven said, looking up and down the street with the desperation of a man under fire. He was breathing hard. Natalie smiled shyly.

'That bad, huh?' she said.

He nodded at the distance.

'Well, next you have two whole hours doing nothing at all,' she said. 'I guessed that you might need a break. I put a little space in the schedule.'

She flicked back her hair and rocked back on her heels, looking away down the street.

'OK. So what?' Steven said, his heart still racing from his dispute with Foley. 'Shall we go and get a bite to eat or something? What? What are you laughing at?'

Natalie was laughing at thin air and she was blushing too.

'I thought we could use this little space to just talk. Get to know each other.'

'Talk?'

'Jesus, Steven. I just thought that maybe we could go

back to your hotel and make conversation. Have you got alcohol in your hotel room?'

Steven said that he had and then stretched out his arm at a passing taxi cab. He wasn't really thinking straight and didn't even notice the look of wild embarrassment on Natalie's face when she climbed into the taxi beside him and said, 'UN Plaza hotel.'

## 2

They talked about the book and the itinerary for four or five minutes. While Natalie asked questions, Steven took the opportunity to put his dirty laundry into a hotel laundry bag. She sat on the bed. Finally, Steven said, 'Listen, Natalie, I'm not sure this is a good time.'

'Good time for what?'

'To talk. I'm pretty tired.'

Natalie patted her clipboard up and down on her lap a few times, disappointed that Steven hadn't already got the message.

'Listen, this is crazy, but I really thought we could do more than talk.'

Steven didn't understand and then he did. He froze for a moment with his hands full of dirty socks and turned to Natalie.

'What, you mean . . . ?'

When he wasn't so preoccupied, he had an instinct for this kind of thing. He could usually follow the map of seduction with his eyes closed. This time, Natalie had fallen on him from the ceiling.

'I never do this kind of thing,' Natalie said. 'Maybe once in five years. My boyfriend is a nice guy. You met him.'

Steven said nothing. He had pushed the last of his socks into the laundry bag and tucked it under the bed.

'You met him in the bookstore,' Natalie said. 'The first one you visited. He was the manager. I fixed it so that you'd go there first. All the stores wanted first bite but I fixed so that you'd start out at his store.'

Steven nodded. Decent, reasonable people like Natalie Kishon being made to act like fools. She was sitting on the bed next to a hero of her own creation, a phantom who didn't exist.

'Well if that's your boyfriend, he seemed like a nice guy,' Steven said. 'You should be OK with him.'

'He is. He's OK.'

'Do you live together?'

'No. We have separate apartments. He says he needs room. He has a lot of books.'

'Yes, I suppose in his line of work he must.'

'And his fish. He keeps fish. They're really beautiful.'

'Yes. Fish are nice.'

Steven put his hands between his knees, a kind of secular prayer that this thing would be over soon.

'I guess the ideal gift for your boyfriend would be a book about fish,' he said and Natalie laughed into her hand.

Steven took a long sip of beer. There were twin beds in the room, two singles.

'I know you do this kind of thing all the time,' Natalie said softly.

'What kind of thing?' Steven said.

'Sleep with strangers. In the book . . . I know you hate talking about it but in the book you say that people cling to each other like wreckage. I loved that image. Sometimes I feel like wreckage myself.'

Natalie shuddered.

'Should I turn the heating up?' Steven said. 'Are you cold?'

He stood up and turned up the thermostat on the wall.

He sat back down on the bed and gave Natalie a warm but formal smile.

'So did you leave your wife to research the book?' Natalie said.

'Yes. I suppose you could say that.'

'What was she like?'

'Blonde. Hard. I always think of polished steel when I think of her.'

'Was she afraid for you? Did she know what you were planning to do?'

'I don't know. We didn't talk about it.'

'That I can believe,' Natalie said and she put her hand on Steven's shoulder.

'Do you want me to leave? I mean is this just the most idiotic thing I've ever done?'

Steven began to search through the pocket of his overcoat, which he had thrown on the bed, and found his packet of cigarettes. He lit one and took a deep drag. Natalie really was pretty.

'Jesus, you are a strange guy,' Natalie said, then she took Steven's cigarette and smoked. She smoked like a twelve-year-old trying to act tough. He knew that she was already screaming at herself for how she was behaving, and loving it too. 'But I'm pretty strange too,' she said, coughing.

There was a long silence and then Natalie said, 'If I had been born a guy, I like to think I would have done what you did.' Then she shook her head at the floor and exclaimed, 'Jesus, I'm such an idiot! Why did I tell you about my boyfriend, like the first thing I say when I sit down!'

Steven knew that he should ask Natalie to leave, but she misunderstood Steven's silence.

'I guess you think I'm some sort of whore, don't you?' she said. 'I mean, I've known you two days and straight away I come up to your room. But it's not like that. It's like I said before, I feel that I know you already. Know you like a lover.'

Steven nodded his head at the window.

'Is that what you think?' she said again.

'What?'

'That I'm a whore?'

Steven turned to her.

'I don't think like that,' he said. 'I really don't think in those terms. That's the truth.'

Steven was about to say that he was tired and needed to rest but Natalie grabbed him around the neck and kissed him on the lips, mostly because she had misunderstood and had imagined that he was being romantic.

'We don't have to talk about the book if you don't want to,' she hissed into his ear.

'OK,' Steven said.

'You are the one who said that life is the needle on the record. The split-second. How do you put it? "The only part of the record that exists is the point where the needle makes contact." I'm crazy like that too.'

Natalie kissed Steven again and Steven found himself kissing her back. They lay back on the bed and Steven closed his eyes.

Then the phone began to ring and he eased himself up on the bed.

'Leave it,' Natalie hissed.

'It might be important . . .'

Natalie took his face tenderly between the palms of her hands. Her hands were wet with sweat. She kissed him so deeply on the lips that something inside began to melt, as if she were sucking all his anxiety out of him.

'There,' she said. 'Now you kiss me back or I swear I will scream.'

The phone was still ringing. Steven kissed Natalie on the lips and she said, 'It's OK, it's OK.'

She took off her glasses and laid them on the bedside table. Without her glasses she looked strange at first, as if she were about to cry, then after a few seconds, she looked prettier than she had before. She didn't have a beautiful face but her sudden passion had changed her. The spectacles were just the last part of the transformation.

'There, it's OK, it's OK,' she whispered again and Steven realized that she was whispering to herself. 'You like me?' she said, her voice a little louder. 'You don't know me but you liked me straight away, didn't you? You can say that . . .'

She spoke in a sing-song voice and then she gave him another depth-charge kiss. It exploded deep inside. Her body felt hot through her clothes and Steven felt a wave of compassion. If he was ever forced to reveal the whole truth, then it would be exquisite torture to reveal it to someone like Natalie, to see so much awe and reverence turn to disgust.

'Why do you do it?' she said. 'Why do you sleep with all those women?' Her voice was shaky, as if she were in a vehicle moving fast over bumpy ground. She kissed him again.

'What women?'

'In the book.'

'Because it's better than the alternative. Better than what's on offer for the next hour. That's all. Please don't give me any *Cosmopolitan* analysis.'

His answer was the truth but it had nothing to do with the women in the book.

'You can say anything you want,' Natalie said. She kissed his neck and the heat of her breath felt like fire. 'We can talk about anything but we don't have to mean it. You can put your lips to my ear and say anything you want.'

He reached out for the ringing phone, lifted it and then

put it back on the hook. She struggled to her knees, her long hair falling on Steven's chest and she began to unbutton his shirt. The phone began to ring again and this time he took it off the hook and left it off the hook. He pushed her hair from her face and she kissed his hand with her eyes closed, as if she had been waiting to feel his hand on her face all her life. If she hadn't done that, he would have carried on. If he had thought that she just wanted to fuck, with him, the guy she had met two days ago, he would have carried on. He took hold of her hand and then gently pushed her over onto the bed.

'You are very nice,' Steven said, knowing that it was the worst thing he could say, knowing that it would be like shifting into reverse at seventy miles an hour. He stroked her face and kissed her cheek.

She lay back with her eyes closed. Steven didn't want to be unkind to Natalie and he knew that she was doing this for the wrong man. But he was fascinated at how elegant she had become. Lying beneath him she had lost all the eager awkwardness she had before she lay down. In her passion she moved slowly, like seaweed in a gentle current. Natalie pushed the side of her face into the pillow and stretched out her arms, waiting for the weight to fall on her from above. After she had waited for longer than was comfortable she said, 'Please don't make a fool of me.'

'That is the last thing I want. I'm going to stop now.'

'You can do anything. Just between now and two o'clock then after that it'll be the same as before. You don't believe me?'

'I have given you the wrong idea. I'm sorry.'

'Be like you are in the book with me. Be like that with me too.'

She looked up at him and stroked his face with her wet palms and Steven grabbed her hands and pushed them onto the bed and held them there.

'Jesus there is no way of doing this, is there?' he said. 'Trying to stop is the same as carrying on.'

She kissed the hand that was holding her own hand to the pillow. Her hair was a little wet by now.

'Natalie, I'm stopping this.'

When he let go of her hands, she put her wet palms on his face again and she touched him so tenderly, as if she were shaping his features out of wet clay. The city was hooting and honking half a mile down below just like before. The pigeons were cooing on the window ledge. 'You've got the wrong man,' Steven said into her eyes. She carried on stroking his face. 'I'm telling you you've got the wrong man, Natalie,' he said again and she sat up on the bed and kissed his neck and then threw her arms around him as if they had been lovers for years.

When she kissed him on the lips for the third time, he pushed her down onto the pillow. She threw her arms open wide. Steven sighed, knowing that the current was too strong for him to swim against it. He began to unbutton her shirt. After he had unfastened all of the buttons he yanked it open and began to unfasten the buttons on her jeans.

'You think you want this?' Steven said.

'Do this to me like the others.'

She arched her back to help him as he pulled her jeans down around her knees. When he pulled them down her pants came down too and Natalie pulled them back up, as if the proper sequence had been broken by mistake. When he put his hand between her legs she stretched out her arms again and sighed, like someone who had just woken from a hundred-year sleep. Since her eyes were so tightly closed Steven could gaze at her body and at her twisted clothes, at the look of deep concentration on her face, the way she was biting so hard on her bottom lip.

'But I really am jealous of him,' Steven said. Natalie opened her eyes lazily and smiled.

'Who?'

'Him. The man you'd do this for.'

She closed her eyes again and began a slow, writhing horizontal dance, as if she were trying to bury herself in the mattress.

'You mean my boyfriend?' she said sleepily. Steven smiled because that wasn't who he meant at all. He leant over her and kissed her on the neck.

'I'll be him until two o'clock,' he said and he pulled Natalie's pants down her short, pretty legs. 'Then after that it'll be the same as before.'

Steven took his weight on his elbow and began to unbutton his shirt and jeans.

'Be like you are,' Natalie kept sighing, her eyes still tightly closed, her face pushed sideways into the pillow.

'You keep saying that. You mean like I am in the book?'

She bit her lip and her hair was tangled with sweat. Her short, dumpy body looked like a sea creature out of its shell. So defenceless, greasy with salt water. Steven was tugging his jeans down his legs, awkwardly. His face fell onto the pillow next to hers.

'Which part?' Steven said, controlling a smile.

'With Lucretia.' She grabbed him and kissed him. 'When you say you'll turn her heroin into perfume and her cocaine into face powder . . .'

'Jesus, how many times have you read that part?'

Natalie screamed with laughter and beat his chest with her fist. Steven was already laughing.

'Don't spoil it, you bastard,' she yelled.

Steven began to kiss her neck and grunted.

'You want me to call you Lucretia?' he said, in a joke deep voice and she groaned and laughed at the same time. She wrapped her legs around his waist.

'One hundred times,' she said. 'I read it one hundred times.'

'And this is your own private fantasy.'

She pointed her finger in his face and growled.

'Don't you spoil this for me,' she said and they both laughed this time. Steven stroked her face and kissed her.

'You don't want it like this?' he said. 'Me laughing? Me joking?'

She grabbed his hand and pushed it between her legs.

'I guess not,' Steven said.

She pushed the back of her head into the pillow. Steven held her hands against the bed and manoeuvred his body on top of her. He had begun to sweat too and dribbles of sweat ran down both his arms. When he looked at her face he could see that she had disappeared into a world of her own, a world that he had created for her. All he had to do now was to get inside it with her. Just until two o'clock.

He went across to the window and closed the curtains on the panoramic view of New York. The room was filled with a pale light that filtered through the curtains. Lying on the bed, Natalie looked as peaceful and inviting as newly fallen snow, her arms and legs outstretched. There was a knock at the door.

'Jesus Christ,' Steven hissed. Natalie didn't seem to have heard it. Another knock and Steven heard a man's voice that he recognized. A dry hiss.

'Mr Hawthorne? You in there? Lobby says you're in there.'

He knocked again. Natalie was just coming round, re-emerging into the world.

'Mr Hawthorne, I tried to call from the lobby but you took the phone off the hook . . .'

'Who is it?' Steven yelled.

'It's Tom Pettman, Mr Hawthorne. NYPD. I need to ask you some questions.'

# Chapter Nine

### 1

Natalie had dressed in a rage and her clothes didn't seem to fit when she put them back on. It was as if her body had expanded with unconsummated passion. She sat on a guest chair near to the bed, straightened her hair, blew a feather from her mouth and then put her clipboard on her lap. Then she put her spectacles back on and the regression was complete. Steven dressed quickly too and opened the door. When Pettman walked in, he raised his chequer-banded trilby at Natalie and looked around the room. The bed was still a pile of twisted sheets.

'Bad time, Mr Hawthorne?' Pettman said, and he pulled open the curtains. He wore an immaculate dark grey suit with shiny brogues and freezing air hung around his overcoat in a cloud. The air inside the room was hot and smelt of sex.

'Yes actually, we were just about to fuck,' Steven said and he rubbed his face. Pettman froze at the window and then turned around with a smile.

'No law against that.' He looked at Natalie, who was blushing into her clipboard.

'You eighteen, young lady?'

If it was meant as a joke, no one laughed, not even Tom Pettman. There was a mean sourness around his blue eyes that Steven remembered from the reading. The hardness in his face was a hardness which had been worked on, beaten in. He took off his hat and sat down near the window, with his legs wide open. He hung his hat over his knee.

'Damn cold day,' he said and Natalie suddenly stood up, her hair covering her face, and said she'd be down in the lobby. Pettman watched her as she left with a look of amused contempt. Steven wanted to hit him, hard.

'What exactly did you want to see me about?' Steven said.

'Any chance of a beer?'

Steven went to the mini-bar, took out a bottle of beer and handed it to him unopened. He looked up.

'Opener,' he said.

Steven handed him the bottle-opener and he opened his bottle and took a swig. Steven sat down on the bed.

'By the way, do you have some sort of ID to come walking in here . . .'

Pettman whipped out an NYPD shield and held it in the air.

'You want me to leave, Mr Hawthorne, that's your right. But I thought maybe we could just have a talk off the record.'

'I have an appointment at two.'

'This won't take more than five minutes. Just something I need to get cleared up.'

'It's one-thirty already.'

'I read your book, Mr Hawthorne. I liked it a lot.'

Pettman stretched his arms and his back clicked. He registered some familiar, old pain inside.

'What do you want, a signed copy?' Steven said.

Pettman pretended to laugh. He turned to look out of the window.

'Hell no, Mr Hawthorne. Just need some information.'

Pettman was looking around the room at Steven's

clothes, at the copies of his book stacked on the hotel desk, at his bag of laundry. He seemed to be looking for something.

'What information?' Steven said, to stop him looking around.

'Well you see, Mr Hawthorne, it's like this. Eight days ago some demolition guys working down on Avenue D turned up a body. Black male, thirty-four, thirty-five years old. Forensic guys say he'd been dead about a year.'

Steven took a swig of his beer which had grown warm beside the bed. He looked at Pettman over his upturned bottle.

'The guy had been shot through the head. Twice. With a 9mm automatic pistol. Then the body had been burnt with kerosene.'

There was silence as Steven finished off the whole bottle in one swig. He remembered Pettman chopping out the distances in the Barnes and Noble bookstore.

'The body was in pretty bad shape but the guy's palate was still intact and we got an ID from his teeth. Traced him to the Big Farm Estate in Salvador, Brazil. The guy's name was De Soto. Raul De Soto. I guess you know where I'm heading, don't you, Mr Hawthorne?'

Steven said, 'No,' even though he did.

'Well, in your book, page 117, you describe how a year ago you witnessed the murder of a black male, thirty-four, thirty-five years old, shot twice through the head with what you confirmed at the bookstore was a 9mm automatic pistol and then burnt with kerosene. The guy you call Pilot. The guy who you say came to America via the Big Farm Estate in Salvador, Brazil. You see where I'm heading now?'

Silence. Finally Steven said, 'I have no idea what you are talking about.'

'What I am saying is that I'm curious to know if the

86

guy you call Pilot in your book was actually called Raul De Soto. It's pretty fucking clear, isn't it, Mr Hawthorne?'

More silence, apart from the cooing of the pigeons roosting on the window ledge. Either this guy was lying or this was a coincidence. The police were winkling half-rotted bodies out of the basements of Alphabet City every day. At least, that's what the papers said. And most of those bodies were the bodies of black males, a lot of them South American or Haitian. And the 9mm was the favoured weapon of the street gangs. Steven had found that out in his research.

'No,' Steven said.

'No what?'

'No that wasn't his real name. Different guy.'

Pettman nodded his head and began to revolve his trilby on the axis of his knee.

'Then would you like to put my mind at ease and tell me what the fuck your guy Pilot *was* called?'

'No. I can't.'

'But it wasn't Raul De Soto.'

'No.'

'You're sure about that?'

'Yes.'

'OK, Mr Hawthorne.'

Pettman began to whistle through his teeth and look all around the room again. He said nothing for a long time.

'So is that it?' Steven said.

'Huh? Oh, I guess so. You're telling me that this is a coincidence, then I guess that's just what it is.'

He waited a few more seconds before he suddenly stood up, holding on to his back and wincing. He flicked his hat back onto his head and headed for the door.

'Sorry to have interrupted you, Mr Hawthorne,' he said, nodding at the bed as he passed. 'You want me to send her back up?'

Steven didn't even answer. Pettman opened the door then hovered in the doorway.

'While I'm here, Mr Hawthorne, when you were living down in Alphabet City, did you ever meet a guy called Coletto Amarillo?'

'Who?'

'Amarillo. He's got a scar down the right side of his face.'

Pettman drew a line down his own dry, sandy face.

'No, I don't think I did,' Steven said.

'You live a whole year in Alphabet and you never met Coletto Amarillo?'

Steven shook his head and Detective Pettman shrugged.

'OK, Mr Hawthorne. You going to be here in this hotel for the next few days?'

'Yes.'

'That's good. Enjoy your stay in New York.'

He turned and closed the door behind him. The moment the door closed, Steven began to work on all the things Pettman had said. Ever since his father's death, coincidences had made Steven uneasy. He didn't even want to think about the odds against so many details matching up like that. The victim's identity, the circumstances of the death, the location. But Pettman had seemed to have been satisfied, and after he had gone, Steven really believed that he would never see Tom Pettman's face again.

**2**

Between red lights, while a record was playing, Foley slipped into the on-air studio and joined Steven and Natalie on the couch. The DJ was leafing through her copy of *Alphabet City*, trying to find a question to ask. It was four p.m., a radio station in Chelsea.

'Steven, sorry to interrupt you like this,' he said with an excited smile, 'but I had to give you the news . . .'

The DJ glanced at the clock on the wall, looked down at Foley sleepily and said if he had something to say he had exactly fifteen seconds to say it or the whole city would hear it.

'OK, Steven it's like this. Eliot at Eagle isn't just interested, he's coming in his pants. They want to make a deal right away. I got them down to two legal people going with you to get the permission signatures in Alphabet City. We get the signatures, Eagle buy the rights. We're looking at a starting price of seven million dollars . . .'

As Steven opened his mouth, the red light came on and the DJ said, 'My guest this afternoon is Steven Hawthorne the author of *Alphabet City*. I understand, Steven, that your book is going to be number six in *The New York Times* list this coming weekend. Is that official yet?'

Foley nodded his head at Steven, his face brimming with pride. Steven leant into the mike and said yes, it was official, and he was really thrilled.

### 3

By the time the interview finished Foley had already slipped away to take Steven's categorical insistence on confidentiality back to Eliot at Eagle. Natalie consulted her itinerary and said that there was one more interview, a guy from the *New England Review*, a little pamphlet that didn't have a big circulation but was prestigious. Steven was due to meet him in the hotel at five. He decided there and then that he would give this one a miss but he didn't tell Natalie. He needed time to think but he couldn't tell

Natalie what it was he needed to think about. She looked at him through her big, round glasses.

'You're worrying about what happened, aren't you?' she said. Steven looked at her with surprise and she prompted him. 'You're thinking about you and me. It's OK, Steven, it's like I said. We carry on just like we were before.' She blushed and said, 'Steven, I'm still in a whirl.'

Steven said that he was still in a whirl too and that it would be best if he went to his final appointment alone. She kissed him chastely on the cheek and then hurried away, leaving Steven standing in the street beside a huge iron urn dispensing turtle soup in great steaming clouds. He bought a cup, blew the steam off it, and then walked slowly towards his hotel, hoping he'd left enough time for the next appointment to fade away.

### 4

Steven didn't get back to the hotel until seven, and to his surprise he found that the guy from the *New England Review* was still waiting in the lobby. At least that's what Steven thought as he approached the front desk, and the podgy, ice cream-faced desk clerk in his tight, blue uniform raised his hands and exclaimed, 'Ah, Mr Hawthorne at last. There's someone here to see you.'

The desk clerk pointed at a dark-haired man in a raincoat who was sitting near to the revolving doors, brooding over a smoked glass table. The desk clerk cleared his throat and raised his eyebrows at the visitor and pointed at Steven's chest with a grin. The dark-haired man stood up and Steven saw straight away that he wasn't what you would expect a New England reviewer to look like. Not at all.

'You Hawthorne?' the man said as he strolled across the lobby. The lobby of the UN Plaza is filled with mirrors and chrome and polished brass and Steven felt that he was being descended upon by a whole crowd of men in raincoats, some enormous in the mirrors, some tiny and bulbous in the rounded butts of brass bannisters. The visitor's face was deep red and pock-marked with scars. 'The guy's a cop,' Steven thought.

'Yes, I'm Hawthorne. You're from Pettman's office, right?'

The guy didn't seem to hear. He grabbed Steven's arm and began to whisper.

'Lemme talk to you a moment. Step outside, I want to talk to you.'

Steven shook his arm free. It wasn't a big gesture but it froze the face of the podgy desk clerk, who instantly bent down behind the counter.

'Are you a cop?' Steven said and at any other time the question would have been hilarious. The guy wore a Rolex, smelt of spicy Cologne, had thick gold rings binding chunky fingers. He put his hand on Steven's shoulder and whispered.

'Come on, come on outside. I just want to talk.' He made a grab for Steven's arm again. 'Come on, just step over here for a moment.'

The guy's accent was hard to place. It was something strange overlain with New York intonation. That breathy urgency that enters the voice of anyone who stays in the city too long.

'Hey come on, Mr Hawthorne, whasswrong?'

'Who are you? If you're a cop I want to see ID.'

The visitor smiled and put his head to one side, a very poor attempt at looking light-hearted. His eyes were almost invisible in the creases of his dark face. Something ugly about the air around him.

'I'm a fan of yours. Of your book. Really. Over here. Lemme have a word with you.'

Steven realized that the visitor's English wasn't good. He could have been Spanish or North African but his clothes were American and expensive. Maybe this was what cops looked like in New York. Whatever he was, a fan or a cop, Steven was in no mood to talk. He turned to the desk clerk who had stood upright again, his face flushed.

'Could I have my key please', Steven said.

'Hey, Mr Hawthorne,' the visitor said and laughed behind Steven's back. Steven heard him say, 'Whasswrong with this guy?'

'My key.'

'Yes, Mr Hawthorne.'

The visitor had his hand on Steven's shoulder and Steven turned around. He now had a copy of Steven's book peeping out of the pocket of his raincoat. He held it up for Steven to see.

'You're the guy who wrote this?' the visitor said and alarm bells began to ring inside Steven's head. This guy wasn't a cop.

'Yes I am. Is that a problem?'

'No sir. No problem. I'm a fan. I loved your book. So did my kids. The whole family loved your book. And I'd just like you to sign my copy. You come over here where we can talk.'

The guy's top lip began to curl. It was like watching a lynx twitching in the moments before it pounced. Steven knew somewhere deep inside that he was in real physical danger. He turned to the clerk, who looked scared.

'Call security,' Steven said. 'I want this guy out of here.'

The clerk picked up a phone and as he did so, by chance one of the uniformed doormen came into the lobby through the revolving doors carrying a suitcase. He put the case down and wiped his forehead. He was a big black guy. The visitor turned and looked at the doorman and at the clerk. Without looking at Steven he pushed his copy of *Alphabet City* back into the pocket of his raincoat and walked quickly towards the revolving door. Steven saw his raincoat flapping as he pushed his way out into the street. Steven took a deep breath.

'Hey, you're famous, Mr Hawthorne,' the clerk said, taking off his spectacles and rubbing his eyes like a rodent.

'Yes. I suppose I must be,' Steven said, still dazed.

The desk clerk put his spectacles back on and peered at Steven, seeing him in a new light.

'You want me to warn security? I mean if this is going to happen a lot we can make arrangements. We have diplomats stay here from the UN, Imams, Sheiks, all kinds.'

Steven nodded his head, still staring at the revolving doors.

'But even if you're not real famous,' the clerk said, 'you should still be careful in this city. This city is full of the weirdest people. If people know your face they kind of like to try and get to you.'

Steven wondered if maybe this might become a feature of his life. Maybe it was true that this level of fame, even fame through a book, would attract the strangest people, would precipitate all kinds of bizarre confrontations. Anton and Zucker had placed four-by-four posters in a lot of the stores in New York, with a photograph of Steven's face. What troubled him most was that the guy with the book hadn't looked like any book-buyer that he'd ever seen. He would have been surprised if the guy could even read. There had been something primitive about him, something blunt and dull that made it hard to imagine him stretching out on a sofa with a book in his hand.

'I have another message for you too,' the clerk said, with great sympathy. He had somehow inferred that all messages were bad news for Steven Hawthorne.

'Was it the cop again?'

'Yes sir. He called three times and said that it was real urgent that you speak to him. You still want your key, Mr Hawthorne?'

Steven took the slip of grey plastic and then spent the evening in his room, with the telephone off the hook and with the door locked and chained.

## Chapter Ten

**1**

By morning, Steven had most of it worked out.

His first priority was to speak to Fiona but he couldn't carry out the delicate task of defusing her over the phone. He'd have to meet her in person. He'd inform Natalie that he had to fly out to London tomorrow and he would return two days later to continue the publicity tour. Getting out of New York City would help to put Pettman off his trail too. When he had woken up, he had placed the phone back on the hook and it rang almost immediately. The desk clerk said that people had been calling from Pettman's office and Stephanie Plater's office and John Cross's office all through the night. He had messages for Steven to call the NYPD in Avenue D and the DEA in the East Village. He was sure that if he disappeared for a few days, the whole thing would blow over.

Leaving the city would put Eagle off his trail too, at least for a while. If Eliot really was creaming in his pants, then maybe if Steven wasn't around, he'd find a way around the rights of portrayal problem for himself. In the past, Steven had always used planes as his favoured method of escape. When things got too hot, you just got the fuck out and flew to another time zone, another hemisphere and put your problems onto the horizon.

When it got light, Steven went out to a travel agency

and booked his air ticket. When he got back there was another message for him from Pettman which he screwed up and pushed into the sand of the elevator ashtray. Until his flight, he would need to spend as little time as possible at the hotel and shuffle his itinerary around in case they contacted Natalie or Foley. If they couldn't get hold of him, then he couldn't speak to them and if he couldn't speak to them, he wouldn't have to lie. When he got back to his room he called Natalie at home. Her boyfriend answered.

'Hello?' he said sleepily.

'Could I talk to Natalie?'

'Who's calling?'

'Steven Hawthorne.'

'Hey Steven. How's New York treating you?'

'It's OK.'

'Your book is just walking out of the store. Maybe I can persuade Natalie to bring you back to sign some more copies . . .'

'Maybe. Is she there?'

'Or maybe you could come round for dinner. Natalie would like that.'

'Yeah. Could I speak to her?'

When Natalie came on the phone she said 'Steven?' with a note of panic in her voice.

'It's OK,' Steven said. 'This is business. Listen, I'm sorry to call you at home like this, but something has come up. I need to change the itinerary.'

Steven explained that there had been a death in the family and he needed to go to London to organize the funeral. Little lies like this no longer seemed important enough to elaborate on. This was the first thing that came into his head, a lie off the peg.

'London?' Natalie said.

'Yes. I have family in London. My mother was English. Didn't I tell you that?'

There was silence. Steven could imagine Natalie glancing furtively at her boyfriend. He could hear the radio playing in the background, imagine the sleepy domestic scene interrupted by Steven's voice. Natalie had a secret now too.

'Well I don't know, Steven, you'll have to talk to Foley. How long will you be gone?'

'Just two days, then I'll be back. And I need you to cancel my appointments for this morning. I need to call some people and break the bad news.'

Natalie lowered her voice and spoke to Steven like a friend, like a lover.

'Steven is this for real?' she hissed.

'Yes it's for real. Jesus Christ.'

'OK, I'm sorry.'

'Just clear it with Foley for me.'

'He'll go crazy.'

'He's already crazy. Believe me, if I don't go to London it'll be worse for all of us.'

Steven guessed that Natalie's boyfriend had left the room because she said softly, 'I've been thinking about what happened . . .'

'Well don't. Remember what we said. Everything is the same as before. Just cancel my appointments this morning and talk to Foley.'

'Can he call you?'

'No. I'll be out.'

'Where, Steven?'

'I don't know. Just do it, Natalie. Lie for me. Trust me . . .'

Her boyfriend must have walked into the room, because she said brightly, 'OK, I'll do what I can. Is everything else OK?'

'Everything's fine, Lucretia,' Steven said with a smile. Natalie said nothing and he put the phone down. Steven knew that Foley would explode when he heard that Steven wanted to change the itinerary, but if he didn't speak to Fiona soon, the whole enterprise would collapse around their ears. He had no idea what he would say to her or if what he said would make any difference. But he had already begun to feel the peculiar tension he always felt when he believed that he was going to meet Fiona. There was a part of his personality that only existed when she was around.

## 2

Steven put on two woollen jerseys, his overcoat, and a hat he'd bought a year before and never worn. It was a leather hat with fur lining. He turned up the collar of his coat. He took the elevator to the lobby and as he walked through the lobby, the clerk called his name but Steven kept on walking. Outside, he saw that there was an NYPD patrol car parked opposite the line of cabs outside the hotel. Steven buried his face into his coat and ducked into the first available yellow cab.

'Where you want?' the driver said. He was African.

'I have no idea,' Steven said. Then he said, 'The Empire State Building.' The cab took off, revolving through 180 degrees right in front of the patrol car.

In the elevator at the Empire State, there was a big-boned family, mother, father, daughter; two Japanese; a blonde woman alone and the elevator operator. The wind whistled through the cavity of the elevator as they rose. Steven still had his ticket to London in his wallet.

Fiona had always been as dogged and relentless as a machine. Her head for statistics and factual data was extraordinary. If she was putting together a dossier, it would be watertight. Steven felt a pressure in his stomach as the elevator climbed. Before he could worry about Fiona, he had to get out of New York City. He stepped out of the elevator and there was the whole of the city spread out before him. He leant against the parapet and felt the icy wind blowing from the other side of the world. From up here, Steven could see the curve of the earth, the intricate map of the city directly below, the galaxies above, the endless frozen blue sky.

'Excuse me,' someone said. It was the mother of the big-boned family. 'Would you mind taking our photograph?'

Daddy and daughter were already frozen into poses against the parapet. Behind them was the mesh wire netting that was riveted to the building to prevent suicides. Daddy and daughter were smiling at the edge. Mother joined them.

Steven held up the camera to take the shot. In the eye of the camera Steven could see the smiles of the family, and beyond that the grey and blue of the city, its buildings looking like natural accretions weathered into marvellous shapes, and above them, airliners circling, waiting to belly-flop down onto the runways of JFK. Only one more day before Steven would be up in the air too. He was about to fire off a shot when someone else stepped into the frame. A big guy in a raincoat with dark hair and leathery skin and those big, pock-marked peasant features. The same guy who'd asked for Steven's signature in the lobby of the UN Plaza. He was in and out of shot in half a second, and then gone around the bend of the tower.

'Hey, what's wrong?' Daddy said, his smile fading. Steven had the camera hanging down by his waist.

'Hey. Did you take it already?'

Steven handed the camera back to Daddy without a word and took off along the parapet. The viewing area

was a hundred yards around and Steven pushed his way
through knots of tourists who were gathered at the ten-
cent telescopes. When he had gone full-circle, he got back
to the big-boned family and they had already found
someone else to take their photograph. The guy in the
raincoat was nowhere to be seen.

### 3

Next, Steven took a cab to the Guggenheim. He had
figured that it would be best to stick to places where there
would be crowds. He arrived just after ten and decided he
could use up the rest of the morning there.

Now he had another coincidence to roll around in his
mind. The big one, the monstrous one with the body in
the basement, and also the guy in the raincoat. Both
coincidences could be rationalized and explained but they
had to be rationalized and explained over and over again,
a murmur at the end of each heartbeat.

Steven was staring at a seven-by-seven canvas, smeared
with red and blue paint, thrown carelessly and left to drip.
Other people came and went and stared at the painting
too, seeing their own phantoms in the curls of paint.
Steven saw Fiona and Pettman and Natalie and the imaginary face of Pilot, which was burning up in a flick of red
pigment. The Guggenheim Gallery is a spiral of white
walls and staircases, rising backwards through the history
of modern art, starting with the daubers and the splashers
at ground level and rising up to the impressionists at the
top. It got more realistic the higher you climbed. If Steven
had been here for any reason other than escape, he would
have climbed straight to the top of the staircase to get
away from the anarchy of the daubers and splashers, the
hideous deceit and pretence of the abstract lower levels.

But since he was hardly seeing the paintings anyway, he simply stood and stared at the first painting he came to.

'So what do you think?' said the young woman who came to stand at his side.

'Of the painting?'

'Yes.'

'I think it is the most idiotic . . . no, no, not idiotic. I think it's just funny. It's funny that it's there on the wall for people to look at.'

'So you don't like abstract,' the woman said.

'This isn't abstract. It's just paint.'

'In art galleries, you're supposed to whisper,' the woman said, and Steven turned to her. Curly blonde hair, a neat face which was also surprisingly hard. Steven nodded, realizing that his anxiety had been making him speak a little too loudly.

'So I guess you prefer the figurative stuff.'

'Yeah I guess I do.'

'You think art should look like life?'

'Something like that.'

'You think art should be based on reality. That there shouldn't be anything from the imagination. It should all be the truth. Paintings, books.'

Steven turned to her again. This time he recognized her face. It was the woman in the second row who had irritated him with questions about Pilot in the Q and A session on East 53rd.

'Especially books,' she said with a curl to her lips. 'You think that everything in books should be the truth. Eyewitness accounts.' Her hard neat face wrinkled into a smile. She was smiling at Steven's look of horror. 'I guess I should introduce myself. I'm Stephanie Plater, from Tom Pettman's office. Can I buy you a coffee?'

They sat in the slate-grey café next to the gallery bookshop, perched on grey, iron chairs. Stephanie Plater was stirring the froth on the top of her coffee and staring down at it, pursing her lips, thinking hard.

'This is a big city, Mr Hawthorne,' she said, and then looked up at him and smiled, 'but we're pretty hot when it comes to finding needles in haystacks.'

'I have nothing to say,' Steven said.

'You don't even know what I want to ask.'

'It's about a body you found. You want me to help identify a body. But I have to tell you that I know nothing about it. That I really can't help you.'

Stephanie was finally ready to sip her coffee. She took a sip and wiped the froth from her lip with her sleeve. It was a suprisingly manly gesture. Maybe cops were like that.

'I know,' she said. 'Tom told me already. But I decided that maybe you'd made a mistake. It happens, Mr Hawthorne. I decided to give you one more chance.'

She reached down and put her purse on the table. She began to sort through it, humming a tune as she did so. Then she produced a stiff-backed envelope and from the envelope she pulled four passport-sized photographs of a black guy with short-cropped hair. They were reduced mug shots, named and numbered.

'This is Raul De Soto. The guy we found in the basement in Avenue D.'

'Really.'

Steven looked at the photos and handed them back.

'Is this man familiar to you?' Stephanie said.

'I never saw him before in my life.'

Stephanie carefully placed the photographs back into the envelope. She put the envelope back into her purse and produced a packet of cigarettes. She offered one to Steven and he suddenly recognized the scene. He recognized her steely coolness, the flippant way she asked important questions, the 'screw you' smile. This was an interrogation scene. These were the cigarettes that the cop offered to the witness. He refused her offer and Stephanie placed the pack on the table. She didn't smoke one herself.

'You're sure about that?' she said, incredulously.

'Dead sure.'

Stephanie looked around the café nonchalantly. Steven couldn't take his eyes off her. She looked like she could be the meanest bitch on God's earth if this coolness were ever challenged.

'But you do remember a guy named Polka,' she said at last.

'Who?'

'Polka. The kids call him Polka. Weird son of a bitch. Everyone knows Polka.'

Steven remembered what the DJ had said three days before about Polo sounding like a weird guy he knew called Polka. He realized that it might be possible that he'd somehow shaped the character of Polo out of some little snippets of conversation he'd had with cab drivers. He wasn't sure which parts of the book had foundations in reality. If Polka was such a character in the area, like the DJ had said, it was possible that someone had mentioned him and Steven had spun him around and turned him into Polo, although he couldn't remember ever consciously basing anyone on anyone.

'No I don't remember anyone called Polka,' Steven said.

'A whole year in Alphabet City . . .'

'I've been through this with Pettman. I don't know any Polka and I don't know any Raul De Soto.'

Stephanie took a sip of coffee and said, 'Well he sure remembers you.'

'Who does?'

'Polka. He told us, "Sure I remember Thomas Bolivar, the Cuban guy. Handsome fellow."' Stephanie's eyes twinkled. 'He was right too, you are a handsome fellow.'

'I told you, I never heard of anyone called Polka. Polka and Polo are different people.'

'Who said anything about Polo?' Stephanie said. 'Is that what you're saying, Polka in real life is Polo in the book?'

Steven pushed his chair back away from the table and the iron legs made a loud scraping sound against the tiled floor. The noise was so loud that some of the other people in the café turned around. Stephanie Plater didn't even blink. She was cuddling her coffee cup.

'Going so soon?' she said.

'I take it that you have no legal right to make me answer questions?' Steven said. Stephanie raised her eyebrows and shook her head.

'Why no legal right at all. We just thought that as a citizen you might want to help us clear this thing up.'

'Well I'm afraid I'm not a great talker,' Steven said. 'Ask anyone.'

'We already did.'

Stephanie's remarks were making Steven angry, even though he was nervous too. Besides, he was sure that she was fishing. He knew for a fact that she was fishing because there was no way that anyone called Polka could have remembered Thomas Bolivar, because Thomas Bolivar had never existed except in the pages of a book. And besides, the DJ had said that the guy Polka was crazy. This whole thing was crazy.

'I have a very busy day,' Steven said, standing up.

'What about a guy named Coletto Amarillo?'

Steven unhooked his overcoat from the back of his chair. Stephanie watched him dispassionately.

'Everyone in the Alphabet knows Coletto,' Stephanie said. 'He says he's an Apache Indian. He's a Mexican but he says he's an Apache Indian. He has a scar right here down his face . . .' Stephanie leant over the table and grabbed Steven's arm as he tried to put it into the sleeve of his overcoat. 'Are you paying attention to me, Mr Hawthorne?'

Steven shook her off and began to button his coat.

'He has a scar right here down the side of his face and, you see, Mr Hawthorne, we were thinking that maybe the bad guy in your book, the guy who pulled the trigger in the basement, that guy you call Emilio, might really be our guy Coletto Amarillo . . . It's like a guessing game we play in the office with your book. We're through guessing and now we need you to give us the answers.'

Steven stopped buttoning his coat and then leant on the table on his fists. He smiled at Stephanie.

'I can assure you', he said softly, 'that all of the people in your investigation and all of the characters in my book are different. As God is my witness. Not just different people, different species, different universe.'

Stephanie reached for a cigarette.

'Some of our smartest people have been playing it. People at Homicide, the DEA, now me. Do you have a light, Mr Hawthorne?'

'This is a no-smoking café.'

'I'm a cop. The rules don't apply to me. You should remember that. Tell me about that night with Coletto Amarillo. Page 117.'

She reached into her bag and Steven thought she was searching for a light. She still had the cigarette between her lips. Instead she produced an ID card.

'Perhaps I should have introduced myself right at the start,' Stephanie said, standing up beside him. 'I'm working out of Pettman's office for this investigation but I'm FBI.'

She was holding out an ID card for Steven to look at. He fumbled with the last of the buttons on his overcoat, not wanting to look up.

'You should look at it, Mr Hawthorne. You should take a good look. You see, I'm not a regular cop. I work on the Witness Protection Programme. I know I look too sweet and pretty but that's what I do. I protect witnesses.'

'Then I suggest . . .'

'I'm talking about you, Mr Hawthorne. You are the witness I am rostered to protect.'

Steven glanced at Stephanie's ID card. A fuzzy portrait shot and a silver shield.

'We know already that Amarillo shot De Soto,' she said. 'We even know why. But we didn't know we had a witness to the murder until someone at the DEA read page 117. The whole thing matches word for word. The problem for you, Mr Hawthorne, is that Coletto Amarillo reads books too. He didn't know that you were hiding down there in the shadows when he shot De Soto, but he sure as hell knows now. You're making him famous, Mr Hawthorne, but he's kind of shy of publicity. And you've got your photo in every bookstore in New York.'

Steven knew lying inside out, and Stephanie didn't sound like someone who was lying. He turned and hurried out of the Guggenheim Gallery and out into the street, where the wind was blowing colder, the first panting breaths of the approaching blizzard that had finally made it all the way down from Alaska.

## 4

Steven walked through Chinatown, getting wet shoes and wet hair in the freezing drizzle and the occasional flurries of snow. The sky over New York had turned slate-grey, and the wind smelt of the ocean. Steven imagined that it smelt of home, wherever that was. He sheltered beneath the canopy of a Chinese food store for a long time, smoking cigarettes and running scenarios through his head, vivid scenarios that had real people and real dialogue in them.

This was how Steven had worked when he had been writing the book. Standing on street corners, or beneath canopies, or sometimes sitting in cafés, taking just the tiniest grain of truth and working on it, like an oyster, spinning it into a pearl. It had become a habit that was hard to break. Then Steven began to run through the murder scene in the basement. The way he had written it, he'd followed Emilio and Polo when they had dragged Pilot out of a bar. He had hidden in the shadows of the basement when Emilio had fired the shots. The flames from Pilot's body had almost given Steven away.

*"I run this street," Emilio bellowed as the flames began to consume Pilot's body. 'Anybody think any different they get a bullet in their thoughts. I put a bullet right into their thoughts.'*

*It was surprising sometimes how lyrical crack-heads could be . . .'*

Steven remembered that he'd got the idea for the murder scene from a cop show on TV. Just the initial idea. After that, it had all been brewed up in his imagination.

'Hey, mister,' came a tiny Chinese voice from the shadows behind where Steven was standing, 'you in my way.'

Steven stepped aside and an old Chinese lady, as small as a child, edged her way around him with a mountain of silk draped over her arm. She looked up at the rain and stole an umbrella from the display rack right beside where Steven was standing. She put the umbrella up, held it over the bundle of silk, and then stepped uneasily into the deluge. Steven made a note in his head that the old lady should be booked for a place in his next book. The whole movement, the silk, the umbrella, the brooding New York dusk, the steady walk, like the walk of a turtle beneath the brightly coloured waterproof shell. That was how lies could be made to work. You made lies out of tiny fragments of truth, like a mosaic, and when you stood far enough back from the fragments, the whole thing looked real. But the real art was in the fragments you chose. You had to choose dull pieces, ordinary, inconsequential fragments that made no sense on their own. And the duller and more ordinary each piece was, the more effective it would be when you fastened it in its place. If the old Chinese lady had stepped into the street and been hit by a taxi cab, he wouldn't have been able to use it. But instead she had just stepped into the rain and disappeared into the shadows. Steven felt pleased with the Chinese lady, and placed her in his mosaic. Who would suspect that beneath her bundle of silk, the old Chinese lady had a silk purse and inside the purse a whole pound of sparkling white, refined opium? And beneath her buttoned-up blue and gold tunic, a silver spoon on a chain and an ornamental dagger. And on her forearm a tattoo of a serpent with a bird between its jaws.

Steven began to walk aimlessly towards his hotel. The overcast sky made it feel like dusk. He caught a glimpse of his own photograph in the window of a bookstore, looking out moodily into the rain, and he thought about what Stephanie had said about Coletto Amarillo. He took his leather hat out of his pocket and pulled it down hard over his head, covering his face.

This was absurd. Even the names, Coletto Amarillo and Polka and De Soto were absurd, but Stephanie and Pettman were real. And if he carried on walking in a certain direction, just a mile and a half, he'd find himself in Alphabet City, amongst its dank fortresses, and that place was real too. Maybe the spirit of Alphabet City had decided to take its vengeance. That would be funny, wouldn't it? And it had been funny when Steven had chosen to set his 'diary' in Alphabet City, because that was private joke of his own. A city made out of letters, a city created from words. Now it was becoming real, coming at him off the page.

When Steven got back to the lobby of his hotel, soaked to the skin and filled with dislocated fears, Natalie was waiting for him. She leapt on him the moment he walked through the revolving doors of the UN Plaza. It was noon, but it felt like midnight already.

'Steven, thank God you're back. We have to go meet Foley.'

'Wait a minute.'

'We can't wait, Steven. He's having some kind of seizure. I couldn't get any sense out of him but he said that if you don't speak to him right away, this whole thing is going to be shot down in flames. Those were his words, Steven. Come on, I got a cab waiting outside.'

## Chapter Eleven

### 1

Foley was pacing the floor of the Anton and Zucker boardroom like a caged bear. When Steven and Natalie walked in, Steven still dripping, Foley was walking and talking to himself in front of the big panoramic view over New York. When he saw Steven he grabbed his arm and eased him down into a seat at the boardroom table.

'Natalie, wait outside,' he said.

She stood her ground for a moment. She had hooks into this thing that Foley didn't understand and she wanted to assert her new authority. But the way Foley glared at her melted her resolve before she said a word and she left. She squeezed Steven's shoulder before she departed. Foley waited longer than was necessary to make sure she was gone. He was still pacing back and forth, analysing the carpet as he walked.

'Steven, I had a call this morning from someone called Siam Drayton . . .'

'Great name.'

Foley glared at Steven and then resumed his patrol of the window.

'Siam Drayton is an investigative reporter on *The New York Times*. They tell me she's the best. She has a reputation.'

He let that fact sink in. He looked like a man laying the foundations of his own execution chamber.

'Siam Drayton informed me that she had been approached by a woman in London called Fiona Van Draken. A woman who claims to be your wife.'

He peeked at Steven to check that this was true. Steven's silence meant that it was true. Another foundation stone laid.

'Fiona Van Draken told Drayton she had documentary evidence that there was no way that you could have spent a year living in Alphabet City. Evidence which proves that you never lived in Alphabet City at all.'

This time Foley didn't peek at Steven to check if this was true and it was an important decision. What Foley needed now was silence. Silence was his only, desperate chance of survival.

'Siam Drayton says that she has now seen a copy of the documentary evidence and believes it to be genuine.'

The ghastly structure was now taking shape.

'She has spent two weeks verifying the information in the dossier and she says that she will corroborate what Fiona Van Draken is alleging.'

Steven thought about his friends, his enemies, his rivals. Some of them may have helped Fiona put it together knowing what she was doing. Anderson could be discounted, maybe not. Maybe Anderson was in on this from the beginning. Maybe Anderson's sympathy had all been phoney . . . 'Fiona, you should have seen his fucking face!'

'And Siam Drayton has made an official request to my department to be given the chance to interview you face to face. To confront you with the evidence. A request which I have refused.'

More silence. Foley did two full widths of the boardroom with his fingers pulling at his lips. Then he came to a halt.

'It is true that Fiona Van Draken is your wife?'

'Yes.'

'The wife you didn't want us to know about.'

'Foley, listen to me . . .'

Foley waved his hand for silence and then began to pace again and took some deep breaths, like an engine overheating and sucking in cool air.

'I have spoken already to our senior attorney and she advised me that I must under no circumstances ask you the next, obvious question. If I ask you whether it is actually true that *Alphabet City* is a hoax and you answer, then Anton and Zucker would be legally implicated. For the moment all we need from you is a number where Fiona Van Draken can be reached.'

Steven started to say that Foley should get hold of himself and calm down but he turned on him, his face bursting with anxiety. He patted the air with his hands to stop Steven from speaking, as if any word from Steven could blow down a whole house of cards.

'You give us her number and her address and we will check out her dossier for ourselves. If the allegations turn out to be false then we carry on as before. Otherwise, we will explore the possibility of reaching some kind of accommodation with her.'

'Accommodation?'

Foley shook his head at some private conversation he was having in his own head. He spoke as if some elaborate self-defence mechanism had already been set into motion. As if an organization as big as Anton and Zucker made provision in advance for every eventuality. Meteorite damage, flood, earthquake. But Foley's face said that this was worse than all of those things put together.

'Natalie tells me that you are leaving the country tomorrow,' he said quickly.

'Yes. Are you talking about offering her money?'

'The fact that you are leaving the country is the only

piece of good news in what has been without doubt the worst morning of my professional career.'

'Foley, you're running way ahead of yourself here,' Steven said. 'I've already made arrangements to speak to Fiona. You've got to remember that the bitch is as jealous as hell of me. I'm leaving for London tomorrow to speak to her myself.'

Foley gasped at this new, final twist of the dagger.

'Natalie told me you had to go to a funeral. That another lie, Mr Hawthorne?'

Unlike Anton and Zucker, Steven didn't have his defence mechanism already in place and he had no position to defend anyway. Foley seemed to be assuming that what Fiona had said was the truth. Steven hadn't expected her to act so swiftly. Part of his mind was still re-running his conversation with Stephanie, which by now seemed almost fictional.

'I cancelled all your remaining engagements until this matter is resolved,' Foley said. 'Until we give you authorization, you speak to no one. Understood? Not a word to anyone.'

Foley suddenly laughed at the madness of it all. There was silence while Foley pushed all the air out of his chest, as if he'd just run a fast sprint. Then he suddenly slammed both his fists down on the boardroom table and yelled, 'Jesus fucking Christ!' He composed himself quickly. 'Leave the number at the front desk,' he said softly. 'That's all I have to say. Now get out of my sight.'

'Foley, I can talk to her . . .'

Foley took Steven by the collar and hissed into his face.

'If this thing screws up my career, you son of a bitch . . .'

Steven suddenly grabbed Foley by the neck and the wispy hair on the back of his head. He lifted him bodily and pushed him with a thud against the window. On the

East River, barges were drifting slowly through the snow. In the distance, Alphabet City was lost in a fuzz of cloud. Steven grabbed Foley's chin and pushed his face against the glass.

'If you just looked out of your fucking window!' Steven yelled. 'If you people had just once looked out of your fucking window.'

Foley was beginning to choke. There was a smear of blood on the glass. Steven let Foley go and he stayed curled against the window, his face ugly with fury and fear. Steven slowly backed away and then turned and walked out of the boardroom. In the reception area, Natalie was waiting dutifully with her clipboard.

'What was it, Steven?' she whispered, standing to attention. Steven walked straight past her and headed for the elevator. She ran after him.

'Was it because you wanted to go to London? Is he letting you go?'

Steven punched the elevator button three times.

'Did he tell you that I asked permission to come with you?'

Steven wanted to tell her the truth but he didn't and for the first time it wasn't for his own benefit, it was for someone else's. He didn't want Natalie's affection to be soiled with this.

She checked her battered itinerary and there were tears in her eyes.

'I got another call from the guy at the NYPD, Steven. Do you think we can get some air-time out of that? I mean maybe they're asking you to lecture to their people . . .'

The elevator doors opened. Steven stepped inside and Natalie said, 'It's something terrible isn't it?' Steven let the doors close without saying a word.

## 2

Eleven minutes to nine in the bar of the UN Plaza hotel. Steven checked the clock every few minutes, counting down the minutes to the moment when his jet plane would leave the tarmac at JFK. It had turned cold outside but according to the weather reports on TV he'd be slipping out just ahead of the blizzard that had been chasing him all the way from the Arctic. The way he saw things now, even the weather was pursuing him.

The bar was made of mirrors and chrome and red plush velvet. There were so many mirrors and the lights were so low that it was hard to tell where the spaces ended and the reflections began. He'd drunk eight beers but he was more sober than he had ever been. The Italian barman had lost interest in trying to make conversation. There were five or six other guys in the bar, all sitting alone, clean-shaven, red-faced, too big for their suits, all sipping mineral water. Steven was too busy looking for ways out to notice them.

He knew that speaking to Fiona would be a pointless exercise, that it would only irritate the rash of anger, but he needed to speak to her anyway. He wanted to look at her face again, even if she would be sneering and laughing at him. He wanted to look into her eyes because she had been his queen once when he had been king. Their love for each other had been buried alive in jealousy but it was still there. That was why it clawed and scratched and screamed so hard. Why else would Fiona have gone to so much trouble? The fact that she had expended so much energy on destroying him cheered him a little, because the thing that he had hated most about their final days in London was that he had become an irrelevance to her.

What he hated was to be ignored by her. He raised his glass and toasted her in beer across three thousand miles of ocean.

Someone came and sat on the bar stool beside him.

'Mr Hawthorne . . .'

'If you know my name I don't want to talk to you.'

'Mr Hawthorne, I came to apologize.'

Steven turned and saw hollow eyes, a thin guy with a bald head who was too skinny for his shirt.

'Who the hell are you?'

'I came to apologize for the behaviour of some of my people. Pettman, Plater.'

Steven waved at the Italian barman for his check. He wasn't ready to go through this again.

'Instead of reassuring you as they should have done, they have scared you. I don't want you to be scared.'

The guy put a bony hand on Steven's hand. It felt like the touch of death. The hand was cold as sleet.

'There is no need to be scared because there are people in this bar who are here for your protection.'

The Italian barman handed Steven his check and the cold, bony hand took it and slipped it into a pocket somewhere in the darkness. Steven turned to him and saw a cold smile.

'What the fuck are you talking about, protection?'

'It's important that you take your time and consider what is at stake. This is my card. You call me when you're ready.'

He placed a card on the bar and then disappeared into the shadows and out into the lobby. Steven looked at the card and saw the words 'John Cross, Drug Enforcement Agency'. Beneath that there was a phone number written in a child's hand. He turned around to look at the guys in the suits who he hadn't even noticed before and it felt like turning to look into the faces of the dead. Each one of them was staring back at him, not even blinking. Steven felt like a man who'd been playing poker with the same hand for three whole days, who had finally decided to throw it in. He stood up and said softly to himself, 'This is insane. I've got to get out of here.'

## Chapter Twelve

### 1

'Have you enjoyed your stay in New York?' the clerk said as he waited for Steven's bill to be printed. It was the same pudgy-faced clerk who'd given him so many messages. Steven looked out through the revolving doors at the early-morning drizzle. It wasn't even light yet but he could see that the street was empty. No cops, no cars except a taxi cab with the driver asleep at the wheel. All the red-faced guys had disappeared and Steven was no longer sure that they had ever been real, or that they had ever really been what he feared they were.

'I saw that guy again,' the clerk said, fussing with some papers. 'The guy who wanted you to sign his book.'

Steven turned around quickly. 'You saw him? Where?'

'Right here last night. He came into the lobby and he walked right back out again. I guess that book of yours is really something. I can't wait to read it myself.'

The clerk was smiling shyly. Steven realized that he was holding a copy of *Alphabet City* and that it was open beneath the print-out of Steven's bill. He handed Steven a pen and Steven signed the book.

'Hey, you'd better sign the bill too.'

After he had signed, he took the bill and stuffed it into his pocket. He hauled his case through the revolving doors and rapped on the window of the cab where the driver was sleeping. He sat to attention and Steven ducked inside the cab. The light outside had already begun to turn grey. The driver was a white guy with an Anglo name. As he pulled away he said, 'Which airline you want?'

'TWA.'

'You in a hurry?'

'Yes.'

'You late for your flight?'

'No. I'm just in a hurry.'

The sun rose grudgingly as they headed for the Manhattan Bridge. On the arc of the bridge, Steven could see the frosty Manhattan skyline emerging from the darkness, the shroud of fog over the river. The driver said that it would snow soon for sure and Steven thought about the flight. He'd been snowed in at JFK before, held back overnight until the ice on the wings of the jet had melted. The driver was complaining about the weather and then he shifted effortlessly from the natural elements to the dangers of driving a cab if you were a white guy in New York City.

'Last year, forty-five cab-drivers were shot dead in New York. Young guys. Night drivers. I don't do nights no more. Don't do nights or Harlem or the South Bronx or Alphabet City. If it's a white guy like you I take them there but I don't pick up. I lock my doors and drive until I'm back in civilization.'

Steven had only ever had four Anglo cab-drivers in the whole time that he was researching his book. They always said the same things, they always knew all the statistics. They were the most likely to carry weapons, the most likely to get nervous and pick a fight, the most likely to be drunk. When they arrived at the ramp of JFK, Steven paid the driver and gave him a big tip and hurried into the airport building. He checked the departures board and saw that the eight o'clock flight to London was delayed by ten minutes. Ten minutes was nothing. It wasn't unusual for a flight to be delayed by an hour or two routinely in winter. But ten minutes was OK.

The airport was quiet. There were a few security guys slouching around the check-in area, and little huddles of bleary-eyed passengers, Japanese, French, English, North African, the whole world returning home, like warrior chieftains leaving Rome. As Steven checked his luggage, he could feel his jaws clamped together. He could still hear the voice inside his head saying 'This is insane, get out of here, get out of here,' and he was obeying that voice to the letter. His daddy had always said that you should sit tight but Steven had hit the ejector button and he knew that he was right to do it. Once he had left New York, the mild furore that his book had caused would die down. This was a big, busy city and his book was a little item, worth one, maybe two days' attention at the bottom of the page. And when he had gone, Pettman would conclude his murder investigation without Steven's help. Some guy shot in Alphabet City, a routine case that would be forgotten in a week or less. And once Steven arrived in London, he would tell Warren that he was making himself unavailable for interview. From now on the book could stand on its own. It was too hot out there in the glare of the lights and Steven wanted to retreat to the shadows. As Steven approached passport control, he allowed himself a sigh of relief. The air in his lungs restored his nerve. He hadn't taken a deep breath for days. He walked into the hot, low-ceilinged corral that led down to departures, flanked on both sides by walls of smoked glass. He handed his passport to a black lady in a black uniform who was sitting inside a small cubicle. She glanced at the photo and then at Steven and Steven met her eye and smiled.

'Enjoy your trip, Mr Hawthorne,' she said.

Then, as Steven walked by her, she leant forward and

pushed a button. A second later, as if connected to the button by wires, two invisible doors in the smoked glass wall flew open. Steven was now a yard beyond the passport control desk, a yard into customs control. First, from the right, he saw two guys in uniform who headed straight for him, then two guys in suits emerging from the left. Then he saw the dry face and the sandy hair of Detective Tom Pettman. Pettman was accompanied by another guy in a suit, who was fat and sweating. One of the uniformed guys took Steven by the arm and Pettman blocked his path.

'This gentleman here,' Pettman said, pointing lazily at the fat sweaty one, 'is a representative of the Bureau of. Alcohol, Tobacco and Firearms.'

The fat man smiled.

'You are now in his custody. And let me tell you, Mr Hawthorne, this is one of the most powerful guys in the whole of the United States, in terms of powers of arrest.'

All this flattery made the fat man blush. The uniformed officers had started talking to each other, laughing, like this was routine business. Some other passengers walked by and stared at what was going on. 'And it seems, Mr Hawthorne,' Pettman said with a laugh, 'that my friend here has gotten it into his head that you may be transporting illegal substances across the frontier. Maybe he read your book. I know that isn't much to go on but you see, with the BAT, suspicion is enough to hold you. He has the power to detain you until he is completely satisfied that you are clean. And in my experience, that can take an awfully long time.'

The uniformed guy who was holding Steven's arm mumbled something and the fat one nodded his head. The uniformed guy let go of Steven's arm.

'And while we are waiting for my friend to conclude his thorough examination of your luggage,' Pettman said, 'I have his permission to talk to you. Just informally. Just to kill the time.'

Steven had crossed the line. He should have been expecting something like this. His daddy always said that you had to use your radar, you had to expect an attack from any angle. He had hit the ejector button and the damn thing had failed to work.

'You agree to talk to me?' Pettman said. Steven said 'No,' and Pettman laughed.

'I'm afraid on the line of the frontier, you have no choice.'

Steven was led to a small interrogation room behind the smoked glass walls. The walls were sealed with brown hardboard, punched full of holes, and behind that there was egg-box soundproofing. The door to the interrogation room was thick and heavy and was sound-proofed too. The air inside was dead, all sound muted. It was hot and Steven began to sweat hard beneath his heavy overcoat. There was a desk and four chairs. He sat down and Pettman swung one of the chairs around and sat on it back to front, leaning against the back rest.

'You look kind of nervous, Mr Hawthorne,' Pettman said. His face looked as if it had been chiselled out of soft stone, and his eyes were milky. The air around him smelt of fresh soap, and in the airless room the smell was overpowering. Steven said nothing.

'You want coffee? Glass of water?'

'I want a lawyer. I want legal representation. Either that or I want to board my flight. It leaves in forty-five minutes. You have no right to detain me. If I miss my flight I will make sure that your department pays for another ticket.'

Pettman rubbed his hand through his hair and chanted a formal explanation in legal language that in this place, which was outside of all federal jurisdiction, Steven had no right to legal representation, no rights of any kind.

'But Steven, you got to understand,' Pettman said, 'I only want to talk. My friend from the BAT, he's pretty thorough. He'll squeeze your toothpaste and drip formaldehyde onto your shaving foam and wash out your clothes and tear open your books. Some of his processes can take half a day, longer. That's a long time to sit in silence.'

The silence in this room was charged with electricity. Maybe it had been designed that way. The air was so still and stale that silence was an obscenity. Perhaps some psychologist had planned this room to make conversation and confession inevitable. Steven shook his head and then looked up at the ceiling, soundproofed too. Pettman reached into the pocket of his jacket and produced a copy of Steven's book. He laid it down on the table and Steven saw the familiar cover design, the silver lettering.

'All that I ask is that we have a conversation about your book,' Pettman said, flicking it open, 'just like I was a reporter from the *Village Voice*.'

There was a phone on the desk and Pettman picked it up and ordered a pot of coffee. Then, to break the silence, he began to read aloud from selected passages.

### 2

*'I remember thinking that it was a silly elaboration to use a silencer out here, out in the wilderness, out among the burnt-out, chewed-up fortresses of Alphabet City. This was a rotten place for Pilot to die. Rotten right down to the core. These places, these waterlogged basements, were the rotten molars at the back of New York City's smile . . .'*

Pettman broke off from his reading to pour the coffee.

Pettman's reading had been awkward and it reminded Steven of how he himself had read aloud from the book in the early days of his publicity tour, before he got his delivery right. He had soon discovered that the delivery that worked best was a kind of halting understatement, flat and unprofessional. If he read it too slick then the impact of the words was lost. If he kept his delivery flat, then any raising or lowering of his voice was more noticeable. He could convey great emotion with just a pause and whisper. Pettman's emphasis had been uniform and dull. He pushed a cup of coffee across the desk.

'You see there you talk about a silencer. And yet later, when the guy Emilio pulls the trigger, you describe a very loud bang. That's kind of an anomaly that I couldn't quite figure.'

Steven didn't touch the coffee and didn't respond. He had decided that even here at the frontier, they couldn't hold him forever. This could take hours, even days, but in the end Pettman would grow weary of the silence and he would be forced to let Steven go. There was another alternative. He could clear his throat right now, and explain in a plain and simple way that the whole of his book, all of it, was a hoax. He could describe to Pettman how he had written the whole thing in his grandmother's house. How he had taken the murder scene in the basement from a TV cop show. How he had used the name 'Pilot' because his father was a pilot. How he'd taken the name 'Polo' from a bottle of after-shave that had been on his desk when he was writing. He could smile and wink at Pettman and say, 'Mr Pettman, what we have here is a coincidence. You're wasting your time.'

'Did the guy Emilio remove the silencer before he shot Pilot?' Pettman said. 'I'm using your names because that way I guess we can talk hypothetically. Hell I know the position you're in. You think I think it's easy to come right out and testify against a guy like Coletto Amarillo? I understand the position you're in, Mr Hawthorne, and I sympathize, but maybe we can just have this conversation about the characters in the book. Like this whole thing was imaginary. That would be easier wouldn't it? So did Emilio remove the silencer?'

Steven laughed at the irony and sipped his coffee. Pettman took some comfort from Steven's laughter. He was speaking softly now.

'He's a mean son of a bitch,' Pettman said and Steven took another sip of coffee and said, 'Who is?' Pettman tried not to show his triumph that Steven had spoken at all.

'Your guy Emilio. The killer. Kind of guy who should be removed from society. You agree with that?'

'Yes I suppose I do.'

'And the guy Pilot, he was just some dude who got confused, wrapped up. Circumstances. He was a friend of yours. And this guy Emilio puts two bullets into his brain. I guess that made you pretty mad.'

Pettman's psychological stalking was clumsy. Like being crept up on by an African elephant.

'Wouldn't it make you feel good to get even with Emilio?'

Steven's deceit made him feel superior, made Pettman look foolish in his eyes. Then Pettman leant across the table and took hold of Steven's shoulder.

'Please don't smile at me like that,' Pettman said.

'Passport and ticket. That's all I need.'

Pettman sat back down heavily.

'OK, let's cut the crap about Emilio and Pilot,' Pettman said. 'In your book you describe how you saw Coletto Amarillo shoot Raul De Soto in the basement of 1124 Avenue D. You saw him shot and then burnt. Let's cut the crap, Mr Hawthorne, because this isn't just some crack-head having what is left of his brains blown away. We both know that. This is a case with far-reaching implications. If you only knew it, smart ass, I'm protecting you from a lot of people way up there who want to have you arrested as a fucking accomplice. There are some high-up people who have been trying to nail Coletto Amarillo's ass for a long, long time. People who have lost buddies in the process. This isn't just a routine investigation, Mr Hawthorne, but I believe you know enough to know that already.'

Pettman stood up and left the room. The soundproofed door locked itself when it closed with a heavy, muffled thud.

## Chapter Thirteen

'Qwuueee, qwueeee, qwueee,' Stephanie Plater said, cupping her hands around her mouth. 'That's the white egret. Female.'

Stephanie had already explained to Steven that she did bird impressions, that she used to do them all the time when she was a kid and bored, when she had nothing else to do. And since Steven was choosing not to say anything, then she had figured that she would go through her repertoire. She had already done the blackbird, the yellow oriole, the sandpiper.

'I do animals too,' she said, raising her eyebrows. 'The mammals of the Mississippi Delta. Here's the possum . . .'

'Stephanie, what do you do if someone in your custody commits suicide out of boredom?' Steven said. Stephanie had already shaped her mouth for the possum, but hesitated.

'Mr Hawthorne, you're not in *my* custody,' she said. 'You're in the custody of the BAT.'

Steven nodded and Stephanie let out a soft, vibrant purr that made her lips tremble. Steven had never heard a possum in the Mississippi Delta but imagined that if he were a male possum, and he had heard that noise, he would be interested.

'Next, I do the alligator.'

Steven waited. The silence was still suffocating. 'Except

alligators don't make a noise. That's my joke. I do jokes too. You want to hear my jokes?'

Stephanie had taken over from Pettman an hour before. It was now after four and Steven's flight had left eight hours ago. Every time the door to the interrogation room opened, Steven could hear the familiar noises of the airport, the murmur of conversation, the gentle roar of aircraft, the ping-pong of departure announcements. But when the door closed, all those sounds were cut off. Then there was just Stephanie and her birds and animals.

'You'll hate my jokes even more than my impressions,' Stephanie said. 'So what do you say we talk instead?'

'I have nothing more to say. I have told you, I didn't witness any murder anywhere at any time.'

'Heard the one about the Italian guy . . .'

'And if I am not on the next flight out of this city . . .'

'Italian guy. Gangster. You know, bang, bang, bang.'

Steven slapped his hand on the desk and the sound of it was flattened by the softness of the walls. Stephanie's eyes didn't flicker. Steven knew that there were no more flights to London until next morning, but he could get a flight to Dublin or Paris and get a connection. In the past two hours he had decided that he couldn't bear silence and had instead answered every question with the statement that he hadn't witnessed any murder, anywhere, at any time, that he had never heard of Raul De Soto and that he had never heard of anyone called Coletto Amarillo. It was the truth, but even as Steven had said it, over and over again, it had begun to sound like a lie. He had told it to Pettman and to Stephanie and they both said with great compassion that they understood why Steven might want to say stuff like that, but circumstances pointed to a different conclusion. The body, the number of bullets, the calibre of the gun used, the physical descriptions of the people involved. Everything matched up. It was too absurd to believe that it was a coincidence. The more Stephanie and Pettman said it, the more Steven had found himself agreeing with them.

Stephanie cooed like a dove.

'Jesus Christ,' Steven said.

'What? You don't like my turtle dove? OK, back to the jokes. Italian guy. Goes into a bar. Except he's not Italian he's chicano. He's a chicano gangster. He's called Coletto Amarillo. Bang, bang, bang.'

Steven put his hands behind his head and stared at Stephanie. He gave her a look of weary contempt which was reflected straight back as if her eyes were made of polished silver.

'Bang, bang, bang. Coletto Amarillo, sells crack cocaine out of a chain of launderettes in Alphabet City. He owns the launderettes and they are run by two guys. Polka and Raul De Soto. You take your clothes in for a wash, and when you go back to collect, you got something extra in your bag. Launderettes get pretty popular. Except De Soto did something wrong. He made Coletto Amarillo mad. So Amarillo shoots him in the basement on Avenue D. That how it was?'

She opened her hands as if this were a real question. The world that Stephanie was describing was pure fiction. It was a world Steven knew nothing about, a world he'd always suspected didn't even exist. But this was the world he had entered, a world with soundproofed walls and stale air. Steven shook his head. The door opened suddenly and Pettman came in. He was smoking a cigarette and the smoke immediately filled the room. He sat down on the edge of the desk with his back to Steven, the cigarette dangling from his lips, the smoke making him narrow his eyes. He took an envelope out of his pocket and laid it down on the desk.

'You got it?' Stephanie said and Pettman nodded, tossing

the cigarette onto the carpeted floor. Stephanie opened the envelope and took out a photograph. She studied it for a few moments before handing it to Steven.

'Is this your guy Emilio?' Pettman said.

Steven studied the photograph. A mug shot of a guy in his early thirties who looked like an Indian. He had long black hair and high cheekbones and deep black eyes. He also had a livid scar down the right side of his face that came out dark grey on the mug shot. Around his neck he had a piece of card with a number scrawled on it and the name 'Coletto Amarillo'. Steven handed the photograph back to Stephanie and said;

'I never saw him before in my life.'

Stephanie handed him a second photograph. A small, weasely guy who looked Mexican.

'Is that your guy Polka?'

Steven hardly looked at it before he handed it back and blinked slowly.

'Never saw him before in my life either.'

Stephanie handed Steven another photograph, the same one she'd shown him in the café of the Guggenheim.

'And this is your guy Pilot,' she said as a statement of fact this time.

'No,' Steven said.

He put the photograph down on the table. The black and white shot stared up at him accusingly. Pettman picked it up and studied it and then put all three photographs back into the hard-backed envelope. Then he pulled out another shot. This time it was a family photograph in colour. He passed it to Steven.

'You recognize the man in this picture?'

The photo had a man, a woman and two small children crushed together and laughing on a sofa, in front of a plain wall and a painting of wild horses splashing in the foam of the ocean. The woman was dark-haired and pretty, the children were pretty too. The man had big peasant features, a pock-marked face, his hand, which he had on the woman's shoulder, was bound with chunky gold rings. The same guy who had asked Steven to sign his copy of the book in the UN Plaza, the same guy who had followed him onto the parapet of the Empire State Building.

'You know this guy,' Pettman said, suddenly animated, seeing a flicker of terror on Steven's face. Steven stared deep into the dark eyes of the peasant.

'He works for Coletto Amarillo,' Stephanie said, sniffing something in the air too. 'He kills people. That's what this guy does. He's a killer.'

'Maybe this is the guy you saw that night,' Pettman said. 'Was this guy in the basement that night, Mr Hawthorne? Was this the guy who pulled the trigger?'

Steven handed the photograph back.

'I never saw the guy before in my life,' he said, and his voice sounded like a broken flute.

Steven's capacity for lying had always been enormous. Suddenly, it had failed him. Pettman and Stephanie exchanged glances and they left the photo on the table to haunt the edge of Steven's vision. They both knew now that they had got inside Steven's shell. The photograph was their way in. It seemed to puzzle them for a few moments. Stephanie leant forward and held the photograph up for Steven to look at.

'What is it about this guy?' Stephanie said.

Pettman stood up and came and stood at Steven's shoulder.

'This the guy who pulled the trigger down in the basement?'

Stephanie was staring directly at Steven's face.

'Maybe not,' she said. 'Maybe you've seen this guy since then. Has this guy approached you, Steven? Has he threatened you? Has he been following you? Is that why you're not talking to us?'

Steven felt as if he'd swallowed a chunk of ice. This fictional world that Stephanie had been describing – absurd, dark, grotesque – was coming to life before his eyes. Its agents had been following him all this time, following him to the top of the Empire State, calling on him in his hotel.

'Can we speak?' Pettman said softly to Stephanie, and he held the door open. They stepped into the doorway and began to whisper to each other. Outside, the noise of the airport was beginning to subside. It was getting late. Steven wiped the sweat from his forehead and put the photograph face down on the table.

Q and A. Q and A.

'Is that really the same guy?'

'You know it is. You know it is. This is insane. Get the fuck out of here.'

Pettman and Stephanie returned, both looking deadly serious. They moved their chairs close to him, one on either side. Before they had chance to speak Steven shouted that they had to let him out of here, that he demanded that they return his passport and allow him to catch the next flight out of the city. Steven's own voice sounded unfamiliar to him. The dead air in the soundproofed room absorbed his voice and Pettman and Stephanie didn't even seem to hear him.

'Mr Hawthorne,' Pettman said with great concern, 'I hardly have to tell you that the situation you are in is very serious.'

Stephanie spoke next. It was as if they had been rehearsing what they were going to say as they stood in the doorway.

'Steven, you have to quit screwing around and get hold of the situation. This thing isn't going to go away just because you close your eyes and pretend it isn't happening to you.'

Pettman took up the thread. He turned over the photograph of the peasant and his family and held it up for Steven to look at.

'You've got to tell us, Mr Hawthorne,' he said, and he sounded truly concerned. 'You've got to tell us if you have seen or spoken to this man. Look at the picture, Mr Hawthorne. Take a real good look.' Steven said nothing.

'If you are refusing to co-operate with this investigation because this man has threatened to kill you, then I can offer you protection,' Stephanie said.

Their two-handed relay seemed to be leading Steven inexorably down into submission, like uneven steps on a staircase. Steven shifted in his seat to give himself room. They were getting so close to him that he could feel the warmth of their breath on his neck and cheeks.

'You've got to let me out of here,' he said aloud but to himself and something seemed to click in the air, as if the air-conditioning had suddenly been switched on or off. Steven looked up at the white strip-light on the ceiling but he could sense that Stephanie and Pettman were communicating with their eyes.

'So this guy has threatened you', Stephanie said.

Steven grabbed the photograph out of Stephanie's hand and slammed it face down on the table.

'No matter how long you keep me here I won't be able to help you,' he said. 'That is the truth. The absolute truth. You have the wrong man and there is nothing I can do to help you.'

There was a long pause and then Pettman puffed out his cheeks and winked in Stephanie's direction.

'What do you say Steph?' Pettman said.

Stephanie glanced at her watch.

'I guess he's right,' she said.

'Guess he is,' Pettman said, then he straightened up suddenly and stretched his back and said, 'OK, Mr Hawthorne, you're free to go.'

Stephanie suddenly stood up too. Steven felt as if a huge boulder was being lifted off his chest. He waited, sensing that something wasn't right. Pettman leant against the wall with both hands and arched his back and his spine made a dry clicking sound. He looked like some strange, dry reptile waking from hibernation. He gasped as his back clicked.

'So you're letting me go?' Steven said.

'Yes sir,' Pettman said, his face red with the exertion of putting his spine back in place. 'Cops've got to sleep too. You are free as a bird.'

Stephanie hoisted her bag onto her shoulder and began to straighten her hair. Steven had an instinct for traps, he could sense them with the hairs on his face and hands.

'So you'll arrange a replacement ticket,' he said, half defiant, half afraid.

'No, Mr Hawthorne, I'm afraid that won't be possible,' Pettman said and he reached for the door.

'What about my baggage and my passport? I have to have them back tonight.'

'No, Mr Hawthorne, I'm afraid that won't be possible,' Pettman said, in the same official tone. The trap snapped shut. 'You see, I spoke to my friend from the BAT half an hour ago. He said he's going to have to keep hold of your passport for a few days. Three, maybe four, perhaps longer. Like I said, those guys have powers me and Steph wouldn't even dream of. According to the BAT you are to remain in the United States until they have concluded their investigation.'

'What fucking investigation?'

Pettman shrugged his shoulders. Steven stood up, an

instinctive reaction to danger. His shirt was soaked with sweat.

'There can't be an investigation,' Steven hissed. 'My luggage was clean and you know it.'

'You're talking to the wrong man,' Pettman said and he grinned as he stuffed the hard-backed envelope into his pocket. 'And that's the truth. The absolute truth. You want your passport back you take it up with the Bureau of Alcohol, Tobacco and Firearms.'

Stephanie nodded at Pettman. He seemed to be taking his cues from her, even though they were trying to make it look like it was the other way round.

'You can't confiscate my passport,' Steven said and he grabbed hold of Pettman's arm. 'I haven't done anything wrong.' He was breathing hard, panting like an animal. 'All I've done is tell a few fucking lies!'

There was a moment's hesitation before Pettman pulled Steven's hand away from his arm.

'Lies?' Pettman said. 'What lies?'

Steven was still breathing hard. The door was open and it was a route of escape. The moment of uncertainty passed.

'You choose to co-operate, we can help,' Stephanie said breezily, sorting through some papers in her shoulder bag. 'You choose to talk to us maybe we can speed those BAT guys up a little. Get your passport back in a day. In the meantime, my budget'll stretch to twenty-four-hour armed guard in any place you choose within the city of New York. All you have to do is sign this piece of paper.'

She pulled a printed form from her purse and held it out for Steven to take. She did it as if she didn't care whether he took it or not.

'Take it,' Stephanie said, 'you don't have to sign it right away. Take it in case you change your mind. It happens, Mr Hawthorne. I can assure you of that.'

Steven took the piece of paper without looking at it.

'Maybe when you've slept on it and thought it over, you'll want to talk this thing through. I'll look you up tomorrow morning, see how we're making out. You have any idea where you're going to be staying tonight?'

Steven didn't say anything, Pettman was already halfway out of the room. He was still rotating his shoulders and Steven thought he saw him punch the palm of his hand.

'You don't have to tell me, Steven,' Stephanie said, joining him in the doorway, 'but like I said, we're pretty hot at finding needles in haystacks.'

Stephanie and Pettman left and the door closed behind them. This time the door didn't lock automatically as it had done before. When Steven opened it, Stephanie and Pettman had already disappeared and he realized that he was free to go, just like Pettman had said. He put the printed form into his pocket without reading it, then spent the next hour walking around the airport, asking anyone in a uniform – janitors, security guards, even guys sweeping the floor – where he could get hold of someone from immigration or from the BAT, or at least how he could get hold of his baggage. They all looked at him as if he was crazy and some of them explained that all flights out of New York had been snowed in by the blizzard. If he didn't believe them, all he had to do was look out of the window.

## Chapter Fourteen

**1**

There was only one car-rental office still open in the airport and the Chinese clerk, who was hoping he'd finished for the night, said he only had two cars left. A little Fiat and a big Mercedes.

Steven drove the big black Mercedes out of the parking bay, which was deserted and covered in fresh snow. Snow was still falling thickly in his headlights and his tracks out onto the airport slip-road were soon covered up. The roads were quiet. It was two a.m.

He followed a salting truck down the Van Wyck Expressway, through the Jamaica district towards Highway 495. That would take him east onto Long Island. He had decided he would call in on his grandmother to pick up some clothes and after that he'd check into a hotel he knew on Long Island. He had left half his belongings at his grandmother's house when he had moved out, but he wasn't sure that his old clothes would fit him any more. In the past six months, he had lost a lot of weight. 'Secrets make you thin,' he said aloud to himself in the rear-view mirror. His face was gaunt and dark, his chin unshaven.

When he picked up his clothes he would also tell his grandmother that she must not, under any circumstances, speak to any reporters who might call. He guessed that Siam Drayton would have her name and number by now and might like to use her as her star witness. She had watched him write it. Telling her not to talk to reporters was a detail that he would have to take care of, along with many others which he would deal with in logical order. He had to think clearly now. He had to step back and work things through, the way his father always taught him he should. His father used to give him little battlefield mottoes that he said could be used in ordinary life. Cover your ass, always make sure you have an avenue of escape, remember that a careless bullet from your own side is as likely to kill you as a bullet from the enemy.

After he had collected some fresh clothes he would carry on up the Long Island Expressway to Montauk where there was a hotel resort he'd often visited. It was too dangerous now to stay in a hotel in New York City. He'd take a room and the minute it got light he'd call the BAT or immigration and register a complaint and get his passport returned. This was the United States, for Christ's sake. He still believed that he could talk his way out of this because he hadn't broken any laws. The snow was falling more thickly.

There were two sides to this thing, like the beating wings of a mighty bird. On one side there was Pettman and Stephanie and that spectre John Cross, trying to prove the book was true, on the other, Fiona and Siam Drayton, trying to prove it was false. This thing had a symmetry which he hadn't noticed until he sat in the driving seat of the Mercedes. Driving on ice gave him a feeling of control. Maybe he could use that symmetry. His father said that a great general will always make his enemies do his work for him.

The 495 was empty of traffic and he drove down the deserted, tree-lined boulevard like a lone venturer in an empty, white vastness. On the car radio they said that the snow was in for the week but that the real blizzard wouldn't hit with its belly until the next day. He drove at ten miles an hour down the Southampton slip-road, driving in the middle of the road to avoid the thickest snow. The small suburban streets around his grandmother's house were as silent and pretty as a Christmas card. When he reached the right turn into her street, he saw a blue light flashing on the snow.

There was a truck with a black and white chequered band across it. Behind that a motorcycle and two patrol cars, nose to nose. All the lights in his grandmother's house were switched on, blazing like a beacon in the darkness, and her front door was wide open. He could see police officers in greatcoats hurrying through the beams of light.

'Who the hell are you?' a cop said from beneath a woollen scarf which he had wrapped around his face.

'I used to live here. This is my grandmother's house. Where is she? What's happened?'

The cop turned towards the house. Steven could see that the curtains had been torn down. He saw a splash of black on the paintwork of the door. Black or red.

'Brook!' the cop yelled. 'I've got a C.O. here!'

Someone pushed their way out of the house. Snow was falling on Steven's hair and on his shirt. He had leapt out of the car so fast that he hadn't bothered to put on his jacket.

'You a relative?' the second cop said. His face and spectacles were almost completely hidden by his upturned collar.

'Yes. Where is she?'

'Relative of Eleanor Hawthorne. The lady who lived here.'

'She's my grandmother, what the fuck is going on here?'

Steven tried to push past but the two cops caught him.

'Hey, hey, hold it right there,' the second cop said. 'Carlos, why don't you go on into the house.'

The cop with the scarf waddled towards the light of the house. Brook took a deep breath. He'd done this kind of thing before and he knew that it was best to be simple and direct.

'Then I'm afraid, sir, that your grandmother is dead.'

Steven looked at his glinting spectacles for a long time through the snow, which fell yellow in the house light. There was a camera flash somewhere inside the house.

'It looks like she was murdered. I'd guess that she disturbed an intruder. It's too early to say. You want to come and sit in the truck and have some coffee?'

Steven didn't say anything. He stared at the lights of the house as if they were a puzzle that would begin to make sense soon.

'Somebody get some hot coffee out here right away!' Brook shouted. Then he began to look into Steven's face as if there were a puzzle to be solved there too.

'I'd guess it happened around eight this evening. Were you anywhere near here around that time?'

Relatives were suspects. Close family were often killers, that's just the way people who love each other are. The cop was only doing his duty. He was studying Steven's face to see if the surprise was genuine. In the darkness it was hard to tell. Steven's hair was white with snow, like the head of a statue.

'What do you say we go sit in the truck and talk,' the cop said. 'Maybe you can help us put this thing together.'


## 2


To confirm Steven's alibi he had to tell the cops about Pettman and Stephanie and about what had happened to him at JFK. Brook wrote the names down on a piece of paper and handed them to a uniformed cop who skipped out of the truck to check Steven's story on his patrol car radio. When he came back he whistled and gave Brook a huge grin.

'This guy's famous,' he said, then handed Brook a handwritten sheet of notes. Brook read it quickly and then looked up at Steven.

'You poor son of a bitch.' He turned to the other cop. 'This right, John Cross is primary on his case?'

The cop nodded and grinned.

'You poor son of a bitch.'

'There is no case,' Steven said, trying to read the sheet of paper. 'I'm not involved in any case.'

'Says here you're on the WPP. It says they want to give you a grade-five protection. We don't catch fish like you in these waters. What is it, the Mob? Hey, don't tell me. Christ, I sure as hell don't want to know.'

The cop had also brought with him a silk scarf which was matted with blood that was so thick it looked like mud. He had it in a cellophane bag. Steven recognized it as a scarf that his grandmother often wore. When he saw it he also saw her, standing in the garden on a summer morning, reaching up on tiptoes to hang a strip of bacon fat on a nail driven into the apple tree. He saw the image vividly when he closed his eyes. When he opened them again, Brook was taking the scarf and hiding it out of sight, giving Steven a brief glance of apology.

'Mr Hawthorne, this information does change things a little,' Brook said. Steven said nothing, his grief just beginning to catch up with his shock. 'If you are on the WPP, then the death of any close relative will automatically be handled by the FBI. Or in this case by John Cross. I guess they'll want to check if there is a connection . . .'

Steven stood up quickly and pushed his way out of the

truck. Outside the birds had just begun a shivery dawn chorus. There were lights on down the street and some neighbours had gathered, wearing overcoats over their pyjamas and nightgowns, to stare in at Eleanor Hawthorne's house. She had never done any harm to anyone. She had fed her birds and sat alone year after year fretting about her family, staring at their smiling faces which peered down at her from her photographs. Steven didn't want to make the connection that the cop had just made. He didn't want to think that maybe her murder had been caused, through an elaborate chain of events, by the decision he had made right there in her study, to tell a little white lie.

This thing that had started as a tiny twist in the truth, a misheard word, a misunderstanding, was now a volcano erupting from the roots of hell.

'Mr Hawthorne, you really should wait here until Cross or Pettman arrive,' Brook said, hopping in pursuit of Steven as he walked quickly towards his car.

'I have nothing to say to them,' Steven yelled.

Brook caught him up and took his arm.

'I can't hold you here, but you really ought to wait.'

Steven shrugged him off and opened his car door.

'Mr Hawthorne, if what the FBI computer told us about you is true, you really shouldn't be driving around alone like this.'

Steven slammed the door and started the engine. As he edged away into the thick wall of snow that had fallen in front of his tyres, he heard Brook call out, 'Mr Hawthorne, you're putting your own life in danger . . .'


**3**


Steven parked the Mercedes right outside the door of the Anton and Zucker offices, in a wall of snow that had been built by a passing snow-plough. He thought about the fact that he was parking illegally and the fact that he had even thought about it made him laugh to himself.

When he reached the reception desk, the receptionist, who had seen him many times before, didn't recognize him, then she finally pieced him together beneath the stubble and the soaking wet hair and the crumpled jacket. He had salt all over his shoes.

'I think Mr Foley is in a meeting,' the receptionist said. Steven put his face close to hers.

'Then get him out of his meeting. Either he comes out or I go in.'

She made a call and then took Steven through to the boardroom, which hadn't been cleared from a previous meeting. There were coffee cups and glasses of half-drunk water all over the table. Steven paced in front of the window. The view of New York was now invisible to him.

'He'll be right in,' the receptionist said. 'Do you want coffee?'

'No.'

Foley arrived with a folder under his arm. He looked scrubbed and pressed and pleased with himself. He was humming a tune under his breath as he walked in. He sat down at the desk as if Steven didn't exist. Steven sat down opposite him.

'Foley, this thing is way, way out of control,' Steven said.

Foley flicked through his papers for a few seconds before looking up.

'You think so?'

'The police . . .'

'Ah yes. Mr Pettman and Mr Cross.'

'You know?'

'They were here in this room an hour ago.'

Steven thought he could smell the soapy cologne that Pettman wore, but before he had dismissed it as his own fevered imagination.

'It's quite a turn of events isn't it, Mr Hawthorne?'

Steven began to put this thing together from Foley's point of view. He began to see why Foley was smiling.

'The police seem to think that I am a witness . . .'

'Mr Hawthorne, I know. They told me everything.'

'And I have to prove to them that I'm not.'

Foley frowned at his papers and then looked up.

'And how do you propose to do that?'

'Fuck, Foley! Holy fuck, somebody killed my grandmother.'

'I heard.'

'This is way out of control.'

'So you keep saying.'

'Did you speak to Fiona?'

'How could I? You didn't leave me her number.'

'Come *on*, Foley. Someone is dead. My grandmother is dead, Foley. Someone I loved.'

'That is why this is now a matter for the police.'

'Did you tell them about Fiona? About the dossier?'

'I told Mr Pettman and Mr Cross about Fiona and about Siam Drayton and they said they would deal with it.'

'They said they would speak to Fiona?'

'They said they would deal with it.'

'Did you tell them that *Alphabet City* is all lies?'

'It is now in the hands of the police. That is all I can tell you.'

Foley patted his papers together and stood up.

'Wait a minute,' Steven said, hating the fact that he needed Foley's attention. Foley sat down again, quite prepared to prolong the torture for as long as Steven cared to take it.

'Did you tell them that *Alphabet City* is lies and that Fiona could prove it, or not?'

Foley relished the silence. Steven wanted to drag him to the window and this time, push him all the way through.

'Mr Cross and Mr Pettman told me that they are working on an extremely important case. They told me that a major part of the case they are putting together relates to an incident described in your factual account . . .'

'But did you tell them about Fiona? Foley, for Christ's sake . . .'

Foley patted the air.

'Before the meeting ended I explained that your wife was alleging that the book was a hoax and that she had some evidence to prove it . . .' Foley looked up for a moment, mock thoughtful. 'I think it was Mr Cross who said that sometimes women are like that. What I mean is, it didn't seem to trouble them unduly. They said they would take care of her.'

It was as if a huge iron girder had smashed through the ceiling and landed with a crash across the varnished oak desk. The only person in the world who had known for a fact that *Alphabet City* was a hoax had been his grandmother. Now she was dead. The only person in the world with the knowledge and motivation to prove it was a hoax was Fiona . . .

'Something seems to be troubling you, Steven,' Foley said.

Steven was thinking hard, hoping that fatigue and grief were making him think insane thoughts, hoping that when the blizzard cleared it would all look different. The cop had said that his grandmother had disturbed an intruder. This was just another coincidence. A conspiracy for sure but not a human conspiracy, a divine one. Fate had sent some crack-head to her bungalow to rob her and she had crept out of bed and he had killed her. It was nothing more than that. It wasn't possible to think that it was anything other than that. Why would Coletto Amarillo want to kill her? Who else would want her dead? It was too soon for this to start making sense but it did have a gruesome shape which Steven could feel with his hands.

'How will they find her?' he said aloud, not meaning to.

'Who?'

'Fiona. How will Cross and Pettman find her?'

'Oh, I don't think they'll have too much trouble, Mr Hawthorne. They have huge resources. And since Fiona Van Draken is now in New York . . .'

Steven looked up from his whirl of possibilities.

'Didn't I tell you that? When I still thought that I was going to have to deal with her, I made some calls and discovered that Siam Drayton has already flown her to New York City to help work on the article . . .'

It was simple, simple, simple. There was some logic to this now and the self-satisfied smile on Foley's face confirmed it. Foley was a man who had been let off the hook. The police needed the book to be true, Foley and Anton and Zucker needed it to be true. Between them they could *make* it true. It didn't matter to anyone what was really true any more, just like it didn't matter to Natalie when she lay down on his bed. He had created this fantasy and now everyone needed it to be real. What chance did Fiona and her dossier stand against their might? She was hard and straight and cool but Steven had unwittingly thrown her to the lions. The king and queen were on the same side again, even though she didn't know it yet, and that was something for Steven to hold on to. That bitch. That poor fucking bitch.

'If she dies, I'll kill you,' Steven said wildly. He had stood up and swept the empty coffee cups off the board-room table. Cross's cup, Pettman's cup. Stephanie Plater's too? Foley watched Steven with curious amusement.

'If she *dies*? Steven, I think you're letting your imagination run away with you.'

'Jesus fucking Christ, I have to get out of here. This is insane! Who *are* you people?'

'No one is going to die, Steven. All that matters is the dossier. The proof. Mr Cross and Mr Pettman simply want to look at it to see if it is genuine. If they find out it is false, as I am now convinced they will, then they will carry on as before . . .'

'And when they find out it's true . . .' Steven yelled, 'they will come to some accommodation. Just like you were going to.'

Foley shrugged. 'It is now a matter for the police. But what really concerned them was your welfare. They said that they just could not allow you to be running loose in New York City unprotected.' Foley checked his watch. 'And your welfare is our first priority too. That's why I had my secretary call them. They should be here any moment now.'

Foley's triumph was complete. He was heading for the door and Steven grabbed him. He brushed Steven off as if his hand were a poisonous spider.

'Are you going to attack me again, Mr Hawthorne?'

'Don't tempt me Foley. Tell me what the fuck is going on.'

'Mr Hawthorne, if you want to know what's going on, why don't you pick up this morning's *New York Times* and read all about it. Didn't you know? You're New York's newest hero.'


**4**


Steven had to run from the building before the police arrived. When he reached the street, he was just in time to see his Mercedes being hoisted onto the back of a tow-truck. Traffic cops. Maybe. He trotted down Madison Avenue, dodging the crowds of commuters, slipping occasionally on the snow, with his collar turned up. He'd left his hat at JFK and it was way too cold to be out on the street. The weather reports had said that the blizzard which was due had already killed fifty people up in Canada, leaving frozen bodies in its wake like some vengeful god. He bought a copy of *The New York Times* and found a café where he could read it.

'ALPHABET CITY AUTHOR GOES INTO HIDING.'

The story said that the author of the best-selling account of life in New York's underworld was about to be taken into protective custody after threats had been made to his life. It said that an account of a murder in the book was being used by police as prima facie evidence against one of Alphabet City's most powerful drug dealers. They didn't name him. Detective Tom Pettman was quoted as saying that Steven Hawthorne's testimony would possibly lead to a conclusion in an investigation which had been going on for six years.

Steven knew that the Anton and Zucker publicity department would have gone into overdrive overnight. They'd provide the papers with the copy, the cops would back it up. Who could say the book was phoney when the FBI said it was true? The article went on to describe how the body of Raul De Soto had been found in a basement in Avenue D and that it was believed that De Soto had been depicted in Hawthorne's book under the name of Pilot.

Would anyone in the whole of New York City not pay a visit to the bookstore this very afternoon to see what all the fuss was about? *Alphabet City* sales would go ballistic. He'd be number one.

Steven spent the day hopping from café to café, heading south along the island of Manhattan, never staying out on the street for more than a few minutes. The wind was so cold that it was hard to breathe the air. In each café he changed a ten-dollar bill for quarters and pumped the phone. He called two dozen hotels in New York, asking to speak to Fiona Van Draken. If they had flown her to New York, Steven figured there was a chance that *The New York Times* would have booked her into a hotel and he'd track her down eventually.

As he made the calls, the screw turned tighter. This was one hell of a story for *The New York Times*, bigger than the story that *Alphabet City* was a hoax. Now that the cops were involved, there would be pressure on Siam Drayton to kill the hoax story. Maybe it had been killed already, maybe they'd already bundled Fiona Van Draken out of town.

Finally, he struck lucky at the Sheraton hotel near to LaGuardia airport. The clerk said that Fiona Van Draken had checked in the day before, but when he connected Steven to her room the phone just rang. All the time it rang, Steven held his breath. He wasn't sure how he'd be when he heard her voice. He only knew that he'd been wrong all this time when he had thought that he hated her. It was a thin line, just like they said, and Steven had been treading it ever since he had left her. It had to be the same for her too.

Finally, the clerk cut in and asked if Steven would care to leave a message. Steven put the phone down, paid his bill and prepared to step out into the blizzard. It was really biting now and Steven could see that the street outside was a canyon of snow and ice. He would take a cab to the Sheraton hotel and wait in the lobby until Fiona showed up. He had nowhere else on earth to go and he'd be close enough to LaGuardia airport to catch a flight if the planes were still flying. It was already dark outside. This day had passed like a flash of lightning.

## Chapter Fifteen

### 1

'You need a cab, sir?' said a voice from inside the wind. A figure had loomed up at him out of the blinding snow. His body had lost all shape beneath layers of clothing and his face was hidden by a scarf and the flaps of his hat.

Steven had only been outside the café for a few seconds but already his toes felt like raw bones in his shoes. The freezing snow was blowing into his eyes, making them stream with tears. It didn't feel like a cold night on earth but a night on some planet that couldn't possibly sustain life.

'LaGuardia . . .' Steven gasped at the figure in front of him. 'Can you get me to the Sheraton at . . .'

The figure had already turned and was waving his arm. When Steven had first stepped outside it looked as if anyone with any sense was waiting until this thing blew over. There were no cabs, no cars. But this shape had loomed out of the whiteness to save his life. He had been on the point of stepping back inside the café himself. Not even a crazy animal would try to defy this blizzard. The wind was howling like a wolf in a trap, and his body had already begun the process of freezing by degrees. He hurried after the figure in the bundle of clothes and they headed for a yellow cab which already had its engine running and its headlights switched on.

Inside the back of the cab Steven gasped and sniffed hard and said, 'Holy Christ.' The cab's wipers were working frantically to clear the snow and the driver pulled away into the whiteness. There was no way of seeing where the street ended and the pavement began. The floor of the cab was two inches deep in freezing black water, the melt-water from other customers' boots. Steven couldn't make out the streets clearly, but he was sure that instead of turning north, the direction of LaGuardia, the driver turned south.

## 2

Five miles an hour was the only practical speed but the black shape in the driving seat seemed anxious to push it to the limit, and the cab kept on heaving towards the curb and sliding across the middle of the road. The blow heater in the back brought Steven's body back to life and he shouted out again that he wanted LaGuardia airport.

'LaGuardia closed,' he thought he heard the driver say. His voice was deep and gravelly, almost indistinguishable from the roar of the engine.

'I don't want the airport itself, I want the Sheraton at LaGuardia.'

'Airport closed,' the driver said again.

'So where are we going?'

The driver put his foot on the gas again. There was no other traffic on the road so the cab had the freedom to swerve onto the sidewalk and skid almost at right angles towards the junction with Third and then Second Avenue.

The black shape leant forward and flicked on the radio. The cab was suddenly filled with deafening music. Steven recognized it as Mozart, screeching and squealing through the broken speakers of the car radio. There was a sweep of violins as the cab suddenly accelerated and glided across the ice, clattering into a streetlight. The impact threw Steven against the perspex window that separated him from the driver. He fell onto one knee in the back seat and, as he did, he caught a glimpse of the Driver ID card hanging from the dashboard.

It said the driver's name was Vlad Bicat, and there was a photograph of a middle-aged Slavic guy with thinning blond hair and a drooping moustache. Steven pushed himself back into his seat as the cab accelerated again into the blizzard. He could only see the back of the driver's head but he could tell through the smudged perspex that the black shape in the driving seat had a thick crown of curly black hair. He felt terror sinking down through his body like a gulp of freezing water. The driver hit the brake too hard and Steven realized that the black shape had never driven a taxi cab before in his life.

'Hey! Hey! Wait a minute!'

Steven hammered on the perspex divide but the driver didn't look around. Steven could hardly hear his own voice above the swirl of music that was making the whole cab rattle and the windows buzz in their frames. He had known for the past two minutes that the cab was heading in the wrong direction. Now the photograph on the dashboard seemed to blink in terror as he looked at it. Then he saw a pair of eyes in the rear-view mirror. The eyes of the peasant from the UN Plaza and the Empire State, the same eyes that had stared at him from Pettman's photograph. When their eyes met, the driver hit the gas and the wheels of the cab spun wildly until they got a grip on the road and they set off at an insane pace across Second Avenue.

Steven tried to dig his fingernails into the edge of the glass to prise it open. He thought that if he could get the dividing window open, he could grab the black shape around the neck and pull him away from the steering wheel. He managed to pull it back a few inches and then the driver braked hard and Steven fell forward. When the driver accelerated again, Steven saw a white figure dart across the headlights and leap for cover. The divide would only open wide enough for dollar bills to be passed forward and Steven put the blade of his hand through the gap and tried to grab a handful of hair with his fingers. He heard the black shape grunt and then lean forward, and as he did, the car swerved wildly and bucked over the curb.

'Son of a bitch,' he heard the driver scream above the wailing of the music and the cab swirled inelegantly, like a swan on ice, back onto the street. When it was straight, the driver hit the gas again.

Steven hammered the divide with his elbow, hoping to smash it out of its frame, and as he did it the music stopped for a few seconds between movements. In the silence, Steven heard the faint wailing of a siren. First Avenue was just a few yards ahead and Steven could see a line of traffic halted by the snow, with drifts beginning to form against the sides of the stationary vehicles. The wailing of the siren became louder, and then the music started up again. The driver seemed intent on crashing straight through the line of traffic ahead but then Steven heard a loud crack beneath his feet. It sounded like a thick steel bar being snapped over a mighty knee, and the whole cab shuddered.

Then the faint orange streetlights and the white lights of the traffic on First Avenue began to swirl around like the lights on a carousel. Steven fell back in the seat and then felt himself floating in mid-air. The car continued to revolve and Steven could see the head of the black shape and the lights beyond and even the patches of swirling snow in the streetlights all turning round and round in slow motion. Cymbals clashed and violins swirled and then the music stopped suddenly as the cab came to rest. All sound was shut off for a few seconds and then Steven could hear the faint moan of the wind which was howling through the broken windscreen and the buckled passenger door. The sound of the wind turned into the sound of a police siren, which took up the chorus and brought it to a gentle climax. After that, the sound of the siren was drowned by a deep buzzing noise. At first, Steven thought it was the sound of the engine starting up again but then he realized that the buzzing was in his head, that it was coming from somewhere between his ears and spilling out. He became fascinated with the idea that the sound of the buzzing in his head was audible outside, that it was so loud that everyone could hear it. The window of the cab door was cracked and Steven thought that melted snow was trickling through the crack and onto his face. He wiped away the water and then saw that the water was black and glistening. There was a flash of blue light and in the blue light he saw that his whole hand was covered in blood. Then he felt a deep thud against the door, as if a bull had just charged against it. Steven closed his eyes and the door was hit again. When he opened his eyes, he thought that he could see the gleaming horns of a black bull goring the side of the cab, tearing it open like a sharp knife cutting through thin aluminium. He tried to sit upright in the seat but his back felt as if it was being held in a steel vice. He didn't feel afraid or cold. He was just curious about the snorting bull and the infernal buzzing in his head, which he was sure was now being broadcast to the whole of New York City. He closed his eyes and felt a pleasant drowsiness that seemed to emanate from the blow heater which was still whirring. The buzzing in his head and the sound of the blow heater became the same thing and Steven blinked away the blood which was pumping out from beneath his leather and fur hat. When he blinked, he realized that the world was upside down, that the cab had landed on its roof.

He then fell into a dream in which he was being transported on the roof of a car through country lanes in England. He was on the roof of his father's car, being driven on an outing to the English seaside. He could even hear his father discussing the journey from inside the car. The speed of the car made the wind blow cold all around him and he spent what seemed like a whole hour trying to build up the courage to leap off the roof of the car to stop himself being so cold. Then there was intense heat near to his face and he woke up from his dream into the dark, frozen interior of the cab. He could see four pairs of legs, the boots lost in thick snow, and between them, like a light through open fingers, a store sign that said, 'Soda, beer, sandwiches'. The blood had all dried on his face and there was a thick puddle of congealed blood swamping the side of his face. He tried to change his position but his body was a long way away. It was a frozen continent, huge and covered in snow, that stretched for a thousand miles into the darkness of the cab. Then the interior was lit up by a faint orange light and by a flashing blue light and by the sparks from an acetylene cutter. When he saw the sparks of the cutter, he heard voices all around him, as if they had just been switched on like a radio.

'You get fuck . . .'

'You got it . . .'

'Take that back to her and tell her . . .'

'The coffee's fucking frozen. Go to a bar and get a kettle full of hot water . . .'

'You watch he don't move and burn his arm.'

Steven had no idea what position his body was in, or where his limbs were. He was only aware of his eyes and the place immediately behind his eyes, which was where his slow, treacly consciousness was beginning to congeal, just like blood. He recognized the legs as the legs of policemen. He saw that a guy with a face-shield was cutting into the door of the yellow cab and he saw that they had set up some kind of blow heater near to the windscreen to pump warm air into the cab. Then he tried to move his fingers, and they felt like thick iron rods, rusted and bolted loosely together at the joints. He realized that the warm air from the heater was bringing him back to life, that he was rising up with the warm air like a hot-air balloon. He grunted and the legs in his eye-line turned into knees and then three faces, all wrapped in scarfs, with snow peaks on their caps and silver badges glinting in the orange light.

'Hey, his eyes are open,' one of the faces said, and the other faces squinted into the interior of the cab. They were all snorting smoky breath out of their nostrils.

'Go tell Steph,' said another of the faces. 'She's in the truck warming her ass.'

Two of the faces disappeared, then three other faces took their place, all looking through the cracked window into the dark interior, like hunters peering down a rabbit hole. Steven grunted again and the pain was switched on. Pain from all over his body, shooting pain and burning pain, burning so hot that he felt that his body was threaded with bare electrical wires all shorting out at the same time. He heard the window of the cab being tapped gently until it cracked. A freezing draught blew snow into the interior. All the sounds from outside got louder, brought in by the draught. The voices seemed to get more urgent.

'You see anything?' someone said.

'Blood both sides.'

'Looks like the bullet went through.'

'You sure?'

'No, I can't be sure but I'd say it's come out through the shoulder.'

Someone stood up and shouted that the doctor thought the bullet had gone clean through. Steven's treacly thought processes slowly absorbed the word 'bullet'. He realized that the white pain was emanating from a place beneath the ball of his shoulder joint. He was conscious enough now to panic and he tried to move his body. He felt his legs and hips and ribs shifting inside something that felt like an oily shell that was too tight for him. He could see that the whole of the inside of the cab was painted with blood. Outside, someone was talking in a soft monotone that sounded like the buzzing of a wasp.

'Exposure probably. We'll need to make the transfusion soon as he's free. How long?'

'Another five minutes we'll have the door off. These son-of-a-bitch chequer cabs are built like armoured cars.'

Steven heard Stephanie's voice approaching from somewhere way off in the wind. He couldn't make out what she was saying but he could tell that she was anxious and angry. The blow heater, which was almost touching his feet through the windscreen, was making him sweat. Finally the door began to twist on its hinges and there was another cold blast of air from outside. With this blast of air, Steven heard someone say, 'Jesus Christ, is that his arm?'

'Quick, quick, get around the other side.'

Then he heard Stephanie's voice, and she sounded as if she was shouting from the top of a high, windswept mountain.

'I fucking told him to hold off,' she said.

There was a grunt and Steven felt two hot hands under his back, and there was a pencil torch shining in his eyes. Stephanie knelt down in the snow to peer into Steven's face and she was close enough for Steven to hear her whisper, 'If he dies, they'll hang Pettman's ass out to dry for this.'

## 3

After that there was only darkness and deafening sound. It was the sound of mighty turbines beneath the snow with pistons that shook the whole city.

*'New York is an indestructable machine, a turbine. When raindrops land on the sidewalk in New York you can almost hear them hiss from the heat that the city generates . . .'*

Steven opened his eyes briefly and recognized the interior of an ambulance, and, hovering above him, he could see Stephanie Plater's face. He could also feel her hand gripping his own. After that there was a rough and uncomfortable darkness and a clammy heat, as if he had been wrapped in a heavy woollen blanket and bound with leather belts. The siren on the ambulance screamed and was then shut off. Each time the ambulance skidded in the snow, Steven felt that he was sliding uncontrollably towards a giddy darkness, a great pool of freezing, stagnant water.

The next time he opened his eyes he saw that there were two men, beating his chest with their fists. There was a crowd of people all shouting at each other and Stephanie Plater was cowering away from them, bent backwards by a howling wind. Someone called out, 'Hands away,' and Steven felt a powerful jolt in the middle of his body. He could even see the rubber tentacles of the defibrillator sucking the skin on his chest. He realized that the screaming and the energy and the distress was only one option. There was another option which was dark but also silent and restful. He considered the silent option carefully as the helicopter left the snow-covered landing pad beside the sluggish East River. The tiny glass bubble of light beneath the rotor blades rose up through the swirling snow and ice and Steven and Stephanie and the furious doctor all looked like tiny cut-out silhouettes, as they were taken closer to the darkness of heaven.

PART TWO

# Truth

## Chapter Sixteen

*'Christopher Isherwood said that "America" is what the neurotic hero dreads. I make no fucking claim to be a hero, not anybody's hero, not even a neurotic one, but I know that dread. I know that mercury of terror sinking through your body when you are confronted with the real thing. The horror of the needle which is poised to pump your veins full of "America", neat and pure and refined. When I went on my odyssey into Alphabet City, fear was my constant companion, like a ferocious dog which I could unleash when the moment called for it. I could whistle and fear would come running and turn me into a dangerous, heathen son of a bitch . . .'*

**1**

When Steven opened his eyes again, he saw a large, leaded window, fringed with heavy, blue velvet curtains. Then he saw a pale blue wall and a white plaster ceiling marbled with hairline cracks. In the middle of the ceiling there was a chandelier and around the modern fitting an ornate plaster cornice, scrolls of roses and leaves. The light from the window hurt his eyes and then a shadow fell over his face.

'Mr Hawthorne, does it feel any easier? You feel this? You feel this in your toe?'

He saw an orange Chinese face above him. The face creased up into a smile.

'My name is Doctor Guo. You hear me?'

Steven nodded and tried to shift his position. He felt that he was held in place by tight wires attached to his flesh by hooks. Guo tutted.

'You rest, Mr Hawthorne. You feel OK for a while but that's just the morphine. I give you morphine for the pain. You go back to sleep now, Mr Hawthorne.'

Steven could hear a fire crackling somewhere near to his feet; he could feel the luxuriant warmth coming off it and smell the woodsmoke. The room he had woken up in had the most exquisite pink and blue detailing, with daisy chains and roses all around the edges of the ceiling. Along with the smell of woodsmoke he could smell mildew and age. Outside, the birds were singing and their song tickled the air like a thousand tiny flutes. He could tell just from the smell of smoke and snowy air, and from the sounds of rooks and of a crackling open fire, that he was somewhere safe and warm, somewhere far away from the cold fury of New York City. He took a deep breath and, as he took the breath, he seemed to suck another presence into the room. He saw Stephanie rushing to his bedside and she knelt down beside him and took hold of his hand. She looked up at Doctor Guo and Guo nodded his head and smiled.

'Did he open his eyes?' he heard Stephanie say and then he heard the Chinese doctor say, 'Sure, he's going to be OK.'

Stephanie squeezed Steven's hand and Steven squeezed her hand as hard as he could. He suddenly remembered that the feeling of her hand in his was familiar and warm. He remembered that he had spent days or months or years holding on to her hand and that it was the squeezing of her hand which had stopped him from falling all the way down through the floorboards and into the engine room of the mighty turbines down below.

Steven closed his eyes and slept, knowing that the hole down which he might have fallen had healed over.

## 2

When his eyes flickered open again, he saw the Chinese doctor and smelt jasmine on his breath.

Doctor Guo was a tiny man with a body that seemed to have been fashioned out of twisted wire. His face was so dark and shiny that it could have been glazed and fired in a kiln.

'So now, Steven, is it easier? Does it feel any easier?'

Stephanie's face appeared behind Doctor Guo's face, eclipsed but shining white.

'Should I slap him again?' Stephanie said.

Steven smiled. He could hear the birds singing.

'You slap me, I'll slap you back,' Steven said through sore, dry lips and Stephanie shrieked. Steven grunted and tasted the inside of his mouth.

Stephanie had hold of his hands and he could clearly see that there were tears in her eyes. And he knew that there were tears in his own eyes too because he could feel them dribbling down his cheeks. He wanted to wipe them away but when he tried to move his right arm he felt tight binding all around his upper arm and shoulder. He raised his left arm to wipe his face but Stephanie caught his fist in mid-air as if it were a little bird. She wiped his eyes for him.

Doctor Guo prodded Steven's belly and said that if they didn't get some solid food inside him straight away his stomach would begin to digest itself. Steven managed to lift himself up in the bed and peer down at his body. His right arm and shoulder were bound with black gauze and tape. His whole abdomen had subsided into a deep hollow.

Stephanie was standing at Doctor Guo's side and he told her to go down to the kitchen and tell the chef to make up some porridge.

'Tell him to make it with water not milk. And no sugar. But lots of salt.'

After Stephanie had gone, Doctor Guo shone his light into Steven's eyes, took his pulse and felt for tiny echoes inside his liver, kidneys and spine. As he gently rolled Steven over, he delivered a formal explanation of his condition, as if he'd prepared it in advance.

'You been shot, Mr Hawthorne,' he said, as he pushed his orange fingers deep beneath Steven's rib cage. 'Also concussion, hypothermia. Lost a lot of blood. You taste metal in your mouth?'

Steven could taste both brass and tin.

'Yes. Who shot me? I don't remember being shot.'

'No one remembers being shot, Mr Hawthorne.'

'Who the hell shot me?'

Steven's voice was weak and wispy. He cleared his throat and looked around the room. He had woken up in some kind of eighteenth-century mansion house, elegant and exquisitely decorated but also buckled and cracked with age. Out of the window he could see a long, snow-covered lawn that seemed to stretch for two miles in all directions, two stone statues beside a frozen fountain and beyond, a line of oak trees laden with snow.

Guo tutted and rolled Steven over onto his front.

'Lucky for you the bullet was spent.' Guo said. 'But you been out a long time, Mr Hawthorne. Take a deep breath.'

'How long?'

'You speak to Stephanie. Take a deep breath.'

Steven breathed deeply and Guo tapped Steven's chest. His upper body was as white and fragile as a chicken carcass beneath the black gauze sling. Guo peered into Steven's eyes and smiled.

'But I guess you're OK now.'

'You think so.'

'Maybe you don't feel so good but your liver is OK. And that metal taste'll go away soon. It's just the morphine. It'll go away when you try some of this porridge they've got warming on the stove downstairs for you.'

'Who have? Where the hell am I?'

Guo pulled Steven up in the bed and gently laid a pillow behind him for support.

'You ask your questions to Stephanie,' he said. 'You're in Stephanie's hands now.' He began to giggle like a child and his face creased up again. 'She's a fine nurse, Mr Hawthorne. She could maybe make it as a doctor if she wasn't already a cop. She took good care of you. She saved your life.'

Steven heard hurried footsteps outside, someone climbing a long flight of uncarpeted stairs at a run. Then Stephanie arrived with the bowl of porridge and Guo took that as a signal to leave. He joined her in the doorway and whispered some instructions and then disappeared into the hall. When Guo opened the door briefly, Steven heard the noises from downstairs. It sounded like two dozen men and women in various parts of a large house, calling out to each other, taking calls, laughing. Maybe there was some kind of celebration going on. From the echoes and the distance of the sound, Steven judged that the house he was in must be enormous, and unfurnished. But beyond the open door he could only see shadows. When Stephanie closed the door, all the sounds were shut off.

'How are you feeling Steven?'

'Like I've just fallen off a twenty-storey building. Where the hell am I?'

167

Steven tried to sit up and felt a strange vertigo that made him want to throw up. Stephanie sat down on the bed with the bowl of porridge on her lap. She looked at him like an indulgent governess.

'Bronxville,' she said. 'Thirty miles north of New York. This is my favourite safe house. Last time anyone got shot in Bronxville it was a guy in a white wig with a musket.'

Steven looked around at the faded elegance of the room.

'Why aren't I in a hospital?' he said.

'This place is better than any hospital. This place is a hospital, a fortress and a hotel and you are the only guest. They say that George Washington slept right here in this room. Two hundred acres of clear ground all around. Guys on the roof, dogs at the fences, cameras, lasers, you name it, it's out there. You must be starved . . .'

The many ragged pieces of Steven's predicament fell back into place. The absurdity of it made him angry for a few seconds, then he felt a great depression roll over him. In his delirium he had been through a whole lifetime of epic nightmares. He had half hoped that the book and the deceit had been one of those nightmares. Now he realized that the worst of the nightmares was the truth, and that he was still inside it.

Stephanie offered him a spoonful of porridge. He took a mouthful and the heat of it made him cough it out.

'Sorry, I put too much on the spoon for baby,' Stephanie said with a grin. She was almost vibrating with suppressed delight that Steven was awake and talking. He coughed again.

'Baby? What the hell happened to you?' he said.

'OK, let's try again. Open your goddamned mouth!'

Steven opened his mouth and Stephanie fed him another spoonful. Swallowing was painful but he was as hungry as hell. For the moment, his hunger was more urgent than his anxiety and he began to gulp the porridge down. He could feel something like an electrical charge rising up through his body, bringing his limbs back to life, making his skin tingle. Stephanie gave him another spoonful and he spilt some of it down his chin. When he wiped his mouth with his good arm he felt a thick growth of beard. The thickness of it terrified him.

'Jesus, how long have I been out?'

'Six days,' Stephanie said. 'Seven if you include the night you died. Come on, open wide and have some of Mama's porridge.'

She blew on the porridge to cool it and then fed it to him as if he were a child. Then she wiped away a dribble with her thumb and stared at Steven's mouth as he ate.

'Six days?' Steven said softly to himself.

'You almost didn't make it. I prayed for you.'

He looked at her with surprise. There was a gentleness in her voice which she was fighting hard to stiffen up.

'Look, if you'd died I would have been fired,' she said. 'It's my job to keep you alive. I'm supposed to be your guardian angel.'

Steven remembered that when he had woken up under the influence of morphine, Stephanie had indeed looked like an angel. He arched his back to dispel some of the stiffness and his shoulder creaked with pain.

'So what happened to me?' Steven asked. 'The doctor said I was shot.'

Stephanie took more care than was necessary in scooping up another spoonful. She held it up to his mouth but Steven turned his head.

'Is that right? Someone shot me?'

'Yes.'

'Christ, I really don't remember any bullet. I remember being in the back of the cab and I remember spinning around. How did it happen? Who shot me?'

Stephanie offered Steven the porridge again.

'Stephanie, who was it who shot me? Was it the guy driving the cab?'

'Come on, open wide.'

'Stephanie?'

'Open wide for Mama.'

'Will you cut this mama stuff. Who the fuck shot me?'

Stephanie put the spoon back into the bowl and sighed.

'It was human error,' she said flatly.

'Which human?'

'We had the café covered. All exits. But the snow made it kind of difficult. The guys on the front door said that visibility was down to three yards. They didn't see you get into the cab and didn't realize there was something wrong until they saw the cab hit the streetlight. Come on, eat.'

Steven pulled the spoon out of her hand and held it up to Stephanie's face like a weapon.

'I asked you who shot me?' he said.

'We did.'

Stephanie took the spoon back for more porridge. Steven's mouth was open and she pushed some food inside it quickly.

'The guys covering the front door had to think on their feet. They radioed Pettman and Pettman gave them permission to break the engine block.'

Stephanie seemed to be prepared to leave her explanation there, even though it was no explanation at all.

'Break what engine block?' Steven said.

'You fire a 9mm into the engine of a vehicle, it'll break the engine block and stop the car. It is standard procedure in hot pursuit since '87. Except in your case it was a little risky. Those chequer cabs are built to last. The bullet ricocheted around inside the engine and then wound up right there in your shoulder. You were unlucky.'

Steven knew enough about firearms to know that firing

a 9mm automatic pistol into a speeding car on an icy road wasn't just risky, it was insanity. He found himself chewing his porridge while staring at the top of Stephanie's head.

'And you are my guardian angel,' he said flatly.

'Not me Steven, Pettman. This is a DEA fuck-up. I'm the one who's been sitting here for six days and nights holding your hand and telling you the story of my god-damned life. Unedited I might add.'

'So Pettman tried to kill me, you save my life. There seems to be a conflict of interest here that maybe I should know about.'

'I told you already, Pettman and me are different departments. I'm FBI. If we had been handling this from the start you would never have been left to walk around New York in the first place.'

Steven shifted uneasily in the bed. His shoulder was stiff but the pain was now an old pain. He peeked down at the dressing on the bullet wound, the kind of wound his father had told him about so often. The impacted fat and flesh, the scorched skin. He'd seen photographs a hundred times but he'd never dreamt he'd ever see one dressed on his own body. His father had a wound in almost exactly the same place that he picked up in Vietnam. He would have been proud.

'I ran out of animal impressions on the first day,' Stephanie was saying. 'So I told you the story of my life in six instalments. Guo said I had to keep talking. I guess you don't remember.'

'No I don't. Sorry, I was pretty busy dying. So you and Pettman . . .'

Stephanie shovelled some more porridge into his mouth.

'. . . you're not working on this thing together?'

'This is a DEA investigation. Long term. We're just helping out. Don't talk with your mouth full. Bad boy.'

'Stephanie, I have a right to know what is going on

here. I have a government bullet in my body, I'd like to return it to its rightful owner.'

Stephanie didn't seem keen to talk. She wiped his mouth and stirred her porridge.

'The bullet is out of your body. It went clean through.'

'Well that makes me feel very happy.'

Steven thought that maybe he still had some morphine in his blood. He was angry and he was acting angry but there was a mad carelessness too. He wanted to grab Stephanie and kiss her on the lips. There was a warmth coming off her that he hadn't felt before, a warmth he would never have believed she was capable of.

'Look, for Christ's sake,' she said at last, 'the guy driving the cab was working for Amarillo. If Pettman hadn't given the order you'd be floating in the East River for the trash barge to pick up. If you're well enough to ask questions you're well enough to feed yourself. Go ahead, the bowl's right there.'

She stood up and stared out of the window, then lit a cigarette. The smoke smelt stale and heavy but nevertheless Steven wanted to smoke too. He asked her for one and she offered him the pack then held Steven's hand steady while he took a light. It made him cough.

'Don't tell Guo I gave you that,' she said. Steven could see that his questions about Pettman had troubled her. It looked as if she'd been asking herself the same questions for six days and still didn't have an answer that fitted. It had never occurred to him that Stephanie and Pettman and John Cross weren't three heads on the same animal.

'He'll be here the day after tomorrow,' Stephanie said as she sat down on the bed. 'Pettman and John Cross. If you have a complaint, make it to John Cross.' She laughed. 'Good luck.'

There was deep foreboding in her voice. Whenever anyone talked about John Cross their voices changed. He remembered the cop in the truck outside his grandmother's house. The guy was obviously something of a celebrity. Thinking about his grandmother served to put all the other elements of this situation into place.

'What they do is their business,' she said, more to herself than to Steven. 'I just keep you alive.'

A wave of nausea made Steven close his eyes. The truth hit him like a poisoned arrow fired from somewhere out there beyond the oak trees. All through his life he had wanted to live behind a mask of harmless fictions. Now one of those masks had melted onto his face and there was nothing he could do to tear it off.

'You had a lady visitor while you were asleep,' Stephanie said, taking a spoonful of porridge herself.

Steven thought about Fiona, his only avenue of escape.

'Natalie Kishon. She said she was from Anton and Zucker.'

Steven closed his eyes again and rested his head against the headboard. He'd noticed a single red rose wilting on the fireplace. He'd guessed already who it was from.

'She brought you some clothes. Nice clothes too.'

'And the flower,' Steven said with his eyes closed.

'Yeah, a flower too. I forgot to put water in the cup. I guess your publishers are pretty pleased with the way this thing has worked out. She cried like a baby when she saw you lying there. Were you screwing her Steven?'

Stephanie didn't seem to be very good at hiding her feelings. Was that a hint of jealousy making her pretend to laugh? All she had to do was put a little water in the cup.

'No I never screwed her,' Steven said. 'That was down to Pettman too. Did I have any other visitors?'

'A guy called Foley. The fucking guy shook your hand while you were unconscious. Can you believe that?'

'Yes.'

'He said to tell you that the rights of portrayal slips were being taken care of. That mean anything to you?'

Steven rubbed his beard and it began to itch.

'I guess he'll sign them himself,' Steven said and Stephanie shrugged, not understanding.

'Anything else happened while I've been sleeping?' Steven said when he opened his eyes.

'Happened to what?'

'The investigation.'

'Not my area. I'm just your bodyguard. And your nurse. And your mama.'

It was impossible to tell how much Stephanie knew. She still had her hard exterior but it was beginning to break up. That recklessness that Steven had always managed to inspire in women was taking effect and it was possible that while she had been tending him for six days and six nights, telling him the story of her life, something had changed between them. Changed without Steven even being conscious. It was possible that a woman like Stephanie would fall for a guy who couldn't eat or speak or move for himself, lying wasted on the sheets waiting to die. A guy in that condition couldn't make mistakes. Steven was an expert on affection and attraction, because he was usually so far removed from the heat of them.

'Has Amarillo been arrested?' Steven said.

'Nope.'

'What about the papers?'

'You're a hero. You're the statue of liberty. People get protective about writers. Beats me why.'

'*New York Times* too?'

'*New York Times* especially.'

'Anything in *The New York Times* by Siam Drayton?'

'Who the hell is that?'

'You heard anything about my wife?'

Stephanie had stood up to gaze out of the window. The mention of Steven's wife made her turn to Steven with a look of surprise, her cover blown for just a fraction of a second.

'Your wife? I thought you were single.'

'It's a big secret, Stephanie. First it was my secret now its everybody's secret. But Pettman knows. John Cross knows too. Strange they didn't tell you.'

Stephanie shook her head and laughed.

'Guo said the drugs would make you a little crazy for a while. You'd better sleep.'

'I've been asleep for six days. Now I'm awake and I'm tired of just letting these things happen to me.'

Stephanie's back was turned and Steven threw off the sheets. He was wearing a white gown, tied at the back. He swung his legs out of bed and a streak of pain shot up the middle of his body. When he put his feet on the floor they felt like two plump bags of blood. He took his weight on his legs and Stephanie turned around.

'Hey, what the hell are you doing?'

She tried to grab him to push him back into bed but he gently pushed her off. His legs felt as weak as a new-born colt's.

'Let me take a look out of the window,' Steven said. She took his arm in her arm and helped him to the window. He put his weight on the ledge and surveyed the snow-covered lawn and the line of oak trees beyond. To the right there was a suburb. Maybe Bronxville, maybe not. He still didn't know for sure that Stephanie could be trusted. Straight ahead was a snow-covered hillside, scattered houses.

'You OK to stand?' she said. 'You want me to pull up a chair?'

'I'm OK to stand. While I've been sleeping, I don't suppose you had chance to read my book?'

'I'd read it already. We all did. Everybody inducted onto the case. I thought it was . . . I don't know, I thought it was pretty weird.'

'Did you think it was true to life? You must know the real *Alphabet City* pretty well.'

'Sure I know it,' she said, and she wiped 'SP' in the condensation from her breath on the window.

'You want to hear something funny about the book?'

'I didn't notice a lot of laughs.'

'No, I mean something really funny. Something that'll make you laugh out loud. It's all lies. I made it up. I wrote it in my grandmother's house. It came straight out of here . . .' Steven tapped his head, his eyes were glistening.

'Steven, you really ought to get some rest.'

'Made the whole thing up out of nothing at all.'

'Steven, look . . .'

His wound had begun to bleed. There was a fresh pink smear on the dressing. When Stephanie went to wipe it he grabbed her arm.

'Do you hear what I'm saying? None of it happened.'

They stared into each other's eyes and Stephanie looked away first.

'Steven, you've still got a lot of drugs going through your veins. You should get back into bed.'

'It's fiction. It should be filed under *fiction*.'

Stephanie dabbed the blood from Steven's wound with a crumpled tissue. She did it with tender care and she stared at the wound to make sure she'd staunched the flow.

'Sure it is, Steven. You get back into bed or you'll bleed to death.'

She tossed the bloody tissue onto the open fire and it was consumed in a burst of flame that made the walls flicker.

176

'I'm telling you the truth, Stephanie. The book is lies and someone is trying to make it real.'

Steven had always believed that the truth, when it was told, would have some kind of unimpeachable authority. The truth had been his enemy for so long now that he was sure that the revelation of it would be accompanied by clarion calls, by the crashing of masonry. But the truth, when it was told, sounded like just another lie. Less believable than a lie.

'Steven, if it was fiction, how come they found the body?' Stephanie said, wiping out her initials on the window.

'Did you see the body yourself?'

'No but . . .'

'Did you count the bullet holes?'

'I'm getting Doctor Guo.'

'Listen to me!'

Shouting made Stephanie's eyes harden. He'd moved too quickly.

'Please listen to me,' he said softly.

'You're crazy.'

'That's not a point I'd argue, but the book is fiction. The whole thing from page one to page 505. How come they found the body? Well that has been bothering me too. Awake and asleep. And the way I figure it, there never was a body. Or maybe they found this guy De Soto's body and moved it to fit the book. How long have they been trying to nail Amarillo?'

'Cross and Pettman? Six years. More if you take it back to Colombia. They showed us a slide show about the guy on day one.'

'Six years. Getting nowhere. Then along comes Steven Hawthorne . . .'

Stephanie laughed as if she'd just figured something out.

'Nice try, Steven,' she said. 'I guess if someone asked me to testify against Amarillo, I'd get pretty jumpy too.'

'I have nothing to testify. I never saw a murder. You don't believe me, ask my wife.'

Stephanie was heading for the door. Steven tried to grab her arm and she gave him a fierce look. He held on to her more tightly and she had to twist her wrist to break free.

'You ever try anything like that again, I'll break your arm in three places.'

She had her thumbs in her belt, her jacket open, her leather holster visible. Steven had to remember he was dealing with the meanest bitch on earth when she wasn't his mama.

'Her name is Fiona Van Draken,' Steven said calmly. 'Six days ago she was in New York and she has proof that the book is a hoax. Pettman and Cross know that and that's why, for all I know, she is floating in the East River herself.'

That possibility made Steven choke a little. Stephanie opened the door, and the sound of cops shouting echoed up the stairs.

'Fiona Van Draken,' Steven said again. 'At least find out if she's still alive. And if you speak to her, ask her if what I'm telling you is true.'

Stephanie hesitated in the door for a moment and then called out, 'Doctor Guo, I think Mr Hawthorne needs some attention.'

She walked away down the landing and Doctor Guo came in and changed Steven's dressing. When Guo mentioned that he could smell cigarette smoke, Steven blamed himself.

## Chapter Seventeen

**1**

After Guo had changed his dressing, Steven fell asleep and he was roused every two hours for Guo to check his wound and administer another injection. Finally he woke up without Guo and it was dark outside and a dog was howling. Steven had no idea what time it was. He could hear movement downstairs, phones ringing, a lot of activity. When he was asleep his nightmares were all about pursuit. Now he was standing at the window, relighting the stubbed-out cigarette that Stephanie had left behind from an ember on the fire.

'Hey, Mr Hawthorne, you shouldn't be out of bed like this.'

Guo came in and took Steven's cigarette between thumb and forefinger and threw it in the fire, which was now just a glow of ash. He took Steven gently around the shoulders. Steven resisted.

'What town is that?' Steven said.

'Over beyond the hill? That's Bronxville. Come on, get back into bed. I want to take a look at the dressing.'

As Guo helped Steven into bed his shoulder began to hum with pain. When he had been unconscious this pain was a dark, hot country which he visited often.

'So do you work for the FBI or the DEA?' Steven said.

Guo began to unfasten the bandage around Steven's

shoulder and tutted. 'You ask your questions to Stephanie.'

'Do they always go to these lengths? How many people do they have downstairs? Sounds like a whole battalion.'

Guo gently prodded the swollen flesh around the stitches in Steven's shoulder and whispered, 'No poison.' Then he began to fasten the dressing against the wound with the bandage again.

'I'd like to take a look around,' Steven said. 'What time is it?'

'Late, Mr Hawthorne. You should get some sleep. Your wound is progressing well but you got to help your body. You sleep, your body works. You fret, your body don't mend so fast.'

'Even so, I'd like to exercise my legs a little.'

'It's three a.m., Mr Hawthorne.'

Guo gently pushed Steven down onto the pillow.

'How long have you known Stephanie Plater?'

Guo's face wrinkled up into a smile.

'I've known Stephanie for a long time now. Maybe two years. Hey, have you got the hots for her?'

'No.'

Guo laughed at some private joke and he put his hand over his mouth to stifle the sound.

'Maybe I'll play cupid,' he said and he adjusted Steven's bandage one last time. 'It's good to have someone like you here for a change. Good for Stephanie too. Most of the guys we deal with are no more than animals. You sleep well, Mr Hawthorne.'

## 2

Next morning, Stephanie took Steven on something she called 'The Grand Tour'.

She said that Steven was fortunate to be holed up in one of the most beautiful and historic houses in the whole of New York State and that while he was here he might as well make the most of it. She devoured most of Steven's breakfast, picking at his plate with her fingers. Then she helped him out onto the landing and he saw below him a huge chamber of sunlight.

'This is my tenth time in this place,' she said. 'When I get the choice I choose this house. Did I tell you that George Washington slept here?'

The staircase wound itself around the chamber of light down to an empty tiled hallway and above there was a glass dome that sparkled with ice. The walls were all bare, with rectangles of vivid blue where paintings had once hung. There seemed to be dozens of doorways and corridors leading away from the central hall.

'Since the government bought this place they're just letting it go to hell,' she said, taking Steven's weight on her shoulder. Ever since he had regained consciousness, she had exuded a gentleness and warmth which made him feel uneasy. His legs were stiff with inactivity but he said he could walk by himself.

The house was a huge empty hulk, stripped of its furnishings. As Stephanie showed him around, he could hear voices behind almost every door, and all the voices echoed. Stephanie pointed out the door to the drawing room and as she did, he heard four or five people bursting into laughter.

'Are these people all here just for me?' Steven said.

'Mostly,' Stephanie said.

'What does that mean?'

'It means that you are part of a larger operation. Come on, come and see the kitchen. You like old places?'

Stephanie explained that the house had been built by a trader who dealt in molasses with Cuba in the early eighteenth century, and that the kitchen and the scullery were original. She led Steven around both rooms and pointed out the places where rough lattice work peeked out through centuries of paint and plaster, like a horny toe sticking through silk stockings.

Then she took Steven back through the central hall, still filled with blinding sunlight, and showed Steven the rooms in the east wing, which, Stephanie explained with great solemnity, had been built on to the original in the 1880s. There were no curtains or blinds in the rooms, and the floorboards gleamed under ancient varnish. Outside Steven could see acres of soft snow, pierced by lines of oak trees and laburnum, and beyond the trees, a fuzzy ice-blue horizon. Beyond the horizon was New York City and Steven imagined he could see the cloud of smoke that hung over it, the colour of gun cotton. Steven had decided that he would never venture into New York again, not even if his life depended on it.

The last room she took Steven to was a vast empty dining room, with broad ledges and the same exquisite hand-painted cornice work that Steven had seen in the bedroom. The air inside smelt like old velvet and the size and brightness of the room seemed to fill Stephanie with delight.

'Can you imagine when the table was set and all the servants came marching through here in a line with all that food?'

Steven said that he could.

'This kind of thing bores you doesn't it?' Stephanie said, still filled with wonder.

'No, but I have other things on my mind. Did you find out about her?'

Steven's voice echoed. The room was a home for ghosts.

'Who?' Stephanie said.

'You know who.'

Stephanie looked around the room as if her mind was elsewhere.

'Beautiful.'

'Stephanie, I need to know either way if you are going to help me.'

She didn't look at him as she said, 'I found out that you do have a wife and that her name is Fiona Van Draken.'

Steven's heart leapt but he didn't want to let his delight show. It wasn't that Stephanie had found out anything, it was the fact that she had tried. To keep Stephanie on his side he had to be cool, he had to reel her in with care.

'This may surprise you, Stephanie, but I knew that already. What else did you find out?'

'I spoke to Pettman.'

'You did what?'

Stephanie shushed him as his voice echoed around the room. The way she lowered her voice made Steven's heart race some more. She was already beginning to act like a conspirator.

'I just mentioned it in passing, like I was curious. I said I thought you were pretty cute and I asked why it was that our records had you down as single. That was when he told me.'

'Told you what?'

'That you had a wife, that she was called Fiona.'

'Did he say he'd spoken to her?'

'Nope. Didn't ask.'

'Jesus Christ!'

'Not my area.'

She peered at Steven's look of exasperation for a long time. Then she smiled.

'You know, this house used to belong to a guy who made guns,' she said. 'Repeating rifles, back in the 1880s. And when he died, his wife went crazy and thought that everyone who had ever been killed by her husband's guns was coming back to haunt her. So do you know what she did?'

'Stephanie, I don't need a history lecture. I need information.'

She opened her hands with mock wonder. 'Did she run out of the house screaming? No she didn't. She had extra rooms built onto the house so that the ghosts of the dead would have somewhere to stay. Kept on building more and more rooms till the day she died. This is one of them. Isn't that a beautiful story? I mean that someone could believe that you can appease the dead with real estate?'

She suddenly put her finger to her lips then said loudly, 'What I'm saying, Steven, is that in a haunted house like this, you never know who might be listening. Why don't we go up to the bathroom. You look like you need a shave.'

Stephanie walked out of the room and Steven had no choice but to follow.

### 3

The bathroom in the house was a recent conversion. The thick, pebbly windows looked original but the plumbing was new, probably courtesy of the FBI. Steven managed to cut off most of his forest of beard with scissors in his left hand but when he tried to apply the razor, he cut himself with the first stroke. Stephanie was standing behind him and spoke to his reflection.

'Do you want me to do that?' she said. 'I used to be a nurse a century and a half ago.'

Stephanie came and stood between Steven and the mirror and dipped the razor in the warm water in the sink behind her back between each stroke. She peered at

Steven's mouth with fierce intensity as she shaved away the foam.

'Are you going to help me find Fiona or not?' Steven said. 'If you're not going to help, I'll have to find another way.'

'Keep your mouth closed or I'll cut your face. Then you won't look so pretty.'

Stephanie washed the blade and then put her hand on Steven's cheek to get a better angle. Steven imagined that he could feel the tenderness coming through her fingers. He tried to speak again but she put her finger on his lips. She lowered her voice.

'I can't find your wife for you Steven. No one can. According to Pettman, she went missing five days ago.'

Steven turned around, startled, and a little dribble of blood trickled down his face.

'I told you to keep still!'

'What do you mean she went missing?'

'I had to pump him like I didn't really give a shit. But the way he said it, as your closest living relative, they were obliged to offer her protection. They heard she was staying at the Sheraton but when they called on her she had disappeared. They have no idea where she is . . .'

Stephanie put Steven's head in a vice-like grip and began to shave his cheek. He stared into her eyes in the reflection. He began to work through all the possibilities.

'Do you think she might be dead?'

'She's not dead, for Christ's sake.'

'How do you know?'

Stephanie hesitated before she replied.

'Because I checked. Took me a whole hour . . . If she'd died in New York it would have been on the register.'

Steven felt Stephanie's body against his back. She felt hot. Each bit of research she had done was another step down into the place where Steven was trapped.

'What else did Pettman say?'

'Keep your mouth closed.'

As she stroked his face with the razor she seemed to make a decision. She glanced briefly over her shoulder at the door.

'Listen, Steven, this stuff about the book . . .' she hissed quickly.

'What about it?'

'I checked the files on the Amarillo investigation. It's like three hundred K of information but I checked the stuff on the last month. They have witnesses, Steven. They have sworn statements from people in Alphabet City who remember you.'

Stephanie looked up from the progress of the blade and stared into Steven's eyes.

'That is just not possible,' Steven said.

'They have sworn testimony.'

'From who?'

'Polka, Azole the guy whose house you lived in on Avenue D. Lucretia the hooker.'

There was a thin stream of blood down Steven's chin now. Stephanie tore a piece of tissue paper and staunched it. The blood and foam mixed pink.

'They are all lying.'

'The whole world's lying except you.'

'Stephanie, you have to believe me.'

'How many times do I have to tell you, this isn't my area.'

As Stephanie continued to work with her blade, Steven tried to figure out what might have happened to Fiona. It was possible that if *The New York Times* had decided to kill the hoax story, she would have taken her dossier elsewhere. It wasn't her style just to give up on it. He tried to put himself in her shoes, which wasn't difficult. They were mirror images of each other. He stared at Stephanie's bowed head in the mirror and an idea came to him. If the *Times* had told her that they weren't prepared to run the story, she would have gone to someone who would.

Anderson!

As far as she was concerned, Anderson was still Steven's mortal enemy and *True Society* would be a good place to break the news of the hoax. A sociological journal with a reputation for puncturing reputations. The queen would have fled to the arms of her poisonous prince. If it had been Steven with the dossier, that is where he would have gone. If she had gone to Anderson's place, then there would be no way that anyone could track her down, because no one but Steven knew of the connection.

Steven was about to yell out Anderson's name but he stopped himself. He still wasn't sure that Stephanie could be trusted. If he told her, he might be leading Pettman straight to the dossier which was now his only way of proving the truth.

'What I'm saying, Steven, is that you have to be careful,' Stephanie said.

'Careful of what?'

'Careful of Pettman and John Cross. Especially Cross. He has a reputation.'

'For what?'

'You'll see for what. Stretch your top lip like this.'

Stephanie stretched her top lip and Steven did the same. She began to work on his moustache. He could see his own face in the mirror, emerging from the husk of hair. He was as thin and gaunt now as he had been when he was a student in London but his eyes were duller and wiser. Stephanie had begun to hum a tune to herself as she worked with the razor and Steven took that as a signal that he shouldn't ask any more questions. He knew that his relationship with her was still a delicate and sickly thing. He needed to find out somehow if he could trust her and to do that he needed to get close to her, to fuel her recklessness. If what she had said so far was true, she had already spent a lot of time checking things through. Steven listened to her humming and realized it was no tune at all.

'You know, with a beard you remind me so much of someone I used to know,' she said at last. 'In fact, I'll be glad when I've got this fur off your face. It's like looking at a ghost.'

'Someone you didn't like?'

'The opposite.'

'Someone you liked a lot?'

'Yep. There, I told you to keep your mouth closed, I cut your cheek.'

Steven put his finger on the cut and Stephanie shaved around it. The blood trickled down his finger and onto the razor. Stephanie began to scratch around Steven's ears with dainty downward strokes.

'You worked it out?' she said, half defiant, half playful.

'Worked what out?'

'The guy you remind me of. I told you all about him when you were unconscious. No subliminal bells ringing?'

Steven smiled and he saw half of his handsome smile in the mirror.

'No, but I'm a pretty good guesser,' he said.

'Clever boy. What d'you work out?'

Stephanie made two more strokes with the razor and moved her head so that Steven could see his full reflection. He was half shaved.

'I remind you of some guy with a beard who was your boyfriend. Your husband maybe.'

Stephanie washed the razor and began to stroke the left side of Steven's face.

188

'He was my boyfriend, someone else's husband.'

'OK. Do you want to tell me about it?'

'I told you all about it already. That's what's so weird.'

'So tell me again.'

Steven flinched. Another cut.

'There, now that's three times,' Stephanie said. 'You're going to be a mess of scars Steven. My boyfriend died. He was killed.'

'I'm sorry.'

'Sure you're sorry. Everyone's sorry. We trained together. He was a cop. Some kid with an assault rifle blew his brains out.'

Stephanie washed the razor again and flicked away the last of the foam. Steven was clean-shaven again and Stephanie studied his reflection in the mirror.

'Was he really this good looking?' Steven said. Stephanie reached into the inside pocket of her jacket. As she did it, Steven saw her gun and holster, buttoned down. She produced a police ID card. There was a portrait photo of a New York policeman with black hair and a black beard. Beneath the photo was the name 'Juan Ramirez'. Steven saw that there was a passing resemblance, nothing remarkable. The ghost was inside Stephanie's head, but Steven thought he understood more now about Stephanie's sudden tenderness towards him.

'When was he shot?' Steven said, as Stephanie put the photo back into her pocket.

'Six months ago.'

'You must still be pretty upset.'

'Well, Steven Hawthorne,' she said with a sigh, 'I guess you'd say I'm just throwing myself into my work. Come on, let's finish the tour. You look like you need some air.'

Stephanie handed Steven a white towel and he began to dab blood from the cuts on his face.

Stephanie helped Steven put on his mohair overcoat before they went outside into the garden. The coat was still stiff with blood and there was dried blood on Steven's face from where Stephanie had shaved him. When they stepped through the french windows onto the lawn, Steven felt the icy grip of the freezing air. The coldness brought back painful memories of rolling over and over in the back of the cab, but somehow the coldness here was different. It was dry and still and the snow sparkled with sunlight. The darkness of New York City seemed to be thousands of miles away even though he could hear its drunken snoring on the horizon.

'You OK? Not too cold?' Stephanie said.

Steven took some deep breaths. He felt as if something was being released. He felt it rising up out of him all the way to the wispy white clouds above. There were rolling hills to the north beyond the line of oak trees and between the hills a shallow river valley, with the foaming blue scrawl of the river cutting through the pure white folds of snow. He could just hear the sound of someone sawing firewood nearby, and the sound of rooks calling in the distance. Stephanie took Steven by the arm and led him away from the house. When Steven looked around, he saw that the house looked like a huge turreted sand castle that had been dumped in the snow.

When they were twenty yards away from the house, Stephanie bent down and picked up a handful of snow. She squeezed it in her fist and let the melted water dribble through her fingers.

'You ever eat snow, Steven?' she said.

'Yeah, why not?' he said and laughed.

Stephanie took a bite of the snow in her hand and crunched it. Her mouth steamed.

'If you close your eyes you can pretend it's ice cream. I just thought you ought to know that.'

'Thank you.'

Steven guessed that this was some private joke that she couldn't share with anyone any more. He felt embarrassed and almost ashamed of himself that he would pump his bizarre good fortune for all it was worth.

'Something else you ought to know,' Stephanie said.

'Tell me.'

'Last night, I made call. I spoke to an old friend of Juan Ramirez who works out of C in Alphabet City. She's a lieutenant. There are three incidents in your book where you say that the police were called. The drug-store robbery where you were look-out, the time when Polo went crazy in the neon-light store and the time with the baking soda. If those incidents had taken place in the places you say they took place, there would have been a record kept of the call-out on the daybook computer in Avenue C. My friend checked all the dates and there was no record of any of those things actually happening. I'm not saying that that means anything but I can't figure out why there is no paperwork or file for any of that stuff if it really happened.'

Stephanie took another mouthful of snow and crunched it with her eyes narrowed.

'You don't ever mention to anyone that I told you that, OK? I'll make some more calls tonight, see what I can find out. There's something weird going on. So like I say, you be careful with Pettman and you be especially careful of John Cross.'

Steven instinctively turned around to look at the house, at the darkness behind the leaded windows and then he turned back to Stephanie with wonder in his eyes. Stephanie smiled.

'You just close your eyes and pretend it's ice cream.'

## Chapter Eighteen

**1**

'For Christ's sake wake up,' Stephanie said. She was shaking him. He had slept for sixteen hours without dreams. Guo had given him tablets and even after so much sleep he could hardly open his eyes.

'It's my job to get you places on time,' she said, and Steven wondered if it was an echo from a dream. She helped him out of bed and handed him his clothes. 'Pettman and Cross are downstairs in the drawing room,' she said as she threw a clean shirt in Steven's face. 'They want to put you through the induction.'

Steven tried to pull on his trousers with his left hand and Stephanie fell to her knees and yanked his fly button closed.

'What induction?'

'Witness induction.'

'I'm not a fucking witness.'

'Just put your pants on.'

Steven waited while Stephanie buttoned his shirt for him. She smelt strongly of perfume and he could see that she had paid special attention to her make-up and hair. He sensed that it was for John Cross's benefit.

They walked down the staircase together into the chamber of sunlight. The door to the drawing room was open and Steven could hear furniture being moved around and he could hear Pettman speaking softly. When they walked into the room, there was darkness and Steven saw that velvet curtains had been pinned up to the windows.

'Good to see you looking so well, Steven,' Pettman said and he offered his hand to shake. Steven glanced down at his sling with disgust and Pettman squeezed Steven's shoulder instead.

'The doc tells me it missed the bone.'

'I was lucky,' Steven said.

'I had to make a decision.'

'Fuck you.'

Stephanie quickly stepped between them and with an open hand pointed at a shadow sitting near to the make-shift curtain.

'This is John Cross,' she said with nervous reverence. 'He is heading the Amarillo investigation.'

The shadow took human form when it lifted from its seat to nod gently in Steven's direction. In the gloom he could only see the whiteness of a shirt, a pale face and the glint of a bald head.

'John and Tom Pettman have been working on the Amarillo investigation for a long time,' Stephanie said with great formality and John Cross laughed.

'Excuse me, did I say something funny?' Stephanie said and the air seemed to crackle. In the gloom all four people looked like shadows with shining faces. Steven noticed that the ceiling of the drawing room was decorated with angels and cherubs blowing silent horns.

'We are going to begin with something John wants you to see,' Stephanie said. 'It's a film show. That's why we've put up the curtains.'

'I want to talk first,' Steven said.

'You watch the film first,' Stephanie said with quiet authority. 'Just watch the film, then we'll talk.'

John Cross grabbed a chair and positioned it facing the

curtains. Pettman flicked on a projector behind Steven's shoulder and the projector cast a vibrant white light onto a screen which had been positioned a few feet from where John Cross was sitting. In the light from the projector, Steven could see some of the features of the room more clearly, the stained portraits on the wall, the edges of a huge and ornate fireplace, the twinkling of an enormous chandelier above John Cross's head. John Cross moved his seat back into the shadows, to get a better view. Pettman cleared his throat and said, 'OK?'

'Why the heck not,' John Cross said, with a warmth and gusto that didn't sit well with the darkness and the shadows. The projector began to whirr and the carousel of slides clunked into position. The first blurred image came onto the screen, a smudge of green, white and black, which Pettman brought into focus as he talked. Steven took his seat beside the projector.

'This is a village called . . . Quiaxaca,' Pettman said. The body of the projector had already grown so hot that the room was beginning to smell of burnt dust and melting celluloid.

'This is one of the villages in Colombia where the leaves are harvested.'

The shot was of a group of children wearing white rags taking in a bright green harvest. They were bent over in a line, putting the green leaves into white sacks. Beyond the line of children there were mountains covered in dense jungle. The next shot was of a coca leaf and the green waxy stem came in and out of focus.

'This is a leaf of the coca plant,' Pettman said.

The machine clunked again and this time there was an aerial shot of a river basin, the thin blue veins of the river cutting through the jungle canopy.

'Another shot of Quiaxaca from above,' Pettman said. He sounded embarrassed, making dumb comments out of

duty. 'And here's a shot of how they distil the leaves into
. . . into the cocaine.'

There was a picture of a primitive distillery, ingenious
and fragile, made out of saplings and twisted vines, with a
pile of kerosene cans beside it hidden deep in black undergrowth. The next shot was another close-up of a coca leaf.

'Same shot of the coca leaf,' Pettman said, pretending
that it wasn't a mistake. The machine clunked again and
this time there was a shot of a house made of mud and
straw, with a hand-painted board above the entrance with
the words 'Drug Enforcement Agency'.

'As you can see,' Pettman mumbled in the darkness, 'we
had to work out there with minimal resources.'

In the reflected light from the screen, Steven could see
the face of John Cross like a black and white photograph.
His eyes were hollows of darkness, his forehead gleamed.
Steven kept looking from the screen to John Cross and
back to the screen again. His expression never changed.
Some more shots came into view and Pettman mumbled
his embarrassed commentary, like a sports master sweating
his way through a sex-education class. He seemed to be
reciting his dialogue from memory.

'The harvest is taken in around October and most of
the leaves are transported by river. To cover an area of
three thousand square miles we have only three helicopters
on the ground.'

John Cross cleared his throat.

'That is to say, they're not on the ground. They're in
the air.'

The carousel clicked and this time there was only a
rectangle of brilliant light on the screen. The new light
filled the room and John Cross reached under his chair.
He handed a new box of slides to Stephanie, who handed
it over Steven's head to Pettman. Steven could hear Pettman loading the carousel with new images.

'Those pictures you've just seen, Mr Hawthorne, were part of an audio-visual presentation we send round to schools and colleges in affected areas. Harlem, the Bronx, Alphabet City . . .'

Steven rubbed his eyes. The light from the projector was as harsh as snow light.

'It gets shown to kids, sometimes eight, nine years old. So it's kind of mild. This next show is the stuff we have been showing to everyone who gets involved in our current investigation. Officers, agents, witnesses . . . during induction. It's kind of graphic, Mr Hawthorne. If you feel the need to throw up, there is a bowl underneath your seat.'

The first image came up. It was a portrait shot of a woman with flowing, long, black hair and shining, black eyes, filled with pain. Her lips were being held apart by the hand of a man. A white man. Her mouth was open to show that all of her teeth had been removed. Where her tongue should have been there were five or six purple lumps. She looked as if she had a mouthful of baby mice.

'This lady is called Maria,' Pettman mumbled, trying to bring the shot into sharper focus. 'Her husband got involved in transporting kerosene downriver to be used in the distillation of the coca leaves. She got scared and told one of the local guys who services our helicopters. The bad guys found out and they pulled all of her teeth out with pliers. Then one of the bad guys bit off her tongue.'

The image was held in silence. Maria reminded Steven of someone he'd known a long time ago. A Turkish woman he'd taken to Paris.

'Maria died two weeks after this shot was taken. She got an infection in her mouth. Turned to gangrene. She was twenty-two years old.'

The next shot was of three small children lying face down beside a dirt track.

'These are Maria's children,' Pettman drawled and the projector whirred. 'All three were shot in the head.'

The carousel clicked and another image came onto the screen. A shot of a bundle of black rags, like two sacks held together by a belt with a silver buckle, and a tangle of silver hair, all thrown against the wheel of a very old truck.

'And this is Maria's mother. They rode over her, reversed, rode over her, reversed, rode over her . . .'

Another click.

'And finally,' Pettman said, with at last a note of drama in his voice, 'the guy himself. The guy who was transporting the kerosene. He tried to tell the bad guys that he was sorry that his wife had gone and talked to the authorities, so the bad guys said, "If you're so sorry, you pull out her teeth." They handed him the pliers and told him to pull out his own wife's teeth. He refused. So this is what they did to him.'

The shot was of what looked like a poor sculpture of a man, made out of black mud, round-headed, leaning up on the crook of an elbow. It looked like the kind of bronze statue of a reclining figure that city corporations commission to decorate their civic buildings. The figure was lying on a patch of blackened grass.

'They burnt him alive,' Pettman said. 'And when we arrived, we found two rats inside his body. Cooked inside him. The bad guys had stuck two live rats up his ass. Tried to eat their way out of him as they cooked him.'

The next shot was of the kerosene man's belly split open, the rats, roasted, curled up inside the cavity of his body. Steven felt the nausea hit him like a wave, like movement inside his own belly, then it subsided. He thought about the snow-covered lawn. The vastness, the freedom beyond the heavy curtains. Pettman was continuing with his sleepy commentary.

'All of this happened in a village on the Lizard River, two hundred miles from Bogota City. There was just me and John Cross to cover the whole area. We got there two days after the massacre. The other people in the village wouldn't speak to us. Hid in the undergrowth when they heard the helicopter. They talk to a helicopter man, same thing's going to happen. The guys who did it . . .'

John Cross shifted in his seat and turned to get Pettman's attention. The sleeping rats came into sharper focus.

'Tell him about the kid,' John Cross said softly.

'Say again, sir?'

'Tell Mr Hawthorne about the kid. The little kid.'

'Maybe you should tell the story yourself, sir.'

'You tell him.'

'We don't have a shot of the kid, sir.'

'Never mind. Tell Mr Hawthorne anyway. He's a writer. He's got an imagination. He can picture it for himself.'

Pettman cleared his throat and told Steven that when the bandits had arrived to massacre Maria's family, one of her sons, six years old, had been out cleaning kerosene cans in the river. He got back just in time to see the bad guys raping his mother then pulling out her teeth. He'd hidden in the bush until they had gone. John Cross and Pettman had taken the kid back with them to the military hospital. That night, the kid had chewed off his own finger. Bit through the bone. The doctors said that he didn't feel a thing because after he'd seen what had happened to his mother, he'd just kind of grazed on coca leaves for two whole days. Ate half his daddy's crop. The slide projector clicked onto pure white.

'Got to change the carousel,' Pettman said.

Pettman was about to load another package of slides when Steven said, 'Wait a minute.'

'Say again, Mr Hawthorne.'

'Wait. There's no need to change the carousel.' There was an astonished silence.

'Mr Hawthorne,' Pettman said, alarmed, 'John Cross asked that we show you the whole AV presentation before we start to talk.'

'There is no need. Mr Cross, there is no need . . .'

For the first time John Cross turned to look directly at Steven. The pure white light of the projector glinted in his eyes and his white shirt glowed phosphorescent.

'What I mean is,' Steven said, 'I get the idea.'

'What idea is that, Mr Hawthorne?' John Cross asked, with the same chuckling, folksy enthusiasm in his voice.

'What I mean is, if this is just to show me how the cocaine cartels operate there really isn't any need. When you hear what I have to say it won't be relevant.'

John Cross's electric stare stopped Steven's speech. There was a long pause in which the projector whirred loudly. Steven turned to look at Stephanie but she was dutifully staring at the blank screen.

'Won't be relevant?' John Cross said, with good-natured disbelief. 'Well OK, Mr Hawthorne, you're the boss.' He had a rounded, drawling Western accent.

Pettman hesitated. 'You don't want me to show him the rest of the pictures?'

'No I don't want you to show him the rest of the pictures,' John Cross said. 'Not if like Mr Hawthorne says it isn't . . . relevant.' He exhaled the last word like a dart from a blow pipe.

The buzzing of the projector was shut off and the room became dark apart from a blade of snow light that came through a crack in the curtains. In the darkness, Steven could see that Stephanie was trying to communicate with her eyes. He felt that he was being initiated into some complex dance or ritual where any missed step could send the whole thing reeling.

'So let's talk,' John Cross said.

'I'd like that,' Steven said and Stephanie cleared her throat.

'Maybe I could talk to my witness before you begin,' she said softly, trying hard to sound casual.

'There'll be no need,' John Cross said. 'You can leave us now, Stephanie. Maybe you could arrange some hot coffee for the three of us. Have one of the boys bring it in. My feet are cold. Huh, Tom? Hot coffee for cold feet. Make it mountain coffee. Nothing like Colombian mountain coffee for cold feet.'

John Cross chuckled and Stephanie gathered up some papers and left the room. She didn't turn around to look at Steven but he could feel the tension in the air around her as she walked by. After she had gone, Pettman grabbed the velvet curtains in his fist and pulled them down with a vicious tug. The room was suddenly flooded with blinding white light. The lawn was quilted with snow and the oak trees in the distance were all laden down with it. In the new light, Steven could see John Cross's face was reflected in the varnish of the drawing room table. He was thin and gaunt and the collar of his shirt was too big for him. He looked sick.

'Damn cold,' John Cross said and he scratched his head and then slapped his knee. There was something crazy about him, something crazy about the air around him.

'Mr Hawthorne wants to talk, Tom,' John Cross said, 'so what should we talk about with Mr Hawthorne? Should we start with the North American Free Trade Agreement? Hell no, Mr Hawthorne got the idea way back. Mr Hawthorne doesn't need to see the rest of the pictures. Hell no. You get the idea of the film show, do you, Mr Hawthorne?'

'I take the point that you're making,' Steven said, terrified by the crazy shadow, silhouetted against the bright light from the lawn. His shoulder began to hurt and he suddenly began to worry that he was defenceless with only one functioning arm. He slipped his arm a little way out of the sling.

'So talk,' John Cross said through a smile. 'Stephanie told us that you had something important to say.'

'She said that?'

'I ain't lying.'

'OK, then I do have something to tell you. You're here because of what you read in my book. You think I witnessed a murder a year ago last April in Avenue D. Well you're wrong. I never witnessed any murder. *Alphabet City* is a hoax. I made it all up.'

John Cross suddenly stood up. Even in the half-light, Steven could see that his crumpled blue suit looked two sizes too big for him. He came and stood beside Steven's chair and whispered in his ear.

'"And it shall come to pass, while my glory passeth by, that I will put thee in a clift of the rock and will cover thee with my hand while I pass by." Exodus, 33:22.'

Steven could feel the silver face of John Cross only inches from his ear and when he turned to face him, he could see the glints of madness in the corners of his eyes.

'You're hurting my shoulder,' Steven said without blinking. 'You see, I got hit by a bullet. From your friend's 9mm automatic.'

John Cross threw back his head and screamed with laughter and the sound of his laughter echoed up to the ceiling. Steven's shoulder had begun to throb and he became angry quickly. He felt that he was being caught up in some kind of amateur theatre, with John Cross playing the dangerous lunatic, Pettman acting as the controlling influence, maybe even Stephanie playing the part of confidante. John Cross walked over to the huge drawing room windows, his hands in his pockets, still laughing in short spurts. Pettman came and stood at Steven's side.

'John's very religious,' Pettman said to Steven, trying hard to sound unruffled. 'He gets kind of . . .'

Pettman shrugged his shoulders. 'Well I guess you can understand, after what we've both been through, he gets a little . . . involved.'

Steven could see that inside his huge, baggy suit, John Cross's shoulders were heaving and it was impossible to tell whether he was still laughing or whether he had begun to cry.

## 2

Coffee was served in the drawing room by a big hairy cop, who carried the exquisite eighteenth-century silver service as if it were a plate of snakes. He placed it delicately down on the drawing room table and left Steven and Pettman and John Cross alone.

'So while John gets his thoughts together,' Pettman said, without a trace of irony, 'perhaps we can just talk about what you've just seen.'

Pettman poured three cups of black coffee. Steven had his wounded arm out of his sling and hooked around the back of his chair. When he twisted his shoulder it cut off some of the blood and that served to ease the pain.

'I don't want to talk about what we've just seen. I want to talk about the book. I want you both to understand that there is no way on God's earth that you can put together a prosecution on the strength of it, because it is all lies. You put me on the witness stand I'll say it out loud. I'm through with lying for good. I also want to talk about these other people who have made statements. Azole and Lucretia and the others. I want to know how the hell you are taking statements from people who don't exist.'

'What I am saying', Pettman said, pouring the coffee, 'is that now you understand a little more what is at stake in this investigation.'

Now that Steven's eyes were accustomed to the snow light, he could see in the distance a watch tower between the line of oak trees. It was a thirty-foot scaffold with a look-out post and a snow-covered timber roof.

'I have known all along what is at stake. That is not the issue, the issue . . .'

Pettman interrupted, as if he'd been given a cue from somewhere, as if Steven's voice was inaudible.

'What is at stake, Steven, is seven years' work, in Colombia and right here in New York. Amarillo is part of a bigger picture. I guess you've worked that out for yourself. It's a kind of a domino effect. If we can convict Amarillo he'll do a deal in return for evidence against the next guy, the next link in the chain. We get the next guy, he'll do a deal for the guy along from him, and so it'll go on. And let me tell you, Steven, that chain that starts right here in this room will stretch all the way to the Lizard River, all the way into the darkest jungle. So do you understand what is at stake? Some small part of what is at stake? You are a white, middle-class witness, Steven. You are a firm foundation to start off the process. We have never, ever before had the chance to take on someone like Amarillo with this kind of ammunition.'

John Cross turned away from the window and joined them at the table. When he walked across the carpet, he made no sound at all. It was as if he were weightless inside his huge crumpled suit. Pettman carried on talking as John Cross took his seat.

'All that John Cross is asking is that you describe to us exactly what you saw on page 117. The murder of Raul

De Soto. John Cross just wants you to describe exactly what you saw and to identify the guy who did it. You do that, Steven, and we can begin to move along the chain.'

'Hey Tom, that's right!' John Cross exclaimed with wonder, as if he'd just worked it out for himself. 'Your book kind of brought the whole thing to life. Couldn't put the book down. Thought, Jesus, this guy knows. He really understands.'

Steven was looking from one to the other.

'But it's all fiction. I made it up,' Steven said. 'You have to understand that.' John Cross didn't seem to hear.

'So beautifully realized,' he said wistfully. 'Each character just alive and crawling off the page. You write like an angel, Mr Hawthorne. I close my eyes and I can see the whole thing in my head.'

Steven looked at the earnest and stony expressions on both of their faces. They were dark agents from another universe, trapped in the brilliant sunlight between one world and the next. Steven could almost smell the lushness of the jungle on them.

'Did you hear what I said, Mr Cross? It's all lies,' Steven said.

John Cross turned to Pettman and said, 'Tom, perhaps you should explain to Mr Hawthorne exactly what the deal is we've worked out for him.'


## 3


John Cross fidgeted with a pencil and looked up at the cherubs and angels, a cue for Pettman to begin.

'OK, Mr Hawthorne,' Pettman said, patrolling the space in front of the window. 'As you can see, we don't have a tape recorder running and so everything I have to say is off the record.'

He waited for the silent approval of John Cross, which came in the form of an almost imperceptible nod and an earnest frown.

'I am not in any way assuming that you have given your assent to help us with our investigation. I am simply empowered at this time to make some proposals and to ask you some simple questions. For now we are proceeding on a kind of "what if" basis. You agree to something like that, Steve?'

'Yes. Just don't call me Steve.'

John Cross looked up at the ceiling and sighed.

'Then that's good,' said Pettman. 'So let me begin by asking you to think of a figure which would in some way go towards recompensing you for the inconvenience which has been caused to you as a result of this investigation. We would like to make you an offer. An offer of compensation which would be paid to you in whatever denomination you choose into any account you choose. On condition, of course, that you continue to co-operate with our investigation. Let's say . . . one hundred thousand dollars . . .'

John Cross suddenly scribbled something down on a piece of paper that he had taken from his pocket and he pushed it across the table to no one in particular. He wrote like a rodent gnawing through rope. Pettman angled his head and read the scrawl on the piece of paper. Then he said, '. . . That's one hundred thousand dollars each year, paid on the first day of January each year for ten years.'

'Million dollars,' John Cross said, then he began to hum under his breath.

Steven felt that at any minute the angels and cherubs above his head could melt like ice cream. There were a few moments of silence before Steven said, 'You have to stop this.'

Pettman blinked quickly in the direction of John Cross, who had folded his hands over his lap and had begun to intone, 'It hath no stalk, the bud shall yield no meal. If so be it the strangers shall swallow it up.'

He repeated the same verse again and Tom Pettman went over to him and put his hand on his shoulder. Steven heard Pettman whisper, 'Get hold of yourself, John.'

Steven wanted to make a break for the drawing room windows. He wanted to burst open the doors and run out into the snow. He realized that something was disintegrating before his eyes. Up until now Pettman had been trying to hold this thing together, whatever the hell it was, but now John Cross was beginning to burn with some uncontrollable passion. Before, Steven had believed that this could all be pure theatre. While that was a possibility, he had been able to keep hold of himself. Now that he knew the actors weren't acting, he was filled with terror.

'You tell him, Tom,' John Cross hissed like a snake. 'You tell him that this is a moral issue. You show him the slides, Tom.'

'Jesus Christ,' Steven said, and he stood up. Tom Pettman glared at him and then pushed him back down into his seat.

'A million dollars,' Pettman said. 'Any denomination.'

'To lie for you.'

'One hundred grand each year, you keep your mouth shut.'

'So you know that it's a lie? Are you saying that you know already that the book is a hoax?'

'You get your passport back, you get help to set up anywhere you please. London, Paris, Rome. Discreet protection. The best. Maybe even Stephanie for the first year and a half. John Cross can authorize anything you want.'

John Cross was no longer listening. It was as if he had been unplugged and was settling into a torpor. The realization came to Steven by degrees. Pettman had been the architect of all of the coincidences, all of the impossible twists. Steven guessed that Pettman had found out the truth when the investigation into the murder of Raul De Soto was already under way, at a time when it had already gone too far down the road to haul it back. But that didn't add up either. Maybe Pettman had known that *Alphabet City* was fiction all along and had set out from day one with the intention of using it for a set-up of some kind. Or maybe the architect was John Cross. Pettman didn't seem to have the intellect.

'How long have you known, Mr Pettman? Did you start out knowing or did you find out?'

Pettman still didn't register Steven's voice. 'Think of it like a movie, Mr Hawthorne,' he said in a whisper. 'To make the book real we've cast the parts like a movie. We've already got some guy to play Polo, some hooker to be Lucretia. They're doing a deal with us in return for supporting your story. Do you remember a guy called Eliot? Eagle Pictures?'

The angels and cherubs above Steven's head all began to blow their horns. The sound was like a hundred taxi cabs all hooting and screeching their brakes.

'What has Eliot got to do with it?'

'He's helping us put the deal together. All the hookers and pimps who take our offer get a hundred grand in return for signing his rights of portrayal slips. It means we don't even have to pay them out of government money. Nothing can be traced back to us. You must see the beauty of this thing.'

Steven wondered who else was in on the conspiracy. Foley? Natalie? Maybe even Stephanie.

'The way we have it figured,' Pettman said, his face close to Steven's face, 'it won't even come to trial. Not if we can show Amarillo that he doesn't stand a chance in court. For that we need you, Mr Hawthorne. If you agree to testify, then Amarillo will do us a deal in return for what he knows about Carlos Pinon. If Pinon knows that Amarillo is testifying, he'll do a deal in return for Langley and Hope. These are just names to you, Steven, but to me and John Cross they are seven years' work in the field. These men are truly evil. Evil like you saw in the slide show. You agree to co-operate with us and you will be doing a fine and decent thing on behalf of the whole of humanity.'

'You mean if I lie. If I say the lie is real.'

'It won't be a lie, because we will make it real.'

'The body you found, was that real?'

'It is all arbitrary. Everything can be made or unmade.'

'What about my grandmother?'

'You decide.'

'Did you kill her because she knew the truth?'

'Everything can be made or unmade. In the beginning there was the word, Mr Hawthorne.'

John Cross suddenly stood up and folded his hands together. He began to squeeze his hands and blink quickly. Pettman suddenly turned on him.

'Jesus Christ, John, will you sit down and get hold of yourself!' he yelled, like a father to a child he loves. John Cross sat down.

'Seven years in the field,' Pettman said softly. 'John Cross was the very best of men, Steven. You take a look at him and see what he gave to fight this evil. And then you decide. You lied before for money, for vanity, because you were ambitious. Now you can lie for us for good reasons.'

Steven studied the thin figure of John Cross. He looked as if his insides had been sucked out of him. He didn't look like a cop but like a tortured prisoner, a witness to unforgettable horror. The fact that John Cross was apparently in charge of this whole enterprise made it not only terrifying but also irrational, and that was worse.

'This whole thing was his idea, wasn't it?' Steven said,

and Pettman didn't answer. 'He's the one who read my book and said he could make it real. He's the one with the imagination. And look what it has done to him. I know how it is for him, because it has done the same to me. You don't understand this, Mr Pettman, but he does. And I can't do it any more. I won't lie for you. I won't lie for anyone.'

Pettman went and sat on the corner of the drawing room table. He took out a pack of cigarettes and lit one. His smoke hung in the winter sunlight.

'You have a choice,' he said softly. 'Simple choice. You co-operate or you don't. You decide not to co-operate, you don't want to be a witness, we have no choice other than to remove your protection. You go back out there alone. You've got your face in every newspaper and every bookstore in the city. Two days, maybe three, Amarillo's people will catch up with you. You see, they think this thing is real too. We know that Amarillo really did shoot Raul De Soto, and we've got him thinking you were hiding right there in the shadows when he did it. So either way, he will have to kill you. You lie for us or you die. Simple.'

Pettman dropped his cigarette onto the gleaming floorboards and let it smoke. He then went over to John Cross and helped him to his feet. He put his arm around John Cross's shoulder and led him towards the door, like a soldier with a wounded comrade. After he had opened the door, Pettman turned around to Steven, who was still sitting in his chair beside the projector.

'What's it to be, Mr Hawthorne?'

'I'm not lying for anyone any more,' Steven said.

'In that case, I'll arrange for a car to take you back into the city. Maybe when you've spent a couple of days in New York, you'll change your mind.'

## Chapter Nineteen

**1**

Outside the air was still and frozen and the cold air hurt Steven's lungs when he breathed. He had removed his sling in disgust, a deep retching disgust at himself. He felt that he had been drunk for years and now at last he was sober. He had walked all the way through the house and found that it was empty, although he could hear raised voices coming from one of the spirit rooms along a darkened corridor. He went out into the garden and sat down on a fallen log, listening to the rooks and the honking of geese overhead. After he had been alone for a few minutes, Stephanie came out and joined him on the fallen log.

'I have orders to escort you back to New York City,' she said to the horizon.

'To be shot.'

'Not my area. I have my instructions, clear as day.'

'Do they have that kind of authority?' Steven asked and Stephanie laughed.

'So who are they?' Steven said.

'Huh? Oh, just . . . guys.'

'I mean, they're not even just DEA, are they?'

No answer. Stephanie's face was contorted with cold and anxiety. There was dewdrop on the end of her nose. 'Kiss her now, see what happens,' said an insane voice inside Steven's head.

'So if they're just guys, who do they work for?'

'Pettman is DEA.'

'And John Cross?'

'John Cross I don't know. I know that he's sick. He was bitten down in Colombia. So they say. A bat or a spider or a snake.'

Steven shivered at the thought of John Cross as a healthy man, John Cross as a man who had his kind of imagination and physical strength. The bat or the snake or the spider had done the world a favour.

'Did they tell you what happened in there?'

'Some. Like I said before, that isn't my area. I'm just a guardian angel. They only told me that your protection is to be terminated. There's a car out front. I have to take you back.'

Suddenly, in the white stillness, a black squirrel appeared, its outline vivid against the snow. The thing had appeared from above their heads and was now scurrying along the fallen log. It sat on its haunches and twitched, keeping one of its eyes on Steven and Stephanie. Then it moved a little closer and groomed its cheeks. Sometime, a long time ago, someone in this house had fed the squirrels on winters days like this one. Someone had cleared the snow and banged a saucepan and the squirrels had come running. This one still remembered those days and it edged a little closer, fear and hunger fighting each other.

'Pretty awful camouflage, don't you think?' Steven said. 'Black squirrel on a snowy day. I thought nature took care of things like that.'

Silence. Stephanie working her way through a whole labyrinth of possibilities.

'But I guess I know how that squirrel feels. I know how it feels to be black on a snowy day. Sitting there like a target for the whole world to see. That's pretty much how it is, isn't it, Stephanie? This is a set-up. I've been set up for something right from the beginning, haven't I?'

The squirrel suddenly darted back onto the log and disappeared up the trunk of a tree. Stephanie didn't say anything. Steven needed to keep on talking because Stephanie was his only chance to get to the truth, even though she wasn't a chance at all. To create intimacy here, on a day with all the sunlight frozen out of it, with so much fear in the air, seemed impossible.

'Stephanie, you've been pretty straight with me. Be straight with me again.'

'I can't.'

'Imagine how it is for me.'

'I am not paid to imagine. My orders are to take you back to New York City.'

'To have a bullet put in my brain.'

Stephanie wiped the dewdrop from her nose inelegantly with her sleeve. She sniffed hard.

'Can't talk like this,' she said with great determination. 'Don't ask, because I can't tell.'

Steven was only now glimpsing the breadth of the conspiracy in which he had become involved. Stephanie looked down at her feet and said, 'Don't you understand anything, Steven?'

'I understand that I have been used by you and by the others for some purpose that I have no knowledge of.'

There was silence, then Stephanie said, 'Look, our friend is back.'

The black squirrel leapt down from the trunk of the tree and began to dig frantically in the snow. Steven waited and waited for Stephanie to continue but she didn't. The squirrel groomed its fat cheeks, as if it knew how cute it looked.

'Hey, I do a pretty good impression of a squirrel,' Stephanie said and laughed in a great cloud of breath.

She was crying too. She reached into her coat and the movement triggered some instinct in the squirrel's mind. It leapt closer, sniffing for food. Stephanie produced a 9mm automatic pistol.

'You know how to use one of these things Steven?' She held it in her open palm for Steven to look at.

'Yes.'

'Sure you do. It's easy. You just release the safety catch ... pull back the chamber ... take aim, and then you squeeze the trigger.'

Stephanie pulled the trigger and the black squirrel's head exploded in the snow. Its body collapsed in on itself. The 9mm had hardly made any noise at all, so the animal's head looked as if it had exploded by itself. There was a spray of dark blood across the snow, like a splash of paint, and the wind blew and ruffled the fur on the squirrel's body. Steven was staring at it with his mouth open. The firing of the gun set off a stampede in Steven's head and he could feel the thundering of hooves. He knew suddenly that he should have been as scared as this all along.

'You'd better take it,' Stephanie said, and she pushed the gun into the inside pocket of Steven's jacket. The thing hung heavily against his chest. 'It was your analogy, Steven, about you being the squirrel. I just finished the analogy off for you. You're a writer. You understand symbolism, don't you?'

He heard a car engine firing at the front of the house. Stephanie stood up and walked through the snow towards the open french windows.


**2**


At the front of the house there was a black limousine with its engine running, the clouds of exhaust fumes frozen into blue smoke. The windows of the limo were blacked out. Pettman appeared from the house wearing a long mohair overcoat and joined Steven and Stephanie at the car. He looked tired, almost deathly.

'Right,' he said.

The front of the house was grey and forbidding, like the front of an asylum. There was smoke coming out of a far chimney, the chimney that led down to Steven's bedroom and Steven imagined John Cross warming himself in front of the flames, taking his place in the bed.

'Get in,' Pettman said.

'No. Not unless you tell me where are we going.'

'Get in, Mr Hawthorne.'

'I demand to know where you are taking me.'

Steven slammed the door of the limo and the sound of the door slamming echoed over the snow, disturbing a flock of rooks down in the oak trees. Steven was breathing hard, not sure if it would be crazy to just make a break for the fence. Pettman rubbed his dry, sandy face, as if this were the last time he would have to put up with Steven's obstinacy.

'Steph and I are heading back for New York and if you want to take a ride with us, that's fine. If you want to walk, New York is that way.'

Pettman pointed in the direction of the sun, which was as dull as a copper coin in a grey sky. Steven turned instinctively to look in the direction of New York and then looked back at Pettman.

'You ready, Steph?' Pettman asked and Stephanie headed for the far door of the limo. Pettman opened his door and was about to get in. Steven grabbed him.

'Wait a minute.'

'It's been nice knowing you, Mr Hawthorne.'

Steven looked over at Stephanie and she hesitated. He could see that she was fighting back tears and he knew that she was trying to control herself for Pettman's benefit. She tried to make her voice sound formal, polite.

'You really should take a ride with us, Steven,' she said.

'There won't be a train into the city until tomorrow morning. And if you try to walk, you'll freeze.'

Stephanie sighed through her tears and looked away. Pettman told her to get in the car and she didn't move.

'Get in the goddamn car, Steph,' Pettman said and he stared at her, incredulous. When she didn't move, he walked all the way around the car, he put his arms around her and he hissed in her ear. She stood stiffly in his arms and Pettman turned around to glare at Steven.

'You gone soft on this guy?' he heard Pettman say and there was something other than anger in his voice.

'You get in the fucking car, Hawthorne,' Pettman shouted, 'and Steph, you shut your goddamn mouth.'


**3**


They drove down a hundred yards of gravel drive, the blackened windows of the limo making it look like twilight outside. Pettman was between Steven and Stephanie. They passed through two steel gates, manned by uniformed policemen, who stood like statues, chins jutting, grave faces. The limo could have been a funeral car taking a military salute. Then they turned into a country lane with high hedges, all daubed carelessly with an emulsion of snow. In the distance there were mountains, in the middle distance horses nuzzling through the snow to get a mouthful of brown grass. After an hour, the fields were replaced by suburbs. When they entered the Lincoln Tunnel, it was twilight for real. When they came out of it, and emerged onto the island of Manhattan, it was already dark, and the huge tower blocks and office buildings were lit up, their heads lost in clouds of snow that had begun to swirl above the city. For all Steven knew, two blizzards had come and gone since he had been shot but the sky was full of another offering. This would go down as the worst winter in New York for centuries, and the whole city seemed tired of it. Even the buildings looked exhausted. The traffic on West 34th Street was almost at a standstill, choked up on stubborn brown sludge. Taxi cabs edged their way across the iced-up roads, limos skidded inelegantly into curbs. The steam of the underworld billowed up through ventilation shafts and Steven wiped away some condensation on his window to see that the stores were all lit up with Christmas lights now. Broadway was a blur of crimson and blue lights, reindeer leaping over the traffic with magical ease. The sidewalks were full of people waddling like penguins, their collars up around their ears. The only people not walking fast to get the hell out of the city were the bums dressed as Santa Claus holding out their plastic cups for change. When the limousine pulled up for traffic lights, the silence inside the car was broken by the sound of Christmas carols being played on PA speakers.

'What date is it?' Steven said. It was the first time anyone had spoken since they had left Bronxville.

'December 10th,' Pettman said. 'Almost Christmas.'

Silence, apart from the hooting of horns and the crackle of Christmas music.

'OK, Mr Pettman, this has gone far enough. If I were to tell you right now that I was prepared to co-operate . . .'

A black Santa Claus approached the window of the limo. He was as thin as matchsticks beneath his heavy red cloak. He tapped the window, held out his plastic cup and mumbled, 'Merry Christmas.'

'Are you saying that you will co-operate?' Pettman said,

holding up his middle finger to Santa Claus. The limo pulled away from the lights, but the street was still choked with people who had stepped off the sidewalk to walk along the snowless tracks left by cars. The city looked frozen and ugly.

'I guess I am saying that,' Steven said. He felt as if he had lost a gallon of water in sweat in the hot air-blow of the interior of the limousine. Someone threw a snowball and it thudded against the side of the limo. Sometimes big shiny cars attract attention.

'Well, Mr Hawthorne, I'd say in reply that you've left it too late.'

The limo turned slowly into East 44th Street. The Christmas lights were broken and they hung in the gloom, making the street seem even darker. The snow was drifting against the sandstone buildings. The limo pulled up outside a bar called 'Freddy's Highball', with a neon sign that flashed on and off.

'Are you saying that even if I said right now that I was prepared to say whatever you wanted, to lie for you, tell you that the book is gospel . . .'

'Gospel,' Pettman said. 'Let me tell you something about the gospels. Let me tell you what John Cross said to me about the gospels. He said the gospel only became gospel when the hero was dead. John Cross has made his decision, Mr Hawthorne. You've made your statement. You've given your testimony. It's right there in your book in black and white. If we can't have you, we will use the book. John Cross has made up his mind.'

Pettman opened the limo door and got out. A blast of ice-cold air blew into the car and the sweat froze under Steven's clothes. Steven's stomach turned over. He turned to Stephanie, whose face was lit only by the flashing light from the bar.

'Stephanie, for Christ's sake, you've got to stop this . . .'

She suddenly produced a screwed-up piece of paper from the pocket of her coat. It looked as though she'd been holding it in her fist the whole journey, waiting for her moment. She handed it to Steven without looking at him. The side of her face was lit by the flashing neon.

'It's my home number. Wait twenty-four hours then call and leave a message telling me where you are.'

Pettman's head reappeared in the window of the car. Steven quickly pocketed the piece of paper and Stephanie snuggled down into the collar of her coat. Steven saw that Pettman was carrying a suitcase. It was the suitcase Steven had left at the check-in desk at JFK. He dumped it in the snow.

'OK, Mr Hawthorne,' Pettman was saying, 'you'd better get out of the car.'

Steven got out and felt the wind blowing up from the East River. The city would freeze over tonight. Everyone was getting out before all the roads were blocked. Fifth Avenue was a stream of humanity, all trudging in the same direction.

'Mr Pettman, you can't do this. If this is a bluff, then it has worked. I have told you that I am prepared to do whatever it takes . . .'

The wind blew around Steven's face. It was so cold that it felt like death whispering in his ears. Pettman pulled up the collar of his coat and went to get back into the car. Steven grabbed his arm.

'My hands are tied, Mr Hawthorne,' Pettman said. 'My orders are to leave you here in New York City and that is what I must do. This case is no longer in my hands.'

He tapped the roof of the limo and the engine fired.

'Wait. I have no money.'

Steven was trying to speak calmly, to stop this thing from getting any more crazy than it already was. He knew that if he shouted or pleaded it would only make Pettman angry.

'At least give me my passport. Or money. I only have fifty dollars ...'

Before he closed the door of the limousine, Pettman said,

'You take good care of yourself, Mr Hawthorne.'

The car pulled away, leaving Steven standing in the street with his suitcase at his feet. As the limo headed down East 44th Street, he saw a cigarette-lighter flicker in the back seat and saw the glowing end of Stephanie's cigarette. Then it disappeared into another New York City blizzard.

## Chapter Twenty

### 1

The girl behind the bar at Freddy's Highball said that someone had said that she could hold a note longer than Whitney Houston. And to prove it she took a deep breath and sang 'I will always love you' and she held the note for half a minute. Steven blinked into his glass of beer the whole time that she held the note, then looked up at her and smiled. Steven was the only customer. Doris was tending the bar alone. She was Afro-American with straight black hair and crimson lips and a smile that seemed out of place in the cool dereliction of a midtown bar on the coldest night of winter so far. On nights like this, Doris had said, the bar could stay empty until closing time. All the regular customers, the guys who came here to take a drink after work with their secretaries, would have set out for home early. She said that the snow made men think of their families, like an instinct. There would be other guys staying the night in hotels, but they wouldn't be coming out till later. Then she had said with a smile that she knew Steven's face from somewhere, that she'd seen it in the papers and she had convinced herself that therefore Steven must be something to do with show-business. That was why she had held the note for thirty seconds. It was an impromptu audition.

'What do you think?'

'You sing very well.'

'And I look good too.'

'Yes, you do.'

'It's driving me crazy where I've seen your face. I know I've seen you in the papers.'

'You have the wrong man.'

Steven had come into the bar to use the phone. He'd already tried Anderson's office three times and there had been no reply. After that he had tried to get hold of Anderson's home number through the operator but Anderson was ex-directory. Anderson was too smart to make himself available to any creep or weirdo who took exception to his opinions.

'You want another beer?'

'Yes.'

'Hey, are you English?'

'Sort of.'

'I can tell by your accent. We have English beer.'

'Anything is fine.'

While Doris poured another beer, Steven tried the phone again. This time he tried to call Natalie on the home number she had given him when he had first arrived in New York but there was no reply. After that, he tried the JFK information desk, even though he had no passport, and he tried LaGuardia, even though he had no money, but the exercise was academic anyway. All flights out of the city had been grounded due to the blizzard. He phoned Grand Central train station and got a recorded message informing him that the last trains out had already left. He figured that it would have been insane to go to either of the airports or the train station anyway. That was just what his killers would be expecting.

While he sat at the bar, listening to Doris sing, he re-ran the conversations he'd had with John Cross and

Stephanie and managed to see everything in a new way. He had been stupid beyond belief not to have worked it out before.

'Hey, you want a whisky to chase that down?' Doris said and Steven nodded without even hearing.

He sipped his whisky and said, 'I'm cold. Could you turn the heating up a little?' He was tapping his foot rhythmically against the bar, staring into an upturned bottle of Jim Beam without seeing it, his hands shaking.

He had seen for himself that all the roads were blocked. The city was snowed in. Even this city, the capital city of the whole world, imprisoned inside its own city limits by a fall of snow. Now everyone was stuck here together and even the phone lines were beginning to freeze. But if he couldn't move around the city, then neither could anyone else. Maybe the blizzard was a blessing, a kind of time-out when the momentum of this thing would be held in check. Doris had her finger on her chin, a coquettish recreation of wonder.

'Maybe you're a movie star. Or you're on TV.'

'No. Please. Don't ask.'

'I got on TV once. I was on *Family Matters* with my brother. We got to meet Bill Cosby. And you know, Mr Cosby told me that I had the sweetest singing voice he'd heard in a long, long time. This was after the show. I went to his dressing room . . .'

Steven asked Doris to change ten dollars into quarters. She took his ten dollar bill to the till.

'Or maybe you're a soccer player. You look kind of sporty.' Doris was sorting coins in the till and turned around. 'That right? You sporty?'

'Look, I'm sorry, I am in a hurry. The quarters.'

Doris was counting out the quarters with a studied nonchalance in her voice and Steven began to imagine that she'd known who he really was all along. This was just some game she was playing. He caught his reflection in the mirror behind the bar. So thin. So dark.

'I did "Don't it make my brown eyes blue" for him,' Doris said.

'For who?'

'Bill Cosby.'

Doris had a handful of quarters. She began to count them out but Steven grabbed them off her. His hands were shaking so much that some of the coins spilled out onto the floor. Doris's smile disappeared and she looked uneasily at the door. Steven went back to the phone and dialled the number for Anton and Zucker. He got a tired duty officer.

'Hello.'

'I need to speak to Foley.'

'Putting you through.'

'Hello.'

'Hello, I need to speak to Foley.'

'I'm afraid Mr Foley has gone home.'

'Then give me his home number.'

'I'm sorry?'

'I need to speak to him now.'

'Who is this calling?'

Steven instinctively turned to look around the empty bar. He looked around like a cornered animal, seeing his own reflection in three split mirrors.

'Steven Hawthorne.'

Silence. Then the voice, filled with wonder, said, 'Steven Hawthorne?'

Steven waited. 'Yes, that's right. Steven Hawthorne. I'm calling from a call-box and I don't have much money. So if you could tell me . . .'

There was another pause for astonishment, perhaps others gathering round the phone.

Silence.

'Mr Hawthorne, could you hold the line for just a moment . . .'

'No I can't hold! Just give me his number.'

He could hear voices raised in the office. It was impossible to say what kind of fortress Foley would have built around himself, what kind of empire he had constructed and here was Steven calling on the phone, like the mythical Sun God, the reason for all those people to be there. Whoever had answered passed the phone to someone else, who solemnly gave Steven the number, as if he were addressing a whole nation.

When he called Foley, the phone rang for a long time. A customer came into the bar. Black, snowy hair, a brief glance around the bar, an exit back out into the wasteland outside. Steven eyed him in the mirror.

'Hello,' said a child's voice. Boy or girl, three or four.

'Hello, I need to speak to Foley . . .'

'Hello,' the child said again.

Steven hadn't spoken to a child for a long time. A year, maybe.

It felt strange, and it made his heart swell with some emotion of longing.

'Hello, could I speak to your daddy?'

'Mommy!' the child shouted and then she giggled and the phone hit something hard with a clatter. Steven could hear a TV in the background and there was jingle playing from a Christmas commercial. Then there was a woman's voice laughing.

'Hi. Sorry, you got Lucy . . . who is this?'

'This is Steven Hawthorne. I need to speak to Foley.'

The woman's voice became serious and she said she'd put him on the upstairs extension but Steven would have to wait a few seconds because David was in the bath. Steven heard Lucy laughing and her Mommy saying shush, shush. He pictured the scene of a warm home, a

fire, snow all around, the child in pyjamas watching TV
with Daddy in the bath, washing away the grime of a
day's work at Anton and Zucker. Doris S. Carlick was
singing and rattling her glasses and the air in the bar was
getting colder.

'Steven?'

'Foley, thank Christ.'

Steven pumped some more quarters into the phone.

'Where the hell are you?'

'I'm in a bar in New York City.'

'Yeah sure . . .'

'I'm serious Foley. They've decided that it's better for
them if I'm dead. They've left me out for Amarillo to
collect like the trash. You don't believe me listen to
this . . .'

Steven held out the phone so that Foley could hear
Doris singing. Foley said nothing. Maybe he knew already.
If he didn't know, he knew enough to believe that what
Steven was saying was true.

'The only person who can save my life now is Fiona. I
need you to tell me where she is.'

Steven could hear the slosh of bath water and water
dripping off some part of Foley's body.

'I can't do anything without speaking to Pettman. This
is in the hands of the police.'

'You are killing me, Foley, just as surely as if you were
pulling the trigger yourself.'

'I can't tell you where she is, because I don't know
where she is. No one does.' Foley was hissing, hoping his
family wouldn't hear.

'What about Siam Drayton. Give me her number and
I'll take it from there.'

'You'd be wasting your time, Steven. Drayton is working for us now. Pettman offered her an exclusive on the
inside story of the Amarillo investigation in return for

dropping the hoax thing. That's why Fiona took off. Pettman has a hundred people looking for her.'

Steven punched the phone with his ring finger as a blade.

'Does she still have the dossier?'

'She has the original. Drayton surrendered her copy to Pettman. Steven, if you find Fiona, tell her to just hand the thing over. Just hand the goddamned thing over. These people . . . Jesus.'

Steven could tell that Foley was scared, that he was out of his depth too. But his fear made him no use. Daddy used to say that fear was like a see-saw, you reached a point in the middle where, if you took one more step, you'd go all the way down. He used to say that a frightened soldier was an enemy soldier. Foley started to say that, Christ, he had no idea that this thing was going to get so out of hand and Steven put the phone down on him, grinding the receiver into the hook of the phone.

He tried Anderson again but there was no reply. He had an instinctive feeling that that was where she had gone. Then he called Natalie. Her boyfriend answered and when he heard who he had on the line, he suddenly became sombre and said quietly and quickly that the people at the store were doing all they could to sell as many copies of *Alphabet City* as possible because it was a mighty courageous thing that Steven was doing. When he heard Natalie's voice, Steven's resolve melted.

'Steven? Is that you? Where are you? Are you OK?'

He was going to try to recruit Natalie to his cause, tell her everything from the beginning and ask her to help him expose the dossier to the press. But when he heard the gentle eagerness in her voice, he knew that he couldn't. The truth now was a fatal virus and anyone who heard it would be infected. His grandmother had died first, now perhaps Fiona and finally Steven, the carrier. If John

Cross and Pettman wanted this case to hold together, they had to be sure that Amarillo's attorney couldn't uncover any star witnesses of their own.

'Natalie? I just called to say hello and to thank you for the clothes.'

'Steven, when I saw you, you looked so bad.'

'I'm fine now. They're taking good care of me.'

'Steven, I told my boyfriend about what happened between us. He's cool.'

'I really can't talk now. I just wanted to tell you that I'm OK.'

'Can we meet again? When this thing is over?'

'Sure we can. I'd like that. I hope I'll see you soon, Natalie.'

Steven put the phone down for the last time. Stephanie had said that he had to wait twenty-four hours before he called her. He didn't know why he had to wait but he would wait anyway, because he was sure now that he could trust her completely.

## 2

As the night wore on, customers came and went, bringing snow and freezing air into the bar with them. A business-man in a suit, a drifter who looked lost and who had just come inside to get warm, a middle-aged man and a young blonde woman who spoke to each other in Russian. Steven could understand most of what they said. His father had made him learn Russian as part of his private education on the air force bases around the world. The two Russians had a long argument about whether they should book one room or two in the hotel. She wanted to have her own room but he said that it would be more economical if they shared. The argument went round and round in circles as they became more and more drunk. The Russian woman said that she was hungry and the man said that they could eat in the bar but that he was afraid that the food would be prepared by the black woman behind the bar. He used the word 'nigger', and they both decided not to eat. Steven figured that they were diplomats from the UN building.

A black guy came into the bar to deliver a box of mixers. He wanted to fool around with Doris but she cut him dead and he looked hurt. Every time a customer had come into the bar, Doris had glanced at Steven surreptitiously, waiting for this to be the moment when she would figure out where she had seen his face. It had changed from being a game into being an obsession and Steven could see that his name was on the tip of her tongue. He tried to avoid her eyes, not wanting to confirm to her that he was vibrating with terror every time the black door onto the street swung open. Between customers, there were periods when the bar was empty. Doris always came to stand in front of Steven, pretending to dry beer glasses, whispering.

'If you're famous, shouldn't you have people with you?'

'Hey ... are you OK? I mean you look kind of nervous.'

'Would I be getting warm if I said that you present some kind of news show, like an anchorman?'

And finally, 'I guess you meet a lot of famous people. You ever meet anyone in the music business who could use a singer ...'

Each time Doris spoke to him, Steven grunted and shook his head. Each time she spoke, she was interrupting a long train of thought, a confusion of voices.

'OK, the guessing game is over,' he said and Doris looked up from her steamy sink of clean glasses.

'What's that you say?'

'The guessing game is over. My name is John McCann.'

'Who?'

'John McCann. I'm a record producer. You've probably seen my photo in the music press. I work out of London. Bowie, Elton John.'

Doris froze and then screamed and put both her hands to her mouth.

'*You* are John McCann?'

'Yep. You heard of me?'

'Well sure I have.'

The ease of the lie. The complicity and the willingness to enter this perfect world.

'Sorry I've been acting so weird,' Steven said, 'but I guess I've had too much . . .'

Steven sniffed the back of his hand and smiled.

'It makes me kind of jumpy.'

Doris said that she knew all about the stuff that made you jumpy. She said she was feeling pretty jumpy herself. Then she took the twenty-dollar bill and Steven said that, since they were the only people left in the bar, maybe they should have a little party. He ordered Jim Beam for them both and asked Doris to run through her repertoire one more time. He had been kind of distracted before. Doris began to sing as sweetly as an angel, song after song, and Steven clapped and grinned and smoked and sipped his whisky. Then he explained that he'd been meaning to fly back to London that night for a session with some new soul band but that his flight had been cancelled and now he had a whole night to kill and he'd spent all of his cash money thinking he would be home soon, and that he didn't believe in credit cards. At two a.m. he asked Doris, who was feeling kind of woozy by then, if she knew of anywhere he could stay.

'Why sure, John,' she said with a huge, lazy grin. 'I got an apartment. I got some of that stuff that makes you jumpy too. It's just a little place but even if we can't get a cab, we can walk there in half an hour.'

It wasn't until they were out in the frozen wastes of First Avenue, praying for a cab to make it through the snow, that Doris explained where her apartment was.

'It's up on East 14th Street. Just down by Alphabet City.'

When a cab finally pulled up, Steven was too cold and too tired to laugh at the irony.

## Chapter Twenty-One

**1**

Steven sat in the middle of the cavernous and dark Cherokee Café on East 14th Street, like Jonah in the belly of the whale. Outside the sun was shining and the snow was beginning to melt. When he'd ordered breakfast, he'd picked a table that had a clear view of both doors, a fast exit to the rest rooms, and within clear sight of the Mexican and Spanish bar staff who were already preparing lunches. He hugged himself to keep out the cold and to stop himself from shaking. His hands trembled so much that he could hardly pick up a cup of coffee. He looked at the Coors Lite clock above the long oak bar and saw that it was eleven minutes to midday. The bar tenders were all shouting out to each other in Spanish above the sound of a Mariachi band playing on the jukebox. It was dark, so no one could see Steven's face too clearly.

Doris appeared from the rest room, her face restored with lipstick and eye-liner. She placed her make-up bag down on the table.

'Are you sure you'll be OK?' she said.

'I'll be fine. You go. You'll be late for work.'

When they had woken up in Doris's apartment, the heating system hadn't been working and so she had suggested that they both go across the street to the Cherokee where there would be hot water. Steven had gone to the rest room first to wash and then Doris had gone to wash and put on her make-up. Doris had said that the cold weather must have frozen the pipes in her apartment but from the way the bar staff had greeted her when she had appeared at the door just as it opened Steven guessed that this was Doris's regular routine. The bar staff seemed to be happy to tolerate her and they didn't seem to be too surprised to see that she was accompanied by a man. A man who was shaking an awful lot.

Steven and Doris had spent the night in Doris's bed, in her apartment above a launderette off East 14th Street, being serenaded by her son, a kid of five or six years old, who lay under blankets in the corner of the room and blew random notes into a mouth organ.

'He's musical, like me,' Doris had whispered in the darkness and Steven had heard the kid giggle then blow some more. His playing was accompanied through the night by a moaning wind that blew in through warped window frames and so Steven hadn't had much sleep. There were only two rooms in the apartment, the bedroom and the bathroom, but the bathroom had been too cold to use even if the hot water had been functioning.

'So, you will listen to the tapes, won't you?' Doris said, putting her make-up bag into her purse. Steven had four cassettes in the pocket of his jacket. Each one was labelled 'Doris S. Carlick – Vocalist'. He promised that the moment he got back to London, he'd play her tapes to some people who might be able to offer her some work as a backing vocalist.

'I'll do what I can,' Steven said.

'Sure. Hey, this is just like my mom said, isn't it? She said she'd seen it clear as light that I'd get my break before Christmas Day.'

Doris stood up, ready to leave.

'Listen, Doris,' Steven said and she sat back down

again. He said nothing for a while and the music from the jukebox stopped right on cue. He took the cassettes out of his pocket and laid them on the table.

'What is it?' she said.

'It's about your tapes.'

'What about them?'

Steven wiped his mouth and looked around.

'You see, the truth is . . .'

'Yeah?'

'Ah it's nothing. I'll do what I can.'

He put the tapes back in his pocket and Doris laughed.

'Is everybody in the music business as weird as you?'

Steven shook his head. She peered at him, her face filled with amused curiosity.

'I mean, last night. We spent the whole night together. How come you didn't try anything?'

Steven said that he had a lot on his mind and Doris nodded her head, still amused, still curious. And when he looked up at her he thought that he could tell from the expression on her face that she hadn't ever really believed a single word of what Steven had said about being in the music business. He thought he could tell that the whole thing had been Doris wanting it to be true. Needing it to be true.

Doris pecked him on the cheek and then handed him an envelope, bulging and folded into quarters.

'What's this?' Steven said.

'It's some of the stuff that makes you jumpy. It's pretty pure. You look like you could use some.'

Steven put the envelope in his pocket as Doris walked out of the Cherokee. After she had gone, Steven took the envelope of cocaine into the rest room, poured a neat pile into his palm and sniffed it up. He'd never actually taken cocaine before but he'd read an awful lot about it and he had decided that, if he was going to make it through to nightfall, he would need the kind of random, senseless energy that it was supposed to provide.

*'My first blast was like a fast car, or like a bug getting hit by a fast car . . .'*

After he had washed his face and hands, he put the envelope back into his inside pocket and waited for the fast car.

## 2

He paid the bill and walked out onto East 14th Street. He began to wander without purpose towards the river, the spirit vapour burning his throat and chest. The snow was beginning to melt all around and the streets were being sluiced down with melt water. The water ran in black torrents all the way to Avenue C and Steven followed the flow of the water, like a piece of floating wreckage.

The buildings either side of him were black and high, like fortresses, and in the arches that led into the dark tenements, children played in the melting snow, hurling snowballs and iceballs up at the windows above. The stores all looked closed, even though they were open behind their steel mesh grills and the cold air rang with the sound of kids screaming. The roads were almost free of traffic and the hunched-up figures who walked by all had their heads pulled down into their collars, blowing steam as they walked. There were other, younger guys, with hollow faces, who didn't seem to have dressed for the weather, young guys in T-shirts and jeans, girls sitting on doorsteps in thin rayon jackets, their hair bundled up into knots on the tops of their heads. Steven didn't notice the way they all stared at him as he walked by, the way they all stopped talking as his shadow fell across them.

He found himself on a street corner, opposite an open-air basketball court with a high fence. Beyond that was a derelict warehouse and a splash of wet greenery where someone had lit a huge bonfire. There was acrid black smoke coming off the fire and six or seven guys in long coats standing around the flames. Steven leant against a streetlight and lit a cigarette. His hands were shaking and his shoulder hurt. When he reached in for his cigarettes, he felt the plump envelope of cocaine and when he bent forward to shield the flame of his match, he felt the weight of his 9mm pistol in his jacket pocket. He began to smile and then he began to laugh out loud.

There was the real conspiracy, the human conspiracy that Pettman and John Cross had set up, but there was also another conspiracy, set up by God or Fate or Justice or Truth. This conspiracy had set all the other elements into motion, just to achieve this one moment of fabulous irony. This place, this dull patch of worn-out urban decay, had attracted Steven to it like a black hole in space. Alphabet City had dragged him here through sheer outrage. Now he was standing under a broken streetlight, ragged and bloody, with a pistol in his pocket and forty dollars' worth of cocaine in a folded envelope. He just couldn't stop himself laughing. He laughed so hard that the guys around the bonfire heard him, turned around to look at him, then angled their heads to bring the strange apparition into their conversation. One of the guys took a flaming stick out of the fire, lit a cigarette with it and then began to hobble in Steven's direction.

'Hey, yo yo,' said a voice. Steven saw that a police car had pulled up by his side. Two cops were getting out of the vehicle. They both had their hands on the holsters of their guns. They were bundled up in chunky dark blue jackets, with the flaps of their hats pulled down over their ears.

'Hey, yo yo,' the cop said again. 'You habla inglés? You speakady English?'

One cop was black, the other looked Hispanic. They approached Steven from opposite directions, their movements following a careful pattern, a stalking manœuvre disguised as a casual approach.

'Yes I speak English.'

'Something funny?' the hispanic cop said. Steven backed away from them and they both clasped their holsters at the same time.

'We saw you laughing, yo yo, something funny?'

'No,' Steven said.

'You got a name, yo yo?'

The guy who had been attending the fire had turned on his heels at the sight of the police car. His companions were collecting their belongings and drifting away into the smoke.

'Steven. Steven Hawthorne.'

'Sure it is. And I'm Peter Pan.'

'You an Anglo?' said the Hispanic cop.

'My grandmother was Bolivian,' Steven said and both cops wiped their mouths and smiled and nodded.

'You're in the wrong part of town, yo yo,' the black cop said. He suddenly stuffed his hand into Steven's inside pocket, fast as a snake. As he did it, the other cop drew his pistol and held it in both hands, pointing directly at Steven's head.

'Just relax, yo yo,' the black cop said, as he felt around in Steven's pocket. He then searched the inside pocket of his overcoat, then he put his hand into the outside pocket and found the bulging envelope.

'Nice coat,' the cop said, squeezing the envelope between his fingers. 'Where d'you get it?'

'In London,' Steven said.

The black cop began to unfold the envelope. The other cop still had his gun aimed directly at Steven's head.

'London, England?'

'Yes.'

'Beautiful coat. Beautiful lining. Got a lot of shit on it though. Is that blood, yo yo?'

The cop now had the envelope open. He wet his finger and put it into the white powder inside. Then he rubbed the powder between his thumb and finger and then spat onto it. He ground the wet powder into his palm. He looked at the other cop and smiled and the cop lowered his gun.

'Like I said, yo yo, you're in the wrong part of town.'

The cop carefully folded the envelope and put it into his jacket pocket. He had just earned himself forty dollars, maybe more if he sold it in the Village.

'You thinking about moving on, yo yo?'

'Yes.'

'That's good. That's real good. You stay round here, we'll meet again soon.'

Steven could feel his heart pounding against the weight of the gun in his inside pocket, the one they hadn't got round to searching. The two cops climbed back into their car and then pulled away.

### 3

Steven had one ten-dollar bill left. He'd spent twenty dollars on booze with Doris, and twenty dollars on a cab the night before. He guessed that it was mid-afternoon and he knew that he would have to call Stephanie soon.

He knew that he should walk or run as fast as he could to the other side of First Avenue but he couldn't get himself to walk in any particular direction. The air had grown cold again and he needed some place warm to make the call. The pay phones in Alphabet City were monuments to optimism, disembowelled and sprayed with exclamations in a hundred languages.

When it began to rain, he found a bar and stepped inside. The bar was a long, narrow room, almost completely dark with only the lights of a jukebox and a fluorescent fly killer winking in the gloom. There were two guys sitting at the bar in baseball caps, identical, twin brothers, and they were talking in rasping Spanish to the barman, who was a fat guy with a bald head. Steven found himself asking for directions to the payphone in Spanish.

'The phone's right over there,' the fat barman replied in Spanish.

Steven asked him to change his ten-dollar bill into quarters.

'Sure, you buy a drink or something and I'll give you change,' the barman said, blinking defiantly. Steven ordered a beer.

One of the two twins turned to Steven and blinked slowly. His face was ruddy and lined and he looked out at Steven from behind decades of booze and worse. He stretched out a hand for Steven to shake then lost his balance and stumbled forward off his stool.

'Whereya from?' he said in English.

'Cuba,' Steven said.

The twin chuckled drunkenly and then sat back down on his stool. Steven's beer arrived and the barman gave him a handful of change. He set off towards the end of the bar to make his call.

'Hey wait a minute,' the other brother said. He seemed more sober and stronger. He twisted round on his stool and grabbed Steven by the arm.

238

'You want to dance with me?'

'What?'

'You want to dance? You buy me a drink and I dance with you. Cheek to cheek.'

His eyes glistened in the half-light. This brother wasn't drunk, but his head was shattered inside by the slow explosion of a thousand chemicals. Steven pushed past him and found the pay-phone. He picked it up and it was dead. He followed the line of the cord and saw that it had been ripped out of the wall. He cursed and put the receiver down. He was going to walk directly out of the bar but the guy on the stool grabbed him again as he walked by.

'You got something for me, Tony?' he hissed.

'My name isn't Tony,' Steven said in Spanish.

'You got some stuff for me?'

Steven shoved his way past and walked out into the street. The light was already beginning to fade. He'd wasted two dollars on a beer he hadn't drunk. He had to get to the other side of First Avenue before it got dark.

He was walking quickly, shivering inside his overcoat. The irony of being here didn't seem so funny any more. He heard a siren somewhere nearby. The sound of it echoed against the high-walled tenements. It sounded like an animal breathing in and out. Steven's breathing matched it. He found himself trotting in the direction of the fading sunlight. It seemed to get dark quickly here, as if the darkness was seeping out of the cracks in the slabs beneath his feet, oozing out of the broken windows in the chocolate-coloured tenements. As he began to half-walk and half-run, the pistol smacked against his chest. Suddenly a figure leapt out in front of him from a darkened doorway. Steven almost fell backwards. The guy was thin and had a mass of twisted, wiry hair spiling out from beneath a woollen hat. He wore faded army fatigues and

239

white tennis shoes. As Steven regained his balance, the guy began to jump up and down in front of him with his hands stuffed deep into his pockets.

'Didn't mean to scare you, sir. You seen the bird?'

Steven stepped back, his hand sneaking slowly into his inside pocket.

'You seen the bird, sir? I spoke to him and sent him up to heaven. Waiting now for him to come back to me with word from God. You seen my bird?'

Steven stepped into the road to get around the guy who was still springing up and down on his toes. But the guy leapt into the road to cut off Steven's escape.

'You seen him, sir?'

Steven shoved him aside and he stumbled. That moment, Steven saw two other guys across the street get to their feet. They had been sitting in a doorway on two beer crates. They were both big guys and they were both wearing long black coats. They stood up and began to approach.

'Hey Rolly!' one of them shouted. 'Hey Rolly, leave the guy alone.'

'Just asking him about my bird.'

'He don't have your goddamned bird. You let him by.'

The two guys were now a few yards from where Steven was standing. Steven produced his 9mm automatic and pointed it at them with his arm outstretched. They both halted and their faces turned to stone.

'Hey, hey, he don't mean no harm,' one of them said. 'Rolly is just crazy in the head. He don't mean no harm.'

Rolly leapt up into the air and shrieked and Steven swung around and pointed the gun at him.

'Mister, he don't mean no harm. You leave him alone.'

The two guys stepped forward and Steven moved so that he was between them and Rolly.

'Rolly, quit jumping or this crazy crack-head'll shoot you. Stay still.'

Rolly suddenly fell to his knees and began to mumble a prayer.

'You see, he's just crazy. You don't have to shoot him for it.'

Steven edged forward and the two guys made way. One of them spat on the ground by his feet.

'Fucking crack-head,' the guy hissed.

'Rolly don't mean you no harm,' the other guy said.

'Put the fucking gun away. There are kids playing around here. Put the fucking gun away.'

Steven lowered the gun and he was breathing hard. Rolly was still on his knees praying and the two guys were glaring into Steven's face.

'Fucking crack-head,' the guy said again. Steven spun on his heels and began to run.

It was dark now. The air smelt of bonfires and the wailing of sirens filled the air. All of the stores and houses seemed to be deserted and there was no traffic on the road. Every fifty yards, Steven ran past patches of waste-ground, and on every patch of wasteground there was a fire burning and he could see thin silhouettes around the flames.

'There is nothing solid in Alphabet City. There is no time to rest. Poverty has a whip and a whistle and it won't allow you to rest. Everything in Alphabet City is firewood and smoke. Lives are short, the music is too loud, there's no place to sit and take stock. Nothing here lasts for more than a minute and a half. A blast of freebase cocaine will make you feel good for exactly ninety seconds, then the endless pursuit begins again . . .'

Another hideous irony. Steven had been right. That was why his deceit had worked. Everything that had spewed out of his imagination was true. It was a work of the devil. There were three guys standing together, sharing a cigarette, shivering on a street corner. They turned as Steven approached and one of the three guys shouted, 'Hey, hey, hey.' Steven ran across the street to get around them and they all howled with laughter. When he turned around he saw that they were standing outside a cab office. They were all drivers looking to pick up fares and they yelled and whistled as Steven ran by.

In East 14th Street there was traffic and Steven stopped running. The stores were all open here, with brightly lit displays of fruit and vegetables. The air was filled with the sound of conversation. Steven stopped to get his bearings and looked up at a street sign.

'Hey, you want some?' said a voice. He turned around and saw a young white guy looking off into the distance with his hands in his pockets.

'I want to get the fuck out of here,' Steven said, as if the thin guy represented the whole neighbourhood.

'This stuff'll get you out of here,' the guy said.

Steven hurried on towards Second Avenue, pushing his way through the crowds of drunks and ladies with babies and early-evening shoppers. He felt that he was tiptoeing on the rim of hell, he could still smell its fires burning in his nostrils. Between Second and Third Avenue, the smell of smoke subsided and his heart stopped beating so fast. He found a bar and he took a deep breath and smoothed his hair before he stepped inside. There were three white guys in suits at the bar. They all turned around as he walked in and two of them stared him down. Steven went to the bar and ordered a glass of water.

One of the three guys was throwing peanuts into his mouth. He threw the last one and then dusted salt off his trousers. He looked Steven up and down and said, 'Lemme, you want us to throw this guy out?'

The barman, who looked old and frail, looked Steven up and down too and then shook his head.

'Nah, he's OK.'

'Looks like a stray to me, Lemme.'

'Nah, he's OK.'

Steven saw that the three guys in suits all had hard, tanned faces and that they were too big for their jackets. This was the frontier and men like these were the guardians who stood between one world and the next. Steven's jet-black hair was matted. His coat was stained with blood and he guessed that he looked like a refugee from the wrong side of the divide. He took off his overcoat because he was sweating and because of the bloodstains. He folded it carefully and as he did so, his jacket fell open.

'I need to use the phone,' Steven said, and the three guys in suits seemed to be surprised at Steven's accent.

'Jees, I thought he was a chicano,' one of them said.

Steven turned on him.

'What was that you said?'

'Hey, nothing friend. Nothing against limeys.'

He smiled and his hard eyes twinkled. There was an Irish tricolour hanging behind the bar and a large, coloured map of the Republic with little red flags stuck into it.

'Phone's by the rest room,' the barman said, pointing vaguely towards the end of the bar.

Stephanie's phone rang six times before the answerphone clicked on. He heard her voice.

'I can't make it to the phone right now. But if you have a message, please speak clearly after the tone.'

'Hello? Hello Stephanie? This is Ste . . .'

She interrupted: 'Steven, are you OK?'

'I'm in a bar called The Jug on East 14th between Second and Third.'

Steven could hear Stephanie making a note.

'The Jug. East 14th.'

'Yes.'

'I know it. It's near to a precinct headquarters. That place is always full of cops.'

'Probably. How long will you be?'

'Half an hour.'

'Make it fast, Stephanie.'

'I will. You be careful in there.'

Steven sat down at the bar. He had a little more than seven dollars left. He ordered a beer. The big guy in the suit turned around on his stool.

'Hey, let me buy that. Sorry I jumped in earlier. No hard feelings. I got the wrong idea.'

Steven smiled weakly at him.

'I'm suspicious by nature. Lemme, get this guy a jug of beer. It's my work makes me suspicious.'

Steven jangled some coins in his pocket. His heart began to race. He remembered what Steph had said. He should have guessed that they were cops. They looked like cops. They drank like cops. Three cops from Alphabet City out on a spree. God or Fate or Truth or Justice chuckled in his throat as a truck rumbled past outside.

'What line of work you in yourself?' the guy in the suit said.

'I'm a writer.'

Steven thought about using the phone again to call Steph and warn her. There was a chance that they might know her or at least recognize her when she walked into the bar but he knew that she would already have left. The air in the bar was hot and clammy.

'You're a writer? What kind of things do you write?'

'Fiction.'

'Would I have heard of any of them?'

'I doubt it.'

The three guys in suits exchanged glances. Steven realized that they had been talking about him while he had been on the phone. All kinds of possibilities presented themselves. There was a chance that they had recognized him but they didn't seem to be the types to read *The New York Times* or frequent bookstores. This was insane. For all they knew he was just a guy taking a drink in a bar but there was the blood on his coat, probably a desperate expression on his face. If they were cops they could probably smell the smoke of Alphabet City on his clothes.

'So how comes if you're a writer you're carrying a pistol?' the big guy in the suit said. He stood up as he said it and the other two guys opened their jackets and put their hands on their hearts.

'Say again?' Steven said.

'Don't fuck with me, friend, I can see the thing through your jacket. What do you say you take it out and let Lemme take care of it.'

Lemme held out his hand.

'I don't object to having you cops in here,' the guy in the suit said, 'but I have a strict rule in my bar that you don't bring firearms in here. You should know that already.'

Steven opened his jacket and the big guy lifted Steven's pistol out of his inside pocket and handed it to the barman. The barman quickly hid it underneath the counter.

'I got good relations with you people but rules are rules. I guess you're new round here.'

'Yes.'

'You undercover in Alphabet City?'

'I can't talk about it.'

'Understood. I got to hand it to you friend, you sure had me fooled. If you make me think you're a chicano pimp you sure as hell would fool anyone else. I'm an expert. You can take that as a compliment.'

The big guy in the suit winked at Steven and Steven

took a long sip of beer. The other two guys relaxed and smiled in admiration.

Stephanie arrived half an hour later. She was wearing a beret and a tightly belted raincoat and she looked like some kind of French resistance fighter. The moment she walked into the bar, Steven scooped up his overcoat and headed for the door. She smiled at him and whispered, 'Are you OK?'

'Sure, I'm on top of the world.'

The guy in the suit called after him.

'Hey, you don't want your you-know-what?'

Lemme put Steven's pistol onto the bar and Steven casually went back and picked it up and put it back into his inside pocket. Stephanie watched with her mouth open. He pushed her towards the door.

'What the hell . . .'

'They think I'm working undercover,' Steven whispered.

'I thought you were through with lying.'

'It wasn't a lie, it was a false assumption. There's a difference. You're not a writer, you wouldn't understand.'

Outside, the rain was falling in sheets. Stephanie's Renault was parked right outside the bar.

## Chapter Twenty-Two

**1**

Steven helped himself to a cigarette from a packet in her glove compartment. He lit two and handed one to Stephanie. The rain was washing away the last of the snow and the windscreen wipers on Stephanie's car were having to work at an absurd pace to keep the glass clear. She drove fast and with aggression.

'Where did you sleep?' Stephanie asked.

'With a soul singer called Doris,' Steven said. Stephanie glanced at him. Horns blared behind them.

'I won't ask,' Stephanie said.

Steven took one of her cassettes out of the pocket of his overcoat. He took it out of its case and slipped it into Stephanie's stereo. Doris's soft, reedy voice filled the car with mellow longing.

'She's good, isn't she?' Steven said.

Stephanie shifted gear with venom.

'When I get out of this mess, I'm going to send her tape to people I know in London.'

'Are you sure you're OK?' Stephanie said.

'No. I am going slowly insane. You want me to switch this thing off?'

'No. I like it. She sounds like Whitney Houston. Did she look like Whitney Houston too?'

Steven lay his head on the head-rest and closed his eyes

with a smile. When he asked Stephanie where they were heading she said that she was taking him to her place.

'I have a couch,' she said quickly. 'You can get some rest.'

'Have you found out anything?'

'Plenty.'

'So?'

'So I can't talk and drive at the same time. Sleep.'

The car hit some traffic and they began to edge forward slowly through the rain. After a few minutes Stephanie wound down her window to pay a toll and they were driving over a bridge. Steven had his eyes closed, because he didn't want to see the slumbering monster of Manhattan disappearing behind them. The rain was falling too heavily to see much anyway. Doris S. Carlick was singing tenderly that she would always love you. Steven turned the music down and Stephanie turned it back up again. A truck rolled by them and the car was hit by a wave of water.

'I slept with her but I didn't fuck her,' Steven said with his eyes closed. 'Do I get a badge?'

## 2

Stephanie's apartment was neat and ordered, just as Steven imagined it would be. Third floor, big rooms, newly built with a thick warm carpet. She drew the curtains before she turned on the light and Steven saw a plump leather sofa, a TV, a tropical fish tank. The walls were decorated with African spears and a brass shield and there was a cabinet filled with trophies and medals. The air smelt of lavender and stale cigarette smoke. There was an open diary and a full ashtray by the phone and it looked out of place in the neat apartment. Stephanie really had been busy. On top of the TV there was a photograph of Stephanie cuddling a big guy with black hair and a droopy moustache and beard. Steven recognized the face from the ID Stephanie had shown him of Juan Ramirez. Now the likeness was more noticeable. Steven studied it as Stephanie went through to make coffee.

'You need a shower?' Stephanie said from the kitchen.

'Later.'

Stephanie appeared with a pot of coffee. When he sipped it, it warmed him like liquor. Steven glanced at the photo and then at Stephanie.

'I see the likeness now.'

'You mean Juan?'

'Is that why you're doing this for me?'

'Go to hell.'

'I've just been.'

Stephanie curled her legs up on the sofa and put a cushion over her belly.

'So what did you find out?' Steven said and Stephanie immediately stood up and fetched a thin folder from on top of the trophy cabinet. She began to flick through her papers, just like Foley used to do.

'OK, smart ass, so I believe you,' she said with a studious expression. 'In the past twenty-four hours I borrowed clearance from two guys who owed me favours to get into the software on the Amarillo case. I also broke a nail forcing a locked drawer. Look.'

She held up a finger for Steven to look at without lifting her head from the paperwork.

'Do you want me to kiss it better?'

She swopped fingers and gave Steven the middle. Steven sat beside her on the sofa and saw a dozen pages, covered in indecipherable notes, initials, words underlined that meant nothing to him. He could feel her body expanding when she breathed.

'Here. take a look.'

She handed him the bottom sheet. It was illegible. Then he saw the words 'Page 117 Society'.

'What the hell does that mean?'

'It means you were right about someone trying to make the book come true.' She looked up at him. 'What I found out scared the shit out of me.'

She left him to read some more of the scrawl.

'It also means the book came first, the body came after. There has been talk ever since John Cross got back from Colombia that he'd gone a little crazy. He got bitten and they call it "kissing bug disease". You get it from a little red jungle spider. He used to be a fat guy. You saw how he is now. Most people in his department except Pettman are getting uneasy. That's how I got two of them to help me. I guess you'd say the DEA in New York is in a kind of transition period.'

She handed him some more pieces of paper to look at.

'Stephanie, I can't even read your fucking hand-writing.'

'OK. I found out that there's a thing called the "Page 117 Society". Pettman, John Cross and two others who I can't get names for. No one below field agent. They call each other after jungle fruit or some crazy DEA thing. The way I figure it, John Cross read page 117 and it struck a chord.'

Steven sifted through some more of Stephanie's papers. They were sitting close now, closer than strangers would be.

'What kind of chord?'

'The burning of the body with kerosene. That's an Amarillo trademark. I guess on page 117 you just accidentally gave a perfect description of an Amarillo hit. Then there was the scar. Wrong side of the face, but Jesus, spooky enough. That's why for a long time I thought you were lying.'

Steven remembered the afternoon when he had written the murder scene on page 117. He'd seen a documentary about the Colombian drug cartels on TV. Maybe the method of disposal of bodies had been described and had stuck somewhere in his head. A lot of his research had come from TV, he'd just sort of recreated the TV world and fed it back to people. He'd added the scar as a literary device, just to make his character Emilio ugly.

'So John Cross decided to check it out. The way I hear it he had two guys searching every basement in Avenue D to find the body and they drew a blank. Two days later Raul De Soto was shot somewhere in Spanish Harlem. I guess the temptation was just too great. Him and Pettman have been after Amarillo for six years. They say Cross only has twelve months to live. He ordered the banana and the orange and the mango fruit to lift the body and put it in the basement. After that, they just had to go through the book page by page and make it real.'

Now that the conspiracy was being unfolded before him in Stephanie's hieroglyphics, it didn't seem so scary. This was just one insane guy against another, John Cross against Steven Hawthorne. Worse than that, John Cross had been lying for a good cause. Steven remembered the picture of the woman in a South American river basin with her teeth pulled out, the story of the kid who bit off his own fingers. Amarillo really was an evil son of a bitch and anything Steven did now would serve to save his skin, keep him on the streets until John Cross could find another ladder to climb down to bring him up from hell. Maybe it was already too late for that, maybe this was John Cross's last throw and he knew it. When Steven looked up, Stephanie's face was close to his. He felt the heat coming off her, so much more enticing because first it had to pass through her cold exterior.

'So can we do something with this?' Steven said, looking at the folder.

'Not a thing,' Stephanie said with a laugh. 'To get this stuff I had to break the law. I'm just an FBI soldier. The FBI and the DEA don't exactly see eye to eye. To nail John Cross I need cast-iron proof to show my superiors. Watertight. You said your wife has a dossier.'

Stephanie handed Steven another handwritten sheet with Fiona's name at the top underlined.

'I checked the DEA's ports and borders register. There is an order to hold her if she tries to leave the country. She's in the US somewhere but no one knows where. Cross can't move on Amarillo until he finds her and destroys the dossier.'

There was a pause while Steven looked up from the sheet.

'And destroys her too?' Steven said. He cursed himself. He had planned to talk about Fiona like she was the meanest bitch on God's earth, which she was, but he wanted to pretend that he still believed he hated her. What he didn't want was for Stephanie to realize that there were two reasons why he wanted to get to Fiona first, two reasons why he wanted her alive. But his ability to lie had started to fail him, just when he needed it most. Stephanie didn't miss a thing. She tidied up her papers.

'Who knows what he'll do to her,' she said breezily and she stood up to get a cigarette. She lit it by the window, striking her match like a man, dragging on her cigarette like a big tough cop.

'I guess the least Cross would want would be a deportation order until the Amarillo trial is over. Jesus, Steven, she must really hate you.'

She turned to him and laughed, as if this were just some weird little detail in this whole thing.

'I mean to put a fucking dossier together to screw up your life. That bitch must be as hot as hell.'

She was trembling a little now. Stephanie had put her career on the line for this, for Steven. Juan Ramirez was still smiling handsomely from on top of the TV.

'Yes, I guess she must hate me,' Steven said softly.

'What did you *do* to her?'

'Lots of things. Other women.'

Stephanie shrieked with mock laughter and flicked her cigarette ash onto the carpet. She looked like the Stephanie Plater who had interrogated him in the Guggenheim.

'A woman scorned,' she said, as if it were a big joke. 'Didn't you know that Steven? Hell hath no fury like a woman scorned.'

Steven looked at her and said, 'I know that Stephanie.'

There was silence for a few moments.

'So do you have any idea where she might be?'

'Yes.'

She glanced at him.

'Have you talked to her?'

'No.'

'So come on. Where?'

'Juan Ramirez had a wife too, didn't he?' Steven said and she laughed as if she didn't understand.

'What has Juan got to do with it?'

'You seem to hate Fiona already.'

'What the hell is that supposed to mean?'

Steven said nothing and Stephanie drew her own conclusions.

'Jesus, who do you think you are, Steven? Who do you think I am? Let me tell you something about Juan that . . .'

Steven broke in: 'I have no idea who you are. That's why I can't tell you where I think Fiona might be.'

Stephanie wasn't used to being interrupted and she

flickered with anger. The photo of Juan Ramirez was a third presence in the room. Six months was no time at all for love to evaporate. She'd been hauling it around all this time and now she was loading it onto Steven. At least, that was what Steven imagined. She had already done more for him than any sane person would have. She pretended to be just interested.

'You know but you can't tell me? Is that what you're really telling me?'

'Not until I'm sure. Stephanie, listen to me . . .' Steven stood up.

'How dare you talk about Juan like that . . .'

Steven grabbed her arms.

'I can't tell you, because I don't trust you.'

She stared into his face.

'I can't trust you,' Steven said. 'I still don't know for sure where Cross and Pettman end and where you begin.'

She struggled out of Steven's arms.

'I tell you what we do, Steven, we put all the stuff I've gathered into the ashtray and we burn it. Then you pick up your coat and you get the fuck out of my life . . . Aaaagh! Jesus fucking Christ!'

She seemed to be trying hard to stay calm. When she became angry she looked as if she were wrestling with a mighty beast, a wild insanity which scared her.

'Tell me about Ramirez.'

'Screw you.'

'Tell me why you're helping me. Tell me why you're risking your career. Because I look like him? Do you believe in ghosts that much, like the lady who owned the house in Bronxville?'

'Yeah, yeah, yeah,' Stephanie was saying, 'go ahead, you know me inside out, go ahead, tell me all about Ramirez and me. You're the expert, Steven, you tell me.'

'I'm not him.'

'Is that it?'

'I have to be sure.'

'She was shaking her head and Steven knew that there was only one way of being sure. He took her in his arms again and she turned the side of her face to his, frozen in his arms.

'OK, so what do I have to do to prove to you that you can trust me?' she said at last.

'Fuck me,' Steven said. She turned back to him. 'Fuck me and I'll know. If you're working for them, if you're using me to get to Fiona, I'll know. I'm no expert, Stephanie, I'm the opposite, but I'll know. The only other reason you would do this for me would be because you want to fuck me, or want to fuck the guy in the photograph, and either way I'll be able to tell. Fuck isn't the word but it will do for now. So fuck me. Take off your clothes.'

### 3

The bedroom was as neat as the lounge, with another tank of tropical fish on the window ledge. The beautiful blue and gold fish swam in their little pool of yellow light, sucking on bubbles. Stephanie took a deep breath and her breath shuddered in her chest, like someone who had been crying. Steven took off his clothes and lay in the bed. He was thin and worn and his wound was still livid with dried blood. He watched as Stephanie unbuttoned her blouse in the light from the fish tank, then she took off her jeans. She sat down in front of her dressing-table mirror, even though there wasn't enough light to see, and she brushed her hair in the darkness. She used the brush like a weapon against herself. When she had brushed her hair she stood up and took off her underwear.

'Are you happy now I feel like a hooker?' she said softly.

255

Her voice had never sounded like that. She lifted the sheets and climbed into bed. She lay on her back.

Steven stroked her hair from her face and kissed her and then began to manipulate her motionless body as if she were a machine that had to be turned on in a certain way, following a certain procedure. He followed the procedure he'd followed so many times before, like adjusting switches and setting gauges and at first the damn machine of her body was just too cold and too rusty and Steven cursed himself. If there was a real hell then he would go to hell for this, but first he had to be sure, because his life depended on it and Fiona's life depended on it too.

Suddenly Stephanie punched his chest and turned her head away and Steven kissed her neck and she scratched his neck as he did it.

'What do I have to do?' she said with a laugh that was filled with fear. 'What do I do to prove it huh? You want this? Or this? This what hookers do?'

She hit him across the face with her fist and he grabbed her arm and pushed it back onto the pillow.

'Do you want me Stephanie?'

'You son of a bitch.'

'Do you want me?'

He tried the procedure again, looking up at the fish drifting in their tank of bubbles. This was the procedure he'd used with Fiona and with everyone else. He kissed her neck and then her breasts and then he took her face in between his hands and she kissed him back for the first time. Her cheeks were wet in the darkness and her tears tasted like the salt water in an oyster.

'You want this?' she hissed and she kissed him back again.

He kissed her body and it looked like gold in the yellow light from the fish tank.

'If you're working undercover for them, Stephanie, I want you to earn your money.'

She hit him hard on the top of the head and he kissed her again and she was as hard as twisted iron. He heaved himself on top of her and took her arms in his hands. She expanded beneath his weight and then he felt her opening her legs. He kissed her neck again and she grabbed his hair and pulled his face away. He lowered his weight onto her body and she began to breathe heavily, as if she were trapped under rubble.

'I can't do this,' she said, with crying in her voice.

'You close your eyes and I'll be someone else. It's easy. Do you want me to be someone else?'

'Get off me Steven.'

'You don't want me Stephanie? Not even in the dark?'

He thought that she was about to struggle from beneath him but she lay back on the pillow and said, 'No,' barely audible.

'Did you say no?'

'I want you. I don't want you to be someone else.'

'Is this what you want?'

'Yes. I want you but not like this.'

'You don't want me like this?'

'I can't do it like this. Not if it's for a reason.'

Stephanie was crying now. She put her fist to her mouth and her whole body began to convulse with tears. Steven looked down on her and then lay back on the bed.

'That's all I wanted to hear,' he said to the ceiling. 'Not like this.'

She was still crying silently.

'You pass the test with flying colours,' he said and he put his arm over his face. 'A good undercover cop would have fucked my brains out and got a medal for it, too.'

They lay side by side for a long time, while Stephanie's tears began to dry. Finally Steven said, 'I'll go and sleep on the couch.' She grabbed him around the waist and pulled him back into the bed. She pushed him down onto the mattress. She was laughing and crying at the same time.

'Do you think that was clever? Huh? Do you?'

He couldn't tell if the look of crazy anger in her eyes was real or play.

'You want me to show you what they teach us in basic training?'

She grabbed a handful of his hair and pushed his head to one side and hissed in his ear. She sounded mad for real.

'I have a gun, Steven. Do you want me to blow your balls off? Do you want me to feed them to the fish? Sure, my little fishes eat balls and they're pretty hungry. It's been six months Steven.'

He felt afraid for a few seconds and then the machine grew soft in his arms. When Stephanie acted crazy it was too real. Especially naked and in the dark. He decided quickly that Stephanie was slightly insane with grief or maybe something more but that that was just his good fortune. If she wasn't insane, she wouldn't be helping him.

'First you people shoot me through the shoulder, now you threaten my balls,' Steven said.

'That was the DEA, I'm FBI, remember? You believe me now?'

Stephanie smiled and kissed the wound on Steven's shoulder. She could fall all the way from rage to feeble devotion in half a second. Steven had learnt that sometimes it was the nakedness and the darkness that made people insane. The straightest people in the light were wild creatures in the dark.

'Do you forgive me?' Steven said.

'Forgive my baby for what?'

'For my little examination.'

'Kiss Mama.'

He kissed her on the lips and this time the kiss was gentle and warm. Outside of the procedure he'd learnt so well, Steven was pretty clumsy and Stephanie yelped when he pinched her skin. She leant away from him and switched on the bedside lamp and they said hello to each other in the light.

'You want me to grow a beard and moustache?' Steven said and Stephanie said, 'Nope. You want me to dye my hair and become a fucking professor?'

'Nope,' Steven said, even though he didn't mean it. Then, in the brighter light of the bedside lamp, Steven's second test began and Stephanie passed that with flying colours too, even though she didn't know that she was still on trial.

They made love for a long time and sometimes, even in the light of the bedside lamp, Stephanie looked at Steven from the corner of her eyes in a way that made him glimpse the darkness inside her head.

## Chapter Twenty-Three

**1**

When Steven woke up, Stephanie had gone. He hadn't slept so soundly for weeks or even months, not since *Alphabet City* had first been published. There was a note on the pillow beside him.

'Steven. I had to report in. I'll go sick and be back by noon. Do you trust me now?

Love Steph.'

Steven grinned at the note. In the daylight the apartment looked bigger. He went into the lounge in Stephanie's dressing gown and opened the curtains. He guessed that he was somewhere in Queens. The last of the snow was melting and the streets were sparkling with winter sun. He opened a window to let out some of the smoke from the night before.

He searched through Stephanie's cupboards and found that there was no food apart from an ancient-looking tin of Vongole sauce. He made himself some coffee and then put the sauce on the stove. He was hungry for the first time in a long time. His wound had begun to itch and Daddy always said that that meant it was beginning to heal. Daddy could go to hell. He ate the sauce with a spoon from the saucepan.

At ten, he called Anderson and finally he was at home. He sounded sleepy.

'Who is this?'

'It's Steven Hawthorne, old friend. How the hell is life in the scandal and exposé business?'

Steven was stretched back on the sofa, his legs sticking out inelegantly from Stephanie's stripey dressing gown. Anderson sounded shocked.

'Steven? Where the hell are you?'

'I'm safe. Nice to know you care, Anderson.'

Steven could hear Anderson shifting around. His voice sounded just woken. Steven needed to get to the point but he didn't want to force it. He didn't want Anderson to get any inkling of what was at stake. No one knows you like an old enemy.

'Anderson, I need to speak to Fiona. Could you put her on the line?'

He said it breezily, as if he was already sure she was there. He held his breath but somehow he knew that now he was on the downslope of something, that the climbing was behind him. Anderson stammered. Steven could imagine him putting on his glasses.

'Put her on, Anderson. She's lying right beside you.'

More silence while the phone was covered up. Steven had guessed that if Fiona had gone to Anderson, she would have done anything at all to get him to print her dossier. Screwing him would have been a detail and Steven just couldn't bring himself to be jealous any more. Anderson would naturally have welcomed her with open arms. He'd know that this story would put *True Society* on the map and he wouldn't be able to resist, in spite of everything he'd said about liking people who told lies more than people who believed them. And neither Anderson nor Fiona could possibly know that the dossier they were working on might be fatal to them both. As far as they were concerned, Steven was still in protective custody, getting fat on the royalties of a book that was selling by the truckload. Anderson would have seen this venture not only as a way of boosting his circulation, but also as a way of taking a swipe at the police. If the rebellious prince had needed any persuasion to betray his old friend, then Fiona would have provided it. Finally, Anderson came back on the line. He sounded as if all the blood had drained out of his body.

'She says she doesn't want to talk to you,' Anderson said. Steven felt a thud of relief which he had to hide with a chuckle down the line.

'Then give her my love.'

'Steven, what is this?'

'Tell her that she wins. Tell her that the queen has the king in checkmate.'

'Steven, are you OK?'

'Anderson, I know when I'm beat. I know that you're going to print the dossier so I've decided to tell the police everything myself before this reaches the papers. You still get the scoop but I have to show the police the dossier or I'll be on a charge myself when they find out. It's over Anderson. Fiona wins. My career as a writer is over as of right now.'

Anderson covered the phone and Steven could half-hear him whispering. He couldn't make out Fiona's voice. A gnawing pain started up somewhere deep inside. Jealousy wasn't that easy to defeat after all. Steven yelled down the phone, as if he were carefree, 'Hey, Anderson! Anderson!'

He came back on the line.

'We'll be with you around two, OK? I'll be with someone from the FBI. Tell Fiona that my humiliation will be complete.'

'But I still get to break the story?' Anderson said quickly.

'You have my word. You break the story. On condition

that you meet us at two. You'd better give me your address.'

Anderson gave Steven an address in Montauk, Long Island. It was the address that the whole of the DEA and half the FBI had been searching for for seven days. Steven wrote it down on a page in Stephanie's diary.


# 2


Half an hour later there was a knock at the door. Steven took his 9mm automatic out of his overcoat and stood in the hall.

'Who is it?'

'Saul and Cotes. Drug Enforcement Agency. We need to speak to Stephanie Plater.'

'She's not here.'

'Open the door.'

Steven could feel fear rising inside him, like a memory from the days before. He had thought he had felt this for the last time.

'I told you she's not here.'

'Open the fucking door,' said a second voice.

Steven had his gun raised to the ceiling.

'I'll get her to call you when she gets back,' Steven said and he heard one of the guys say, 'Who the fuck is this guy anyway?' He heard them checking some papers, then the first guy said lazily, 'Open the door or we kick it down.'

Steven put the pistol into the pocket of Stephanie's dressing gown, which was deep enough to take it. Then he opened the door a little way and the two guys pushed their way in. They were in the hall and past him before he could move. One was fat with a white shirt that split between buttons. The other was younger and meaner.

'Who the fuck are you?' the fat guy said.

'I'm a friend.'

'Frienda who?' said the young, mean one. Steven had to stay out of these guys' eyeline, had to work this thing through quickly.

'A friend of Stephanie's.'

'Boyfriend?'

'Kind of.'

The young guy suddenly pinned Steven to the wall. He had to turn his body so that the young guy wouldn't feel the weight of the gun in his pocket. If Steven had been just a boyfriend, he would get angry, so he had to pretend to get angry.

'Hey what the hell is this!' he shouted and pushed his way out of the young guy's grip. They were both surveying the room. 'Show me some fucking ID.'

The two DEA detectives ignored him.

'You a kind of boyfriend? What kind of boyfriend?'

'A new kind of boyfriend.'

'Steph's fucking you? Jesus. Nice dressing gown. What's your name, boyfriend?'

'Thomas. Thomas Bolivar.'

'Fucking spik. Steph fucking you?'

'I want to see some ID.'

The fat cop had begun to wander around the room. He walked near to the telephone. Stephanie's diary was still open, with the address in Montauk on the open page. He was jangling change in his pocket.

'Has she got a thing for spiks? First Ramirez now you.'

The fat cop was devouring the whole room, taking in every detail. Soon he would see the open diary. He wandered closer to the phone.

'We have bigger penises,' Steven said. 'You want to see?'

It was a gamble. Steven couldn't let the fat guy get any

nearer to the address book, so he had to get his attention somehow. The fat guy laughed without humour. Then he hit Steven in the belly and Steven doubled up. He had to grab the gun in his pocket to stop it droping out as he fell. He glared at the fat guy. He had a thin, pencil moustache.

'You want me to cut your penis off?'

Steven didn't answer. The young guy spotted something.

'Hey, hey, what's this?' He took hold of Steven's dressing gown and pulled it open. 'You been shot, Mr boyfriend?'

Steven's dressing gown had fallen open and his wound was visible. The young guy touched the wound.

'That look like a bullet to you?' the young guy said. The fat guy studied the scar on Steven's shoulder. 'Where d'you catch a bullet, boyfriend?'

Steven gasped with the pain in his stomach. This lie had to come straight out of the chamber, like pulling a trigger. 'I'm US Air Force,' he said. 'Serial number 44 stroke 33. I got it in weapons drill training. I'm on rest and recoup.'

Steven held his belly, not wanting to look up.

'Where you based?' the fat guy said, just curious.

'Fort Calhoun. Some fucking Portuguese trainee put a 9mm bullet into me.'

There was silence. Steven straightened up.

'What rank are you?' Steven said to the fat guy. He sneered. 'I asked you a question.'

'Fuck you.'

'If you are anything below lieutenant you're on a charge for assaulting an officer. DEA are covered by Section Fifteen.'

The fat guy laughed but he wasn't sure any more. Steven had no idea what Section Fifteen was, or if there was any such thing, but they didn't know either and it sounded right. People will believe if it sounds right and you sound sure enough. He pushed himself away from the wall.

'You ever strike a major in the US Air Force before, fat man?'

The young guy was about to say something, but Steven pulled his gun from his pocket.

'Major Thomas Bolivar. You want to salute my service pistol, fat man?'

They both backed away. It was as if they were looking into a strong wind. Steven's ability to fabricate was suddenly a glorious and beautiful thing. It swept him towards them.

'You want to suck my barrel, fat man?'

He herded them towards the door.

'Hey look . . .'

'Fuck you!' Steven yelled. 'You don't come in here and criticize my dressing gown, OK, fat man? I get very sensitive about my clothes. You want to tell me your name?'

'We just want to leave a message for Stephanie Plater.'

'Go ahead.'

'We need to talk to her.'

'About what?'

'We need to talk to her right away. Tell her that John Cross and Tom Pettman need to see her. Right away.'

Steven's cover was almost blown at the mention of their names. Somehow, they had found out something and were on Stephanie's trail. Steven lifted his leg and kicked the fat guy towards the door.

'I see your face again, I'll put you on a charge,' Steven said. 'Section Fifteen. Now get the fuck out of here.'

At that moment, Steven heard a key turning in the door and his stomach turned over. All three of them turned to see Stephanie walking in. Her mouth fell open when she saw Steven holding his gun to the fat guy's head.

'It's OK, Stephanie,' Steven yelled, 'you don't have to speak to either of them. I outrank both of them . . .'

Stephanie recognized the two DEA guys and they recognized her.

'What the hell are you doing here?' she said to them. She had a bag of groceries in her arms.

'We came to pick you up, Steph,' the fat guy said. 'John wants to talk with you like right now. We came in here and this crazy Air Force guy . . .'

'Air Force?' Stephanie said. Steven knew that if he swopped looks with her now the whole thing would fall to pieces. He kept on staring at the fat guy.

'I don't know who these people are, Steph, but if they're DEA then I outrank both of them. I'm a major. I take jurisdiction. Now both of you, get out of here.'

The door was still open and Steven pointed at it with his gun. The fat guy turned to Stephanie.

'We'll be downstairs. We'll wait for you. Cross is real anxious that . . .'

Steven suddenly yelled and pushed both of them through the door and slammed it. He took a deep breath and Stephanie and Steven held each other for a few seconds.

'What happened?' Stephanie whispered. Steven had already set off for the bedroom. He hopped into his trousers and buttoned his shirt.

'We've got to go right now. Pretty soon they'll put two and two together. They saw the bullet wound.'

Steven tucked his pistol into his jacket pocket and then went into the lounge to collect the address from the diary.

'Steven, wait, if John Cross is asking for me . . .'

'. . . It means he knows something. We've got to get to Fiona before he does.'

Steven headed for the door, opened it and looked away down the corridor. Stephanie followed him out.

'They'll be waiting downstairs,' she said. 'They'll follow us.'

'No they won't,' Steven said.


### 3


They got into Stephanie's Renault and pulled up onto the ramp that led up from the underground carpark beneath the apartments. The two DEA guys were waiting in an unmarked car just where the shadow of the carpark met the bright sunlight outside.

'Pull up beside them,' Steven said.

Stephanie pulled up and Steven produced his gun.

'Jesus Christ,' Stephanie yelled, 'you can't just shoot them!'

Steven lowered his window, engaged his pistol and fired two shots into each of the nearside tyres. They exploded like cannons. The two DEA guys had already ducked down into their seats.

'OK, move!' Steven said.


### 4


They drove down the Long Island Expressway, the same route Steven had taken when he had driven through the snow to his grandmother's place. Now the road was clear and the sun was shining bright. Stephanie drove fast, anxious and silent behind her sunglasses. She peeked at the address on Steven's lap.

'Is that near the Montauk Air Force Station?' Stephanie said.

'It's up on Montauk Point,' Steven said. 'I know the area.'

'How long a drive?'

Steven thought about it.

'Two hours if you drive. Hour and a half if I drive. Why?'

Stephanie laughed and said nothing.

'What is it?'

'Nothing. It's OK. I'll hold out.'

'Hold out for what?'

'I need to go to the bathroom for Christ's sake, OK? But it's OK, I'll hold out.'

'Pull over.'

'Don't be crazy, we don't have time.'

'We have time. They still have no idea where Fiona is.'

They drove on some more in silence. There was no turn-off for the next five miles. Finally, Stephanie sighed and said, 'OK, I lied.'

'About what?'

'About needing to go to the bathroom. I mean, I do, but that's not why I want to pull over.'

She laughed into her hand and the car veered across the highway.

'What's funny?' Steven said, wondering if he should grab the wheel.

'The real reason I want to pull over is because I didn't have time to check my face.'

'Your face?'

'My warpaint. I don't want to meet her looking like this.'

She glanced into the rear-view mirror.

'Isn't that insane?' she said flatly.

'You mean you want to pull over so that you can put on some make-up.'

'Yes. Forget it. Forget I spoke.'

Steven spent a few minutes trying to somehow make sense of it and then gave up. When they reached the next turn-off, Stephanie whimpered and Steven said, 'Just do it.'

Stephanie spent ten minutes inside a diner somewhere in the suburbs of the Hamptons, while Steven sat in the car and listened to Doris S. Carlick singing the blues.


## 5


An hour and a half later they were approaching Montauk Point, the eastern tip of Long Island. Steven knew that they were close because the jet fighters that use the Point as a launch pad for sorties over the Atlantic were dipping low over the highway, their throaty, shocking roar filling Steven with something approaching pride. The highway took them through the Montauk Downs State Park and the huge banks of trees on either side looked black and skeletal. Steven had driven down here in summer and the whole world seemed to be alive with leaves and wind. The sky now looked as if it were made of sea water. Soon the road would run out and there would be just ocean.

Anderson had a house on the cliffs, a development of white, stone, angular houses that looked newly built. There were four or five apartments, all with huge rectangular windows looking out over the ocean, clinging to the cliffs like gulls' nests. Steven followed the Highway 27 until it disappeared and then took a smaller road that led up to the back of the apartments. The new houses looked untouched by wind or rain, as if they had just been dropped from the sky and embedded into the cliffs. Once upon a time, Anderson had said he would never live anywhere where you couldn't put your head out of the window and hear a saxophone play. He had always been full of shit like that. His driveway even had a sign saying 'Private Property, Keep Out'.

They pulled up outside the door and Stephanie straightened her hair in the rear-view mirror. Steven looked at her.

'What are you doing?'

'Nothing.'

'Why are you straightening your hair?'

'The window was open, it got blown around.'

Steven laughed and checked his face in the rear-view mirror too. Somehow, without ever doing anything in particular, Fiona had always had a way of turning a meeting with her into an audience. Even people who had never met her sensed something from the way that people spoke about her. Now even Stpehanie had been drawn into the enchanted arena. Fiona had a way of inspiring violent emotion and often Steven had blamed her memory for getting him into this situation in the first place. *Alphabet City* had been an offering. Now she was going to help him to escape from it.

Stephanie was giving Steven a hard stare.

'Screw yourself,' she said.

'What's the matter with you?'

'You want to look nice for her? After what she did to you?'

They both got out of the car. Steven knocked on the door and a dog barked.

'We get the dossier and we leave, OK?' Stephanie said.

'Whatever you say. You look beautiful. Fiona will be as jealous as hell.'

'If she's good looking, I'll blow her brains out.'

Steven could hear Anderson approaching the door. The three of them, Steven, Anderson and Fiona, hadn't been together since the day Steven had dropped out of college.

## 6

The door was opened a few inches and Anderson's head appeared. He looked like a suburban father opening the door to an unwanted salesman. He seemed even older here, at home, without his shoes. He was leaning down to switch off a security device.

'This is Stephanie Plater,' Steven said. 'She's the FBI agent I told you about.'

Stephanie flashed her ID. Anderson said nothing and opened the door.

Inside there was only one open space, split in the middle by a huge fireplace with a brass surround. There was a log smouldering in the grate and the wind from the ocean moaned down the chimney stack. At the far end of the room there was an enormous sliding window with a balcony which looked out over the ocean, two hundred feet below. They called this new development Whale Point, because in the summer, you could see the whales feeding in the warm water before they swam back to the Caribbean.

Anderson was wearing a knitted sweater and corduroy trousers. He mumbled something about coffee and neither Steven nor Stephanie said anything. Stephanie scanned the room, a professional habit which she couldn't break. It might have seemed that Anderson was alone in the house, if it hadn't been for the huge, silent presence in the air. The expectation. Steven and Stephanie were waiting for Fiona Van Draken to appear like penitents waiting for a vision of the Virgin. There were seagulls wheeling so close to the window that Steven could see the yellow of their eyes.

'Where is she?' Steven said, standing in front of the fire.

Anderson gestured at the staircase, which led up from the main room into the stripped-pine gloom above. The whole house smelt of newness. Stephanie unbelted her raincoat.

'Shall we get it over with?' she said and there was a creak of a freshly fitted floorboard from upstairs. They all turned to look at the stairs. Fiona Van Draken came down, barefoot. Feet, legs, a swathe of silk, then long black hair and a smile.

She looked as if she were made from stripped pine too. Steven noticed her dyed hair first, then he saw that her body was slimmer than he remembered, and her eyes were clear blue. She was wearing a Japanese dressing gown with a peacock woven into the silk. He took in every detail. Under her arm she was carrying a folder.

'Hello Steven,' she said.

'Hello. Your hair's different.'

She came and stood in front of the fire. Her composure would have been convincing if it hadn't been for the way her hand trembled slightly when she leant against the brass fireplace.

'You have something for us,' Steven said.

Fiona placed the dossier down on the coffee table that was between her and Stephanie. It was a brown cardboard folder, bound with yellow string. It looked battered and worn, but nothing remarkable.

'Is that the only copy?' Stephanie said.

Fiona nodded.

Anderson stepped nearer to the fire. 'There are some things that Fiona wants to get cleared up,' he said and his hand shook over his hip. Steven felt a sudden unease. 'Some things that she wants to get straight before we move any further.' He talked as if he were Fiona's agent and he turned to Fiona for approval. In the presence of a real life FBI agent, Anderson wasn't sure how far he could push things. His assaults on authority had always

273

been made from the comfort of his swivel chair. His hand still shook, and when Stephanie looked at him he tried to give her his hardest smile.

'Who the hell is this guy?'

'He is the friend of the friendless and champion of lost causes,' Steven said. 'His name is Anderson.'

'How much does he know?' Stephanie said.

Fiona said, 'He knows everything. He and I are working together on this.'

Fiona finally looked at Steven and he knew that he had been right. She had dragged herself half-way around the world, stepped into Anderson's bed, worked for months alone, just because love and hate were the same thing. What Steven wanted to do now was to say out loud to her that he loved her, because it was so outrageous, because it was the last thing that anyone would expect and that was the kind of thing that Fiona had always admired. Suddenly the whole of the last six months was a private joke between the two of them, played on the rest of the world. Anderson, as always, was the cringing spectator, looking after the details. Steven felt that he had regained his throne.

'Do you mind if I take a look?' Stephanie said.

'Not at all,' Fiona said, still looking at Steven. Her black hair was suddenly a puzzle. Was it some kind of disguise? If it was, then maybe she knew that half of New York was looking for her.

Stephanie leafed through the pages and Steven looked at it over her shoulder. The pages were all blank. They both looked up at Fiona.

'As Mr Anderson told you,' Fiona said, 'there are some things we need to get cleared up before I can give you what you came for. I had that ready to burn in case you came in here with the cavalry. Why don't you both sit down.'

Stephanie turned to Steven and said, 'Is this bitch . . .'

and Steven shushed her. Stephanie's eyes glinted with anger, but when Steven sat down, she sat down beside him. Fiona stood over them.

'I'm sorry I didn't catch your name,' Fiona said and Stephanie just stared at her.

'Her name is Stephanie,' Steven said. 'She's an FBI agent and she's in a hurry. I am too.'

'That's what bothers me,' Fiona said and Anderson said, 'Fiona, just go easy with this.'

'What bothers me, Steven, is that Anderson said you phoned this morning to surrender.'

Anderson whispered in her ear. 'I didn't say that word Fiona, I said . . .'

'That's dead right,' Steven said. 'My exact words were, I know when I'm beat. That's why we're here. I want to show Stephanie the proof that *Alphabet City* is a lie. Then we can all go home.'

'This is my home,' Fiona said, and the wind moaned down the chimney stack. Fiona would use any weapon to hand, even Anderson, if it made Steven's guts turn over.

'I'm very pleased for you both,' Steven said, smiling at Anderson, who was wilting at Fiona's side. It looked like this was news to him too.

'So let me tell you why your unconditional surrender makes me uneasy,' Fiona said. 'You see, I know you, Steven, and I know that you wouldn't give in this easily. You may be many awful things but you've always been a trier . . .'

Anderson said, 'Fiona, can we talk for a moment?' from the edge of the scene but Fiona didn't listen.

'The way I see it,' she said, 'I mean, feel free to correct me if I've worked this out wrong, but the way I see it, the only reason you would want me to hand over the dossier is because you have decided that you really have gone too far this time and you need a fast and easy exit. You want me to save you, probably from something worse than professional suicide. Am I right about that, Stephanie? You don't talk much, do you? Has my husband got himself into more trouble than he can handle?'

Stephanie turned deliberately to Steven and said loudly, 'OK, I'll take this for ten more seconds.'

'I'll deal with it,' Steven hissed and Fiona opened her mouth wide for a silent 'Ah.'

'Oh, I see, I see,' she said, tapping the brass hood of the fireplace with her knuckle. 'God, I'm getting so slow, he's fucking you, isn't he? Anderson, do you see that? Steven is screwing the lady from the FBI. You must get extra points for that, don't you Steven?'

Fiona turned and picked up the poker beside the fire and rolled the log over in the grate to expose its glowing underbelly. She knew that all eyes were on her.

'It's OK, Stephanie, you don't have to tell me,' she said, standing up again, pulling her dressing gown tight around her body. 'I can read my husband like a book, no pun intended. Is that a pun? No, it's just a joke in very poor taste, but you see, Stephanie, when my husband is screwing someone, he has a certain look in his eyes when he speaks to them. He looks like a small terrier that hasn't been fed recently. I'm sorry, Steven, you were saying you would deal with it.'

Silence. Fiona had been trying so hard not to let her anger spoil her performance but she looked as if she were about to lose control. Anderson took her arm and tried to whisper to her but she peeled his hand off without looking at him.

'So go on, Steven,' she said, 'deal with it. Perhaps your friend would like to come to your aid at this point.'

Stephanie shook her head in disbelief and Steven hoped that she wasn't counting under her breath.

'Well, someone say something,' Fiona said, as if this

were a funny, awkward pause at the dinner table. 'I'm fascinated to hear what sort of trap my husband has put his foot into. I mean I read the papers but we all know that you can't believe anything you read, so perhaps one of the two of you would care to tell me exactly why it is that you suddenly have a desperate urge to tell the world the truth.'

Stephanie said the word 'ten' out loud. Then she reached into the inside pocket of Steven's jacket and pulled out his 9mm automatic pistol. Before Steven had had the chance to ask what she was doing, she engaged it and said, 'I'm bored with this.'

Then she closed one eye like a child in a fairground shooting gallery and shot Anderson through the head. Steven thought that she was going to point the gun and say 'bang, bang' with her mouth as some kind of joke, but she pulled the trigger for real and Anderson fell forward. The bark of the gun echoed for a long time and Anderson fell dead, as if his body had never known life. She then pointed the gun at Fiona and said calmly, 'Fiona, I really don't have a lot of time.'

Anderson had fallen forward onto his knees and his body had adopted the position of a supplicant bowing down to his master or to a god. There was blood soaking into the carpet but apart from the blood his head was intact. His presence, the presence of death still in the shape of life, was like a silent scream that filled the room. A huge gull hovered near the window and screeched at the echo of the gunshot. Fiona had her hands to her mouth. Steven had stood up as if he'd been lifted on wires.

*'When you see your first dead body, it scares you to death because you realize that you don't give a fuck. Your first response is primeval, instinctive, and back when we were monkeys, killing was*

*a way of filling a dull afternoon. The grief and the horror come later, when your civilized mind catches up . . .'*

At first Steven didn't think that it had happened for real because the room hadn't collapsed, the ceiling hadn't fallen in. Everything was the same as it had been a few seconds before but now there were only three people in the room. Anderson was gone. Where he had gone to was nothing more than a puzzle. Steven's first logical thought was that he should grab Fiona and drag her out of the room. Anderson was dead and Stephanie was suddenly transformed into a creature from the roots of the volcano.

'So is the real dossier here?' Stephanie said in her ordinary voice but Fiona was frozen, looking down at Anderson's dead body. 'Anybody home?' Stephanie said, getting to her feet, staring at Fiona. 'What is it with this woman? Can you hear me?'

Stephanie suddenly shrieked.

'Come on! Snap! Snap! Snap!' She clicked her fingers in Fiona's face. 'You don't have time to think, just do as I say! Come on . . .'

Stephanie turned to Steven with her pistol lowered. 'Is this lady with you? I mean, does anybody want to help me get through to her little noodle? Jesus! You want to talk to your wife, Steven, and make her snap out of it?'

Stephanie sighed as if this was the last straw on a really busy day. Then she whispered gently into Fiona's ear, 'Come on, baby, it's OK, just do as I say and you'll be fine. Get it for me. The real thing this time.'

She yelled, 'Hey! Move!' and Fiona jumped. Steven realized this was some sort of procedure, a procedure which Stephanie knew so well that she could go through with it here, with Anderson dead and bleeding. He had begun to shake his head.

'No, Stephanie. No, no. For Christ's sake . . .'

Steven found himself moving towards them. Stephanie grabbed Fiona's long black hair in her fist and twisted it around. She whispered gently. 'Come on, baby, you do as I say and I won't hurt you. You're in a nightmare, just sleepwalk . . . where? Show me . . . show me where you've hidden it.'

Fiona suddenly sobbed with her hands to her mouth. Steven tried to grab Stephanie's arm but she turned the gun on him and her eyes were like shards of ice.

'Stephanie, wait a minute, you have this all wrong . . . Stephanie, I can deal with Fiona. Fiona it's OK, it's OK.'

Stephanie hissed into Fiona's ear like a snake. 'Tell me where. Three seconds. One . . . two . . .'

'There . . .' Fiona said, pointing to the window. There was a glass dome on top of a brand new dark-wood cabinet with an iron handle and a lock, with the key hanging out of it.

'Where? The dinky little cabinet? In the cabinet? Come on, baby, I ain't going to hurt you.'

Stephanie jerked Fiona's head back. Steven made a grab for Stephanie's gun arm and she hit the side of his face with the gun and then pushed it directly into Fiona's temple.

'You just relax, Mr Hawthorne. Just relax or I do the same to her.'

Stephanie pushed Fiona towards the cabinet by the window. Steven walked beside them, the three of them stepping sideways in a grotesque dance around the fire-place. It was ugly because the gun, a tiny thing, was making them all co-operate. When they reached the cabinet, Stephanie reached down towards the lock and as she did so she pushed Fiona away so that she fell into Steven's arms in a desperate embrace. Stephanie got down on her knees, pulled a pile of papers out of the cabinet and began to sift through them feverishly.

'Let me see here . . .' she said to herself. 'Let me see what we have here . . .'

She scanned the first few pages then looked up at Fiona. Steven had her head in his arms and she was trembling.

'Is this it?' Stephanie said. 'This all of it? Speak, sweetheart. Speak and you won't be hurt. Is this all of it?'

Fiona nodded.

'Speak!'

'Yes.'

'Only copy?'

'Yes.'

'Cross your heart and hope to die?'

'Yes.'

'Then that's just fine. That's just . . . what do you English say? That's just spiffing. Just fucking spiffing.'

Stephanie got to her feet with the bundle of papers in her hand. All of Fiona's venom distilled was now made to look puny against this monstrosity. Fiona and Steven were kneeling now, Fiona with her head resting on the crook of his arm. Behind them, Anderson was still bowing into a puddle of his own blood.

Steven thought that Stephanie was about to hand over the dossier for him to look at. She was still whispering to herself, 'Just fucking spiffing,' as she slid open the huge window behind her. She had to heave it open because the fitting had already begun to rust in the corrosive sea air and when Steven moved, she pointed the gun at him. When she had got the window open, the wind howled and the air in the room grew icy cold. Stephanie leant out onto the balcony and then threw the pile of papers into the wind. For a few seconds some of the sheets floated and stuck against the glass but finally they all drifted slowly two hundred feet down to the ocean below.

As she slid the window closed, Steven leapt on her from behind and wrestled her to the floor, knowing the truth now and not caring if he lived or died. Fiona scuttled towards them like a dog, on all fours. They wrestled for position silently, their violent desire to kill looking like a frantic copulation. Steven was strong and insane with fury and he held Stephanie in a good neck lock, the kind his father had taught him to do many times when they wrestled each other to the floor. But Stephanie still had the gun and it exploded somewhere deep inside his chest. He felt a fog forming all around his head like a crown or a halo and then the fog began to buzz and he felt himself slipping down a long dark tube that seemed to lead all the way down to the ocean.

Before he lost consciousness, he heard the gun being fired one more time.

## Postscript

Steven took a book in his left hand and raised his right. It was a book of rumours and half-truths.

'I promise to tell the truth, the whole truth and nothing but the truth, so help me God,' he said and he lowered his right hand and the book was taken away from him.

Coletto Amarillo, his long black hair tied into a pony tail, sat flanked by his attorneys and helpers. Stephanie Plater sat near to the front of the gallery. John Cross and Tom Pettman further back, their hands folded over their laps, their lightweight suits neatly pressed. The air-conditioning was blowing full blast but still the heat from outside was making the courtroom uncomfortable. The whole of New York City was panting in a heat wave like a sick old dog.

'Is your name Steven Hawthorne?'

'It is.'

'Is it true that on the night of 15 April last year you were in the basement of 1124 Avenue D, Alphabet City?'

'It is.'

'Is it true that on that night, you clearly saw Raul De Soto shot twice through the head and then partially burnt with kerosene?'

'Yes.'

'Is the man who fired those shots in this courtroom?'

'He is.'

'Could you point him out to the court?'

Amarillo was whispering something to his attorney. He really did look like an evil son of a bitch. Steven knew so much more about him now, after six months of intensive briefings. The wound in his chest had healed slowly, since he really had no desire to live, now that Fiona was dead. He realized as he hovered on the edge of extinction that Fiona had always been his real motivation and without her, he was a ship with sails and a rudder and a mast, but without a destination. In the end he had decided to live just for this moment, the moment when he would be asked to stand up in court and testify the truth.

They'd told him that this whole thing had been done in a good and noble cause, that the people who got hurt along the way had died for the greater good. Fiona and Anderson had been tidied away as the victims of a bloody lovers' quarrel, not a suicide pact but a fight to the death with no winner. It had been explained to Steven as he slowly regained his strength in his bed in Bronxville that if Amarillo stayed on the loose, the body count would be in the high fifties within a year, more if you counted all the kids who would die smoking his lethal white smoke. So this whole thing had been evil in pursuit of good.

Steven was a hero. *Alphabet City* had broken all sales records at Anton and Zucker. Foley sent cheques and Natalie sent more red roses.

He knew more about Stephanie now, too. She had been working with Pettman and John Cross all along. When Steven had been shot the first time, they hadn't been sure if he would co-operate when he came round. And they had the secondary problem of Fiona and the dossier. That was when John Cross had his big idea. They'd use the two variables against each other, they'd use Steven to get to Fiona and in the process make sure that he came on side. It was John Cross who had spotted the symmetry of it and he had chosen Stephanie to get into Steven's confidence, because she'd done that kind of work lots of times before.

The whole conspiracy had been orchestrated by John Cross and he had created his fictional world with a subtlety and precision that was beyond Steven's capabilities. Even his acting like a crazy man was a cover. There had been lots of meetings within the DEA, casting sessions, discussions on story-lines, plot-progression, the development of fictional characters. He admired John Cross's technique and especially the way he always chose dull and ordinary pieces to put together his mosaic. Steven had now been offered two million dollars to testify and a new identity. Foley suggested that he'd still be able to write more books for Anton and Zucker under his real name but that he'd have to live the rest of his life under a pseudonym. Didn't Steven see the fabulous irony in that?

The courtroom waited for Steven Hawthorne to point the finger.

'There's no need to point to the guy who pulled the trigger,' Steven said, and the courtroom fell silent. 'Because I did it. I shot him. It was me.'

Pettman and Stephanie Plater both stood up at the same time. Only John Cross sat motionless. Steven Hawthorne stared into the hollow eyes of John Cross.

'You see, Your Honour, for six months these people have been telling me to say that it was Amarillo, but the truth is, it was me. I shot De Soto. I fired the gun. There was only me and Amarillo and Polka down there and so only we know the truth. That's right, isn't it, Mr Amarillo?'

Amarillo and his attorneys looked as if they were made of stone. Steven turned to stare at John Cross again as the murmuring in the courtroom began to build.

'Nothing you can do about that is there, Mr Cross?' Steven said, raising his voice. 'Can you hear me John

Cross? *I* was in the basement, that's all true, but it was me who pulled the trigger. Mr Amarillo is innocent. That really is the truth. It was me who decided to kill Pilot, and lots of other people too.'

Steven smiled through the wave of incomprehension from the gallery that hit him like a hail of bullets. Because he hated John Cross and Tom Pettman so much, because he hated Stephanie Plater so much, because he had really loved Fiona Van Draken. He had told his most wicked lie and it would end them all.

# Discover more about our forthcoming books through Penguin's FREE newspaper...

# READ MORE IN PENGUIN

In every corner of the world, on every subject under the sun, Penguin represents quality and variety – the very best in publishing today.

For complete information about books available from Penguin – including Puffins, Penguin Classics and Arkana – and how to order them, write to us at the appropriate address below. Please note that for copyright reasons the selection of books varies from country to country.

**In the United Kingdom**: Please write to *Dept. JC, Penguin Books Ltd, FREEPOST, West Drayton, Middlesex UB7 OBR.*

If you have any difficulty in obtaining a title, please send your order with the correct money, plus ten per cent for postage and packaging, to *PO Box No. 11, West Drayton, Middlesex UB7 OBR*

**In the United States**: Please write to *Consumer Sales, Penguin USA, P.O. Box 999, Dept. 17109, Bergenfield, New Jersey 07621-0120.* VISA and MasterCard holders call 1-800-253-6476 to order all Penguin titles

**In Canada**: Please write to *Penguin Books Canada Ltd, 10 Alcorn Avenue, Suite 300, Toronto, Ontario M4V 3B2*

**In Australia**: Please write to *Penguin Books Australia Ltd, P.O. Box 257, Ringwood, Victoria 3134*

**In New Zealand**: Please write to *Penguin Books (NZ) Ltd, Private Bag 102902, North Shore Mail Centre, Auckland 10*

**In India**: Please write to *Penguin Books India Pvt Ltd, 706 Eros Apartments, 56 Nehru Place, New Delhi 110 019*

**In the Netherlands**: Please write to *Penguin Books Netherlands bv, Postbus 3507, NL-1001 AH Amsterdam*

**In Germany**: Please write to *Penguin Books Deutschland GmbH, Metzlerstrasse 26, 60594 Frankfurt am Main*

**In Spain**: Please write to *Penguin Books S. A., Bravo Murillo 19, 1° B, 28015 Madrid*

**In Italy**: Please write to *Penguin Italia s.r.l., Via Felice Casati 20, I–20124 Milano*

**In France**: Please write to *Penguin France S. A., 17 rue Lejeune, F–31000 Toulouse*

**In Japan**: Please write to *Penguin Books Japan, Ishikiribashi Building, 2–5–4, Suido, Bunkyo-ku, Tokyo 112*

**In Greece**: Please write to *Penguin Hellas Ltd, Dimocritou 3, GR–106 71 Athens*

**In South Africa**: Please write to *Longman Penguin Southern Africa (Pty) Ltd, Private Bag X08, Bertsham 2013*

# PENGUIN AUDIOBOOKS

Penguin Books has always led the field in quality publishing. Now you can listen at leisure to your favourite books, read to you by familiar voices from radio, stage and screen. Penguin Audiobooks are ideal as gifts, for when you are travelling or simply to enjoy at home. They are edited, abridged and produced to an excellent standard, and are always faithful to the original texts. From thrillers to classic literature, biography to humour, with a wealth of titles in between, Penguin Audiobooks offer you quality, entertainment and the chance to re-discover the pleasure of listening.

*Published or forthcoming:*

**Persuasion** by Jane Austen, read by Fiona Shaw

**Pride and Prejudice** by Jane Austen, read by Joanna David

**Jericho** by Dirk Bogarde, read by the author

**A Period of Adjustment** by Dirk Bogarde, read by the author

**A Postillion Struck by Lightning** by Dirk Bogarde, read by the author

**A Short Walk from Harrods** by Dirk Bogarde, read by the author

**The Blue Afternoon** by William Boyd, read by Kate Harper

**Brazzaville Beach** by William Boyd, read by Fiona Shaw

**A Good Man in Africa** by William Boyd, read by Timothy Spall

**The Road to Welville** by T. Coraghessan Boyle, read by the author

**Jane Eyre** by Charlotte Brontë, read by Juliet Stevenson

**Wuthering Heights** by Emily Brontë, read by Juliet Stevenson

**Great Expectations** by Charles Dickens, read by Hugh Laurie

**Hard Times** by Charles Dickens, read by Michael Pennington

**Middlemarch** by George Eliot, read by Harriet Walter

**Zlata's Diary** by Zlata Filipovič, read by Dorota Puzio

**Decider** by Dick Francis, read by Robert Powell

**Wild Horses** by Dick Francis, read by Michael Maloney

**I Dreamed of Africa** by Kuki Gallmann, read by Isabella Rossellini

**The Prophet** by Kahlil Gibran, read by Renu Setna

# PENGUIN AUDIOBOOKS

**Virtual Light** by William Gibson, read by Peter Weller

**Having It All** by Maeve Haran, read by Belinda Lang

**Scenes from the Sex War** by Maeve Haran, read by Belinda Lang

**Thunderpoint** by Jack Higgins, read by Roger Moore

**The Iliad** by Homer, read by Derek Jacobi

**More Please** by Barry Humphries, read by the author

**Four Past Midnight: The Sun Dog** by Stephen King, read by Tim Sample

**Nightmares and Dreamscapes** by Stephen King, read by Whoopi Goldberg, Rob Lowe, Stephen King et al

**Two Past Midnight: Secret Window, Secret Garden** by Stephen King, read by James Woods

**Shadow over Babylon** by David Mason, read by Bob Peck

**Hotel Pastis** by Peter Mayle, read by Tim Pigott-Smith

**Waiting to Exhale** by Terry McMillan, read by the author

**Murderers and Other Friends** by John Mortimer, read by the author

**Under the Hammer** by John Mortimer, read by Tim Pigott-Smith

**Bitter Medicine** by Sara Paretsky, read by Christine Lahti

**Guardian Angel** by Sara Paretsky, read by Jane Kaczmarek

**History: The Home Movie** by Craig Raine, read by the author

**First Offence** by Nancy Taylor Rosenberg, read by Lindsay Crouse

**Frankenstein** by Mary Shelley, read by Richard Pasco

**I Shudder at Your Touch** by Michele Slung, read by Stephen King et al

**The Devil's Juggler** by Murray Smith, read by Kenneth Cranham

**Kidnapped** by Robert Louis Stevenson, read by Robbie Coltrane

**The Secret History** by Donna Tartt, read by Robert Sean Leonard

**Bad Girls, Good Women** by Rosie Thomas, read by Jenny Agutter

**Asta's Book** by Barbara Vine, read by Jane Lapotaire

**A Dark-Adapted Eye** by Barbara Vine, read by Sophie Ward

**No Night is Too Long** by Barbara Vine, read by Alan Cumming

# READ MORE IN PENGUIN

## A CHOICE OF BESTSELLERS

**Paradise News**  David Lodge

'Lodge could never be solemn and the book crackles with good jokes . . . leaves you with a mild and thoughtful glow of happiness' – *Sunday Telegraph*. 'Amusing, accessible, intelligent . . . the story rolls, the sparks fly' – *Financial Times*

**Pleading Guilty**  Scott Turow

When over $5 million goes missing from the coffers of law firm Gage and Griswell's largest client, Mack Malloy is dispatched to find G & G's maverick missing partner, Bert Kamin. 'Extravagant with danger, sex and especially money – and full of surprises to the end' – *Independent on Sunday*

**Devices and Desires**  P. D. James

'Like the wind-lashed Norfolk headland buffeted by the sea, which is so tangily evoked, *Devices and Desires* always has an intensely bracing chill to its atmosphere' – *Sunday Times*

**Doctor Criminale**  Malcolm Bradbury

'The best novel so far about post-modernism. With grace and wit its author deconstructs fifty years of European thought and history' – *Observer*. 'Bradbury has produced something even rarer and trickier than a good comedy of manners: *Doctor Criminale* is a bracing comedy of ideas' – *GQ*

**Hotel Pastis**  Peter Mayle

Forty-two-year-old adman Simon Shaw is rich, successful, newly divorced and bored. Yearning for a life free of complications, he escapes to the bright skies and vivid landscapes of Provence. '*Hotel Pastis* is great entertainment and a rattling good yarn . . . Peter Mayle has once more created his own world which thousands will enjoy' – *Literary Review*

# READ MORE IN PENGUIN

## A CHOICE OF BESTSELLERS

**Brightness Falls**   Jay McInerney

'The story of a disintegrating marriage set in New York in the frenzied few months leading up to the Wall Street crash of 1987. It is his biggest, most ambitious novel yet – a sort of *Bonfire of the Vanities* with the added advantage of believable, likeable characters' – *Independent on Sunday*

**The Burden of Proof**   Scott Turow

One afternoon in late March Sandy Stern, the brilliant, quixotic defence lawyer in *Presumed Innocent*, returns home to find his wife Clara dead in the garage. 'Rarely has a plot as political, as sexual, as criminal, as moral, so lip-smackingly thickened ... A wonderful read from tight start to taut end' – *Mail on Sunday*

**The Russian Girl**   Kingsley Amis

'Dazzling skill with dialogue and ... no less dazzling ability to conjure up minor characters – policemen, academics, businessmen, Russian émigrés – who, for all their hilarious oddity, somehow remain believable' – *Evening Standard*

**The Children of Men**   P. D. James

The year is 2021. For twenty-five years no child has been born. Nor will there be any more children for infertility has spread like a plague and the human race faces extinction. 'The central images haunt the mind terrifyingly ... It has extraordinary power and visionary passion' – *Observer*

**Pronto**   Elmore Leonard

'The American crime master moves to Italy and stays on top of his form in a cracking tale of small-time criminals' – *Independent*. 'Elmore Leonard keeps you holding your breath as usual, and your heart pounding' – Alec Guinness

# READ MORE IN PENGUIN

## A CHOICE OF BESTSELLERS

**The Stories of Eva Luna**  Isabelle Allende

'Vibrant and colourful ... twenty-three magical tales of anger that changes to laughter and revenge that turns into love' – *Literary Review*. 'Like a plate of hors-d'oeuvres, each one tempting, some as exquisite as caviare ... stunning' – *The New York Times Book Review*

**Love in the Time of Cholera**  Gabriel García Márquez

'Rich and brilliant with emotion – an extraordinary poeticization of old age. It brings everything close: the disabling heat, the presence of the sea, the storms ... It suggests that true love is not blind, but sees all the faults and does not mind' – *Observer*

**The Blue Afternoon**  William Boyd
Winner of the 1993 *Sunday Express* Book of the Year Award

Kay Fischer, a young, independent and ambitious architect, is shadowed by an enigmatic stranger who claims to be her father. Within weeks of their meeting, Kay will join him for an extraordinary journey into the old man's past, initially in search of a murderer, but finally in celebration of a glorious, undying love.

**The Fourteen Sisters of Emilio Montez O'Brien**  Oscar Hijuelos

'Hijuelos weaves another magical literary spell in his evocation of a loving, Edenic childhood' – *Independent on Sunday*. 'A capacious, marvellously complicated novel that is Mr Hijuelos's paean to femininity and to family life as it is actually lived' – *The New York Times Book Review*

**Brazil**  John Updike

Tristão Raposo, a nineteen-year-old black child of the Rio slums, spies Isabel Leme, an upper-class white girl, across the hot sands of Copacabana Beach, and presents her with a ring. Their flight into marriage takes them from urban banality to the farthest reaches of Brazil's wild west. 'A brilliant performance' – *Independent on Sunday*

# READ MORE IN PENGUIN

## A CHOICE OF BESTSELLERS

### The Secret History   Donna Tartt

'*The Secret History* tells the story of a group of classics students at an élite American college, who are cerebral, obsessive and finally murderous ... it is a haunting, compelling and brilliant piece of fiction' – *The Times*

### Memories of the Ford Administration   John Updike

'Quintessential Updike, an exploration of a modern American terrain of desire, guilt and moral ambiguity that he has made distinctly his own' – *The New York Times Book Review*

### Virtual Light   William Gibson

'In an alert and often graceful prose, Gibson charts a nightmare landscape with surprising flashes of humour and beauty ... Cyberpunk doesn't come any more stylish than this' – *Sunday Telegraph*. 'Sheer inventive zest' – *Independent on Sunday*

### The Devil's Juggler   Murray Smith

A lone corpse in New York's Grand Central Station; an SAS soldier missing on active service during the Gulf War; and hideous unseen carnage in a South American cemetery – the deaths demand vengeance ... 'A damn good read ... tense, topical and brutally authentic' – Frederick Forsyth

### The New Confessions   William Boyd

The outrageous, extraordinary, hilarious and heartbreaking autobiography of John James Todd, a Scotsman born in 1899 and one of the great self-appointed (and failed) geniuses of the twentieth century. 'Boyd has written funny novels and clever novels. *The New Confessions* one can confidently call a great novel' – *Listener*

# READ MORE IN PENGUIN

## A SELECTION OF CLASSIC CRIME

**The Daughter of Time**  Josephine Tey

Now established as one of the most popular and enduring of crime classics, *The Daughter of Time* investigates the questions that surround the reign of Richard III, the most hated King of England. Both detective story and enthralling mystery, *The Daughter of Time* is one of the most original pieces of historical fiction ever written.

**Beast in View**  Margaret Millar
Winner of the Edgar Allen Poe Award

'On one level, *Beast in View* is a dazzling conjuring trick. On another it offers a glimpse of bright-eyed madness as disquieting as a shriek in the night. In the whole of crime fiction's distinguished sisterhood there is no one quite like Margaret Millar' – Matthew Coady

**Fen Country**  Edmund Crispin

Gervase Fen, Oxford don, vain and eccentric amateur detective, together with the self-effacing Detective Inspector Humbleby, solve some of the most bizarre cases in the annals of crime.

**The Wisdom of Father Brown**  G. K. Chesterton

Voodoo, political scandal, murder, the follies of man – the shabby little cleric confronts them all with his characteristic blend of mischievous humour, deceptive simplicity and moral insight.

**The Allingham Case-Book**  Margery Allingham

*The Allingham Case-Book* records eighteen crimes – from the seedy and sinister to the fashionable and frivolous. All are curious and some seem downright impossible. They feature the exploits of the famous detective Albert Campion and his friends the policemen Charlie Luke and Stanislaus Oates.

# READ MORE IN PENGUIN

## A SELECTION OF CLASSIC CRIME

**Wall of Eyes**  Margaret Millar

Kelsey has become bitter since the accident that left her blind. She was driving the car that night. Geraldine did die, and Kelsey will never see again. But that was two long years ago. Time enough to heal. So why would Kelsey now want to end her life with a grain of morphine? 'She is in the very top rank of crime writers' – Julian Symons

**Sweet Danger**  Margery Allingham

'That was the beauty of Campion; one never knew where he was going to turn up next – at the Third Levée or swinging from a chandelier . . .' *Sweet Danger* is perfectly crafted, full of surprising twists and turns. What starts as a light-hearted, slightly crazy wild-goose chase becomes something much more dangerous, nasty and sinister.

**Operation Pax**  Michael Innes

Something rich and rotten is going on behind the discreet façade of a very private Oxfordshire clinic. Meanwhile Sir John Appleby has been summoned to Oxford to investigate the disappearance of an undergraduate from Bede's. Almost accidentally he, and a host of others, stumble on the sinister secrets of Operation Pax . . .

**The Franchise Affair**  Josephine Tey

The Franchise is the name of a large country house in which Marion Sharpe and her mother live. The Affair concerns the accusation by a fifteen-year-old schoolgirl that these two apparently respectable ladies kept her locked up in their attic for a month, beat her, and starved her.

# READ MORE IN PENGUIN

## A SELECTION OF CRIME AND MYSTERY

**Devices and Desires**  P. D. James

When Commander Adam Dalgliesh becomes involved in the hunt for the killer in a remote area of the Norfolk coast, he finds himself caught up in the dangerous secrets of the headland community. And then one moonlit night it becomes chillingly apparent that there is more than one killer at work in Larsoken . . .

**Gallowglass**  Barbara Vine

When Sandor saves little Joe from the path of a London tube train he claims his life for himself. In adoration and gratitude, Joe willingly offers himself to him, becoming Sandor's *gallowglass*, servant to the chief. 'Of all living writers, she can enter most convincingly into the criminal, or even pathological, mind' – *Sunday Times*

**Death among the Dons**  Janet Neel

'*Death among the Dons* is probably the best crime novel set in a women's college since Dorothy Sayers's *Gaudy Night*' – T. J. Binyon. 'Janet Neel sets her nerve-tingling plot in a wonderfully alive and intelligent collegiate milieu' – *Sunday Times*

**Pleading Guilty**  Scott Turow

Gage and Griswell is a large law firm with an even larger problem: $5.6 million has suddenly vanished from the coffers of its largest client. 'Extravagant with danger, sex and especially money – and full of surprises to the end' – *Independent on Sunday*

**The Big Sleep**  Raymond Chandler

Millionaire General Sternwood, a paralysed old man, is already two-thirds dead. He has two beautiful daughters – one a gambler, the other a degenerate – and an elusive adventurer as a son-in-law. The General is being blackmailed, and Marlowe's assignment is to get the blackmailer off his back. As it turns out, there's a lot more at stake . . .

# READ MORE IN PENGUIN

## A SELECTION OF CRIME AND MYSTERY

**Paper Doll**  Robert B. Parker

Olivia Nelson had almost been a candidate for sainthood – perfect wife, perfect mother with a perfect home in the best part of Boston. Too perfect, perhaps. Because someone murdered her. But when Spenser sets out to solve the case, nothing – least of all the life and death of the victim – is what it seems . . .

**This Way Out**  Sheila Radley

The thought of doing away with his mother-in-law would never have entered Derek Cartwright's head, if he had not begun to suffer from bad dreams – and if he had not met Hugh Packer. Sheila Radley's spine-chilling story traces the descent of an upright husband and citizen into blunder, nightmare and murder. 'Here is an author who can be bracketed with the best' – *Observer*

**Fatlands**  Sarah Dunant

'Make way for Hannah Wolfe, one of the best private eyes, either sex, either side of the Atlantic' – *Daily Telegraph*. Hannah's latest brief is to mind teenage rebel Mattie Shepherd. But what began as a Knightsbridge shopping trip ends in an act of explosive violence.

**Guardian Angel**  Sara Paretsky

When a friend of Mr Contreras, Vic Warshawski's loyal neighbour, claims that he has some information that will make him a rich man – and then turns up dead in the canal, Vic knows it's no coincidence. 'The richest and most engaging yet of Ms Paretsky's thrillers' – *The New York Times*

**Berlin Noir**  Philip Kerr

Ex-policeman Bernie Gunther thought he'd seen everything on the streets of 1930s Berlin. But then he went freelance and with each case he tackled he became sucked further into the grisly excesses of Nazi sub-culture. And even after the war, amidst the decayed, imperial splendour of Vienna, Bernie uncovered a legacy that made the wartime atrocities look lily-white by comparison . . .

# BY THE SAME AUTHOR

**The Movie House**

Karl Stone's comedy scripts have bombed, his wife's left him for an adman and a slow death from brandy poisoning seems like the future's only hope. Until Karl finds himself adopted by Hollywood producer G. F. Benelli and whisked off to the sunshine of the Florida Keys.

Holed up in the tumbledown Movie House, overlooking Key West's boundless ocean, our hero begins to hammer out the movie script that will change his life and make Benelli's fortune. But something about the plot just doesn't ring true . . .

Why does the Chief of Police think he's a criminal? Who is the one-time starlet Scarlet Timberley – and why is he falling in love with her? Caught up in a whirlwind of dark and sinister events, Karl Stone has to act to save his sanity – and maybe even his life . . .